PRAISE FOR

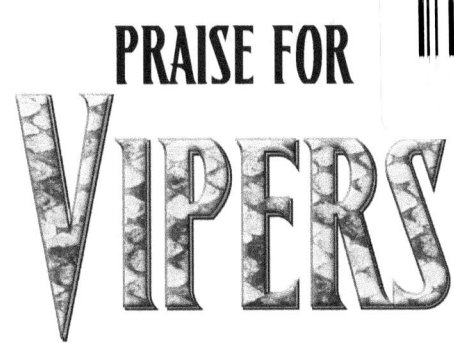

"Add ambitious evil spirits to a marathon game of *Grand Theft Auto* and you have this breakneck made-for-the-movies celebration of bloody carnage and black scheming . . . fans of summer blockbusters will be happy to crunch popcorn through the car chases, explosions, and brutality."
—*Publishers Weekly*

"Lawrence C. Connolly's *Vipers* is to his *Veins* what Coppola's *Godfather II* was to *The Godfather*; he's . . . deepened its themes, expanded its vision, and reached near-operatic levels of grandeur, terror, and complexity. Simply jaw-dropping, *Vipers* must be read by any serious follower of horror, crime, and dark fantasy who wants to see the next step in the cross-genre revolution."
—**Gary A. Braunbeck,** International Horror Guild and five-time Bram Stoker Award-winning author of *To Each Their Darkness* and *A Cracked and Broken Path*

"Connolly shows us once again just how imaginative, intelligent and skillful a writer he is. Deftly weaving together mythology, edge-of-seat action sequences, more characters than most authors would dare try to control in a single narrative, terror and a real sense of an encroaching apocalypse, he delivers a novel that is at once gleeful, unpredictable and entirely ominous."
—**Simon Kurt Unsworth,** author of *Lost Places*

"Lawrence C. Connolly has the rare ability to completely transport the reader. . . . But beware—as you race along the dusty, backcountry roads with the characters, with the thrill of speed comes something else, something deadly and far from human. Connolly delivers a taut novel of horror and suspense that will have you reading chapter after chapter long after you meant to go to sleep."
—**Alice Henderson,** author of *Voracious*

PRAISE FOR VEINS

"One of the joys of my days at *Twilight Zone* was encountering the work of an extraordinarily subtle and imaginative writer, Lawrence C. Connolly, who brought enormous power to the shortest of stories. And now, in *Veins*, he's created something equally extraordinary—a supernatural novel that brings Native American magic to a crime thriller as intense and fast-moving as a Tarantino movie."
—**T.E.D. Klein,** World Fantasy and British Fantasy Society Award-winning author of *The Ceremonies* and *Dark Gods*

"*Veins* is haunting work, meticulously crafted by one of the genre's most masterful storytellers, writing at the top of his game. A tremendous and unforgettable read."
—**Michael Arnzen,** Bram Stoker Award-winning author of *100 Jolts*

"*Veins* is both spiritual and physical, blending both this world and the world of that beyond with seamless grace. Connolly is a writer to follow, and his work a thing to savor."
—**Mary SanGiovanni,** author of *The Hollower*

"Much like the souped-up vintage Mustang that cuts through the heart of the story, *Veins* starts fast, accelerates quickly, and finishes with a flourish, fulfilling all the promise at novel length that Lawrence C. Connolly has been flashing for years in his outstanding short stories."
—**Robert Morrish,** fiction editor of *Cemetery Dance*, the World Fantasy Award-winning magazine of horror, dark mystery, and suspense

"Feels like some of the best magic realism that's been written lately . . . highly readable."
—**BookSpotCentral.com**

"With . . . expert imagery, Lawrence C. Connolly takes a reader on a different kind of magical mystery tour . . . about what drives people to extremes, and how destiny ultimately intervenes."
—**HellNotes.com**

"[S]ubtly haunting, bringing together Native American Okwe myth with a crime thriller. The plot is fast and intense and the characters are wonderfully real."
—**Laura Lehman,** *BellaOnline.com*

AWARD NOMINATIONS FOR VEINS

Finalist for the 2009 Eric Hoffer Award.

Appeared on the Preliminary Ballot for the 2009 Bram Stoker Award for Superior Achievement in a First Novel.

Nominated for the 2nd Annual Black Quill Award for Best Small-Press Chill by the editors of Dark Scribe Magazine.

PRAISE FOR VORTEX

"Few writers understand their characters with the same depth, and empathy, that Connolly does. He leaves me in awe. Every time. I am a Connolly fan through and through."
—**Joe McKinney**, Bram Stoker Award-winning author of *Dead City* and *Plague of the Undead*

"Writing with power and precision, Connolly evokes sights and sounds that haunt us. *Vortex* is a book you won't be able to put down."
—**Jon Sprunk**, author of *Blood & Iron*

"Unbridled imagination meets impeccable storytelling. Connolly is amazing that way, like the bull and the matador rolled into one."
—**John Dixon,** author of *Phoenix Island*

"[*Vortex*] will lose readers in a mystical and frightening world that they won't want to slither out of."
—**Stephanie M. Wytovich,** author of *Hysteria*

"This is gleeful, intelligent stuff that deserves the widest audience possible. It's a hell of a ride, and I cannot wait to see where Connolly takes us next."
—**Simon Kurt Unsworth**, World-Fantasy-Award-Nominated author of *The Devil's Detective*, forthcoming from Doubleday

ALSO BY LAWRENCE C. CONNOLLY

The Veins Cycle

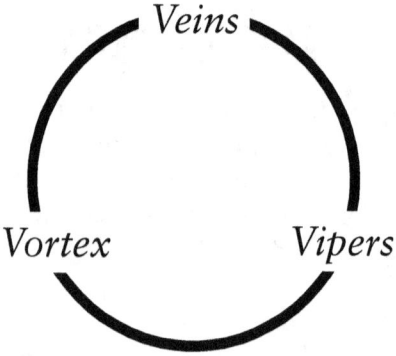

Veins

Vortex *Vipers*

Short Story Collections
Visions: Short Fantasy & SF
Voices: Tales of Horror

From Ash-Tree Press
This Way to Egress

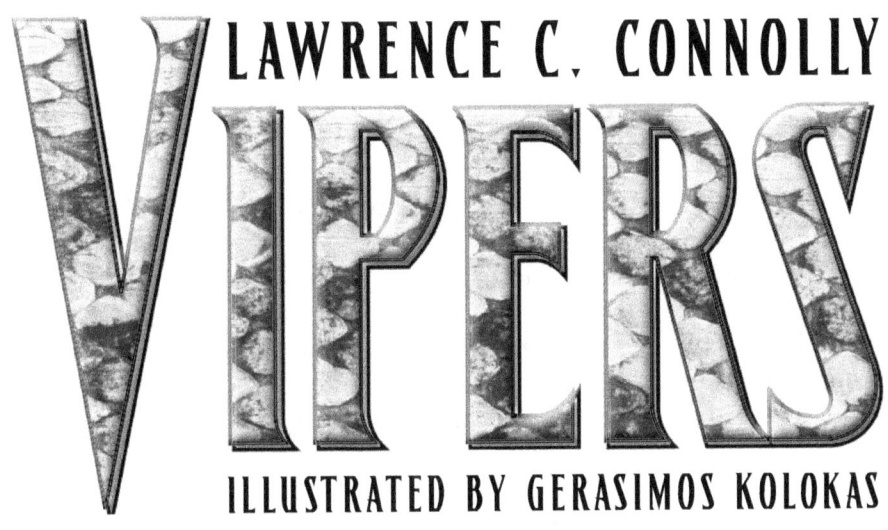

LAWRENCE C. CONNOLLY

VIPERS

ILLUSTRATED BY GERASIMOS KOLOKAS

Fantasist
Enterprises

WILMINGTON, DELAWARE

Designed by W. H. Horner Editorial & Design

Published by
Fantasist Enterprises
PO Box 9381
Wilmington, DE 19809
www.FEBooks.net

Vipers

Trade Paperback:
ISBN 13: 978-1-934571-03-3
ISBN 10: 1-934571-03-2

ePub:
ISBN 13: 978-1-934571-07-1
ISBN 10: 1-934571-07-5

FIRST EDITION
September 2010

SECOND PRINTING
July 2014

10 9 8 7 6 5 4 3 2 1

For my father.

ACKNOWLEDGEMENTS:

I would like to thank David Shifren, formerly of the Baldwin Borough Police Department, Pennsylvania, for his invaluable help in crafting the police scenes featured in this book; Will and Meesh Horner of Fantasist Enterprises for their exacting editing and careful guidance during the drafting and revision process; Christina Stitt and Paul Popiel of FE, and Greg Schauer of Between Books, for their eyes; Dave Tournay for trusting me behind the wheel of his Dodge Viper; and geologist, friend, and brother-in-law Tim Kuntz for listening to my questions and pointing me in all the right directions. Without their help and assistance, this book would not have been possible.

And when he had gathered a bundle of sticks,
and laid them on the fire, there came a viper
out of the heat, and fastened on his hand.
—Book of Acts

And the high mountains shall be shaken,
And the high hills shall be made low,
And they shall melt like wax before the flame.
—Book of Enoch

But with an overrunning flood
he will make an utter end of the place . . .
and darkness shall pursue his enemies.
—Book of Nahum

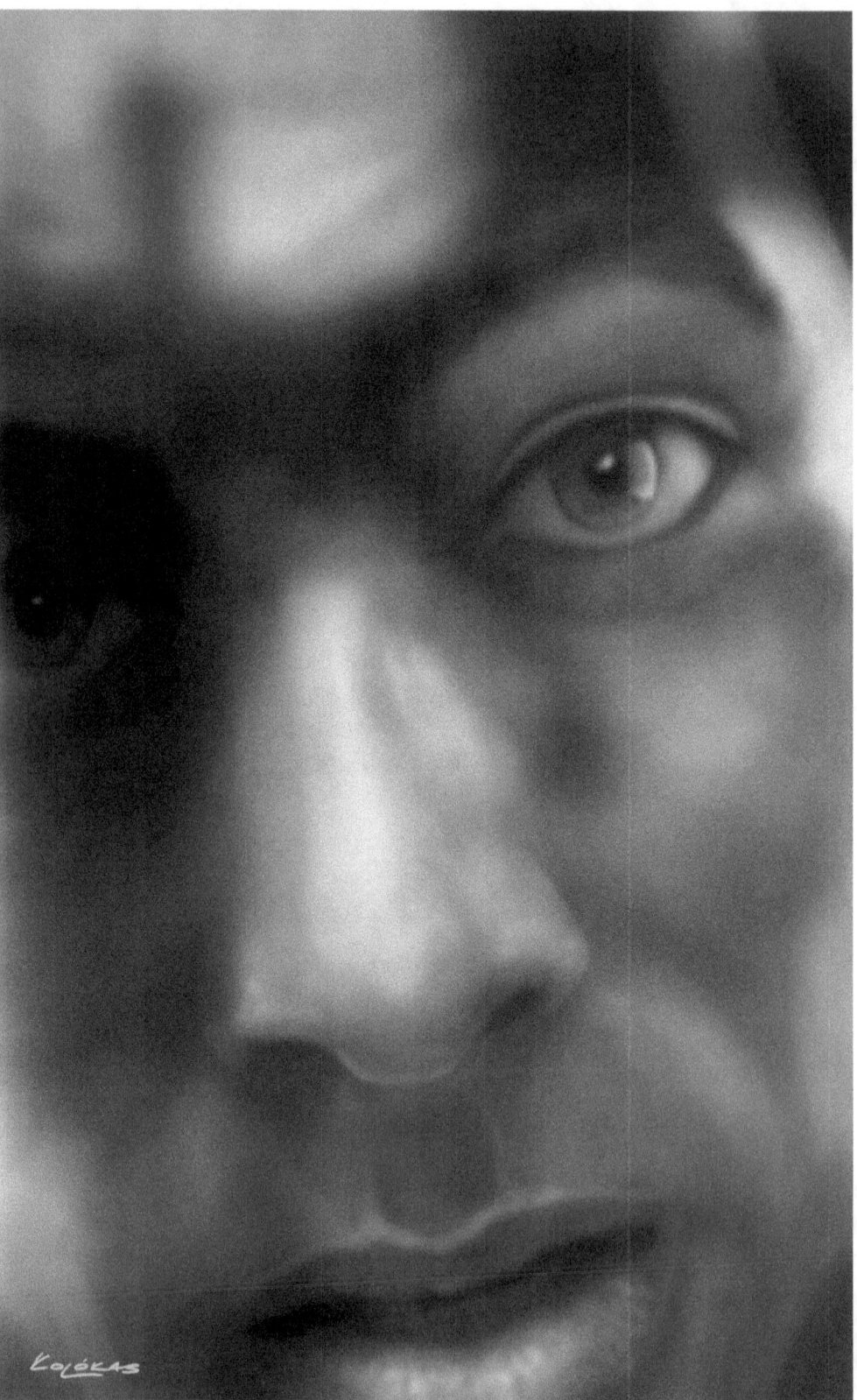

PROLOGUE

When his dead girlfriend's car broke down three miles from the West Virginia line, Dalton Davies got out, jumped the guardrail, and walked into the Pennsylvania forest.

He didn't have a plan, didn't know where he was going. He simply knew he needed to keep moving, putting distance between himself and the mess he'd left behind in Pittsburgh.

The sun was low over the hills as he entered the trees, shining yellow against the trunks and vines. It occurred to him that his clothes—T-shirt, cutoffs, and threadbare sneakers—were all wrong for a night in the woods, but he couldn't return to the highway. He needed to be elsewhere before the cops found the car. It would be simpler that way.

He came upon a coal-hauling road, humped in the middle, patched with weeds. He followed it to a ravine strewn with appliances, car parts, scrap wood, bottles, wire coat hangers, and something that looked like the rusted frame of a backyard swing set. It was Polly's kind of place. She'd been a junk artist before she went psycho, and he wondered if finding a dump on this particular evening was some kind of omen.

Dalton trusted omens.

Polly used to kid him about that, back in the days when she'd still had a sense of humor.

"You're a mystic, Dalton. A Sariputra in need of *bodhi*."

"Body?"

"*Bodhi*. It's like *satori*."

"The hell's that?"

"It's what you're looking for, my Sariputra."

"And what's a *sorry poochra*?"

She laughed. "That'd be you, Dalton." She punched his shoulder. "You're the *sorry poochra*. Definitely the *sorriest poochra* I've ever seen."

She had been like that when they'd first met, peppering her insults with

Eastern mysticism, always talking in circles and jagging him around—but in good ways. Those had been happy times. Even now, after all the crap that had gone down, he cherished those memories. And now here he was, on the day of her death, running away and stumbling upon a cache of junk that at one time would have had Polly jumping with anticipation.

"Damn," he said, speaking to her memory. "Wish you could see this place, Polly."

Sorry, Dalton. I can't see anything. Her words seemed to come from outside his head, emanating from the hiss and babble of a creek running through the ravine. *You killed me, remember?*

"I didn't kill you."

You didn't help me. It's the same thing.

"What could I have done?"

Anything but run away. Damnit, Dalton. When things get tough, you run like a pustule.

"So what should I have done?"

The creek babbled, flowing south. No words now. No answer. Just the sound of flowing water. Maybe that was because there was no answer. Or maybe because the only answer was one he didn't want to consider: that it was time to stop running, turn back, alert the authorities. He'd been ignoring that answer all morning, telling himself that his only option was getting away to a place where he could forget he had ever had a relationship with a manic-depressive junk artist whose final work had been painting the floor with her open wrists. "Angels!" she had said, looking up at him from the stained carpet, blood smeared like red wings. "I see angels! What do you see?" That was it. Her last words.

What do you see?

"I couldn't stop you, Polly."

Angels.

"I couldn't save you."

I see angels. What do you see?

Maybe his only option was to return to the car, tie something white to the door, and wait for the cops to check on him. When they did, he could tell them how he hadn't really stolen the car, just borrowed it. He could explain that he hadn't meant to bolt without calling 911, it was just that he'd been confused. It was like something had snapped when he saw all that blood.

Whose blood? The cop would say.

"My girlfriend's."

What happened?

"It's complicated."

Wind stirred the trees. Dalton shivered, sunlight shifted, and suddenly, near the base of the slope, he saw Polly lying in a drift of rotting leaves.

"Jesus!"

He stepped back, heart racing. This was crazy. She couldn't be here. And yet—

What do you see?

He stepped forward again, squinting, focusing, determining that it really was there. But it wasn't Polly. It wasn't even a real body.

"A mannequin!" His shivers deepened. "A sign!"

This one had to mean something.

He descended the slope.

The painted eyes seemed to follow him, staring from a face that looked more like Polly the closer he got. Wide eyes, straight nose, high cheeks, narrow jaw—it resembled the woman she had been *before* her junk-art mania had succumbed to depression, before her features had darkened and her gaze turned toward the angels in her head.

I see angels.

The slope was steeper than it looked, and more slippery. Halfway down he lost his footing, fell, and slid the rest of the way. Rocks and junk clawed at him, scraping his legs, pummeling his butt, covering his cutoffs with a muddy smear before he careened to a stop at the edge of the creek. The mannequin was beside him now. He looked toward it, and that's when he saw the other set of eyes.

What do you see?

The other eyes were real, alive, and looking right at him. They peered from the shadow of the mannequin's head: fixed, unblinking—snake eyes.

"Aw, shit!" He backed away.

The snake didn't move. It just sat there: body coiled, neck cocked, eyes staring. Its head wasn't much larger than the tip of Dalton's thumb, but the shape of its eyes and the banded colors of its body marked it as a copperhead.

He scooted away.

The snake moved now, turning its head, tracking his motion, tasting the air with its hair-thin tongue.

Dalton rose to his feet. He took a step backward, intending to turn and climb out of the ravine when something struck the back of his leg, thumping a few inches above the heel. He looked around.

A second snake recoiled behind him. This one was larger than the first. Had it bitten him? The thump hadn't felt like much, just a tap. Maybe it was a warning tap. Did snakes do that?

He moved away, sidestepping now.

Both snakes watched, eyes fixed, tongues darting.

A rotting log angled over the creek, one end resting in the water. Dalton sat on it, looked at his leg, checked the ankle. The bite marks were there, two of them. They were like pimples, beads of welling blood. He touched one. It broke and flowed, dribbling down, staining his shoe.

The big snake kept staring.

"You son of a bitch! I wasn't even bothering you."

The snake flicked its tongue.

Dalton's leg was hurting now, pain spreading in waves. He tried getting up. The leg cramped. He stumbled and went down hard. And suddenly there were more snakes, a nest of babies emerging from the log. They struck at his hands. He recoiled. One of the snakes held on, clamping the soft flesh between thumb and finger. He tried shaking it away. The ropy body coiled, flexing against his palm.

"Goddamnit!"

He slammed the hand against the log, rubbing hard, reducing the body to a pulpy skid. But the head held on, jaws pulsing, eyes staring as Dalton pried it loose. The fangs retracted. They were nasty-looking: curved, smeared with blood, dripping venom. He tossed the head away, but the other snakes were on him now, biting his limbs, riddling them with punctures that oozed and smeared as he crawled backward through weeds. And then he was up, on his feet, and running along the creek. That was what he did best. When things got crazy, when the world turned shitty, he ran. Get away, that was his strategy. But why was he following the creek when he needed to get back to the road, flag down a car, scream for help?

He turned toward the slope, threw himself against it, and started to climb. His throat tightened. He couldn't catch his breath, feared he might pass out, but then he emerged: out of the hollow and into the presence of . . . not an omen . . . but a *miracle*.

A farmhouse stood before him: gabled eaves, covered porch, open door.

"Hey!" He stumbled forward. "Help!" He fell. A shadow streaked the ground in front of him, racing away on a gust of wind. He looked up. Nothing there. No clouds. Only the sun resting low atop the trees.

He stood, winced at the fire in his foot, and resumed his stumbling gait toward the house.

The door was open. Someone had to be home.

"Hey! Help me. I've been snake bit!"

He fell toward the porch steps, grabbed the banister, and nearly blacked out as his bitten hand spasmed from the pressure. He fell to his knees, everything hurting now, pain burning inside him as he crawled up the stairs and onto the porch. Then he knelt, blinking, clearing his vision. He'd been wrong about the door. It wasn't open. Not in the usual sense. He forced himself to stand, lurching forward, past a pair of dangling hinges, looking inside to see the door lying on a rotting carpet, dusted with years of grit. Weeds had taken root, spreading onto the floor, rising tall and spindly beneath the exposed beams of a fallen roof.

The house was in ruin, deserted. But still he pushed forward, entering the main room where wood, shingles, and flooring lay in a massive drift against the parlor wall. And beyond the drift, framed within a water-stained arch, he saw another room whose walls bore the outlines of a stove, sink, and refrigerator. The appliances were gone, and now other things stood in their place: strange constructions—incongruous. They didn't belong in a kitchen.

Are they really there?

He blinked.

Please be real.

He fell to his knees, rubbed his eyes, looked again.

What do you see?

The constructions remained fixed in his vision. One was a collection of books stacked in a case of cinderblocks and boards. The other was a bed of newspapers and cardboard sheeting. No dust on any of it. No weeds. The space looked clean.

Someone lives here.

"Hey! Can you hear me?"

The flying shadow returned, streaking through the open roof, blurring across the floor.

Dalton looked up, squinting at an exposed patch of sky. Something was up there . . . flying . . . circling. Dalton tried standing, but pain pushed him down again, onto his back, flat against the fibers of the rotting carpet.

I'm dying.

He clawed at his throat, staring straight up as the shadow came again . . . only this time it stopped, landed on a cornice, and looked down. Its head twitched between curving wings. Its eyes glowed.

Not real.

Dalton blinked.

I see angels. What do you see?

The thing slipped from the cornice and glided down to a second-floor beam.

It resembled a man . . . a winged man with legs bent in too many places. Dalton couldn't see its face, only its eyes—sloe-shaped, glowing from within. "Are you real?" Dalton asked.

The creature stepped from the beam and dropped onto the fallen roof. It was close now. Too close. But Dalton couldn't move. Couldn't breathe. He could only watch as the creature tensed, arched its wings, and dove.

Officer Sharo Jenkins heard the blast while cruising south past Silver Lake. It had the cadence of rolling thunder, a slow and steady rumble that echoed through the predawn hills. She slowed as smoke rose above the trees. There wasn't anything out there to cause an explosion, just Pennsylvania forest, dirt trails, and the wasted remnants of the Windslow Surface Mine—the abandoned hollow that locals called *the crater*.

She checked the dashboard's digital clock. Her shift was coming to an end, and this was one morning she needed to get home. Jordan was running a fever, and all night she had been thinking about how he had pleaded as she left the house, holding his infected ear with one hand, reaching for her with the other. "Mommy!"

She had almost turned back right then, but her own mother waved her on. "Go, Sharo! Grandma's got him."

Good old Grandma. She'd been a godsend since the divorce. But Grandma worked mornings, and Sharo needed to be off duty in time to take over.

The smoke darkened as Sharo drove toward it, blotting the thin light of a predawn moon.

Please let this be nothing.

She hit her flashers and took the mike from the dash. "Car Two-Eleven. South on Cliff Mine. Looking at a ten-seven-three near the crater."

"Roger, Two-Eleven."

The dispatch operator was Becky Yakulis, a local girl who'd become a Windslow celebrity after winning the Pittsburgh Marathon a few years back. That had been before a jackknifing trailer on I-79 took both her legs and part of her hip. Since then, working dispatch had become Becky's life.

Sharo heard the hum of Becky's chair turning toward the station window. "I see it!" Becky said. "Over Windslow Mine. That's smoke all right!"

A pair of floodlights flashed by on Sharo's left, the beams illuminating the entrance to a resort community that investors were building along the shore of Silver Lake. So far, only a few waterfront homes had been sold, but press releases claimed that the others would be snatched up as soon as construction broke ground on the new casino and entertainment center a mile to the south. The investors had made other promises too, about how casino revenue would improve roads, utilities, community services, and schools. But Sharo had her doubts. She'd been around long enough to see how things worked.

The rich get richer. The poor get screwed.

The fire station's alarm echoed through the hills as the entrance to Lakeside Estates slid from her side mirror. Windslow was a small town. Police, fire, and EMS shared the same frequency. Sharo's report of smoke had alerted the VFD, and now the fire siren was blaring: swelling, falling back, swelling again.

Sharo thought of Jordan, his bedroom less than a block from the fire station. If he'd been sleeping, he was awake now.

Don't cry, baby. Mommy's coming.

She glanced at the clock.

Real soon.

Her rooftop red-and-blues streaked the trees as she sped past Old River Trail. Unlit and unmarked, the gravel road led to the face of Silver Lake's earthen dam, a sloping wall of clay, shale, and riprap that was supposed to have been replaced before ground broke on any of the lakefront properties. So much for promises. A dozen homes and a boathouse had already been built, and more were under construction.

She kept driving, away from the dam, toward the smoke, and into the glare of approaching headlights. It was a pickup truck, accelerating around the uphill lane.

Sharo flashed her beams.

The driver kept coming, highballing well over the limit.

She glanced toward the side window, making eye contact with the driver. Then he was gone, shaking the cruiser in his wake.

Any other night she'd have given chase, but she was almost under the smoke now. It looked thick, full of particulate.

Chemical fire?

Grit fell from the cloud. She snapped on the wipers, smearing the windshield, cutting her speed until the washer fluid did its work.

That's when she saw the broken plastic, bits of shattered taillight strewn across the road. The shards looked fresh, the edges sharp, the pieces spread in a widening wedge across the asphalt.

Looks like someone was just here, raising hell.

She stopped and studied the skid marks. There were multiple sets. One started in the uphill lane, crossing the center as if the driver had slammed his brakes while cutting a U-ie over the double-yellow line. To the left of those skids, the road's shoulder was all torn up, plowed and gouged.

Sharo reversed, cut her wheels, and eased forward until the cruiser's lights shined into the forest, illuminating a coal-hauling trail that ran off toward the rising smoke.

"Two-Eleven. That old coal trail off Cliff Mine, half a mile below the dam. Can you check the big map, tell me if it goes to the crater?"

"Copy that, Two-Eleven. Stand by."

Sharo waited, studying the trail, its surface marked with the fossil tracks of coal trucks. But there were newer marks too. She saw a fresh scar in the dirt where a car had banged its oil pan, bottomed out on hard clay.

She put the details together.

A car leaves Cliff Mine at a high rate of speed, descends the slope, slams the trail, keeps moving. Then a second car follows. But where were they going? And what about the broken taillight?

She checked her sideview, looking again at the bits of plastic. The debris appeared to have come from a vehicle leaving the scene, one that slammed the guardrail while swerving into the downhill lane.

"Car Two-One-One?"

"Go ahead, Becky."

"That trail goes to the crater, all right. But the lower half is chained off. Private property."

"Office of Surface Mining?"

"No. Not no more. You might see OSM signs, but it's been sold to Mountain Downs."

Sharo angled her spotlight along the trail. Something flashed, a patch of glare among the trees.

Becky kept talking. "To reach the mine, your best bet is to take Cliff Mine south to Coals Hollow. Follow Windslow Road to the extension."

"Thanks, but I'm not going to the mine. Not now." Sharo kept moving the light, centering it on the thing at the end of the trail. "I've got something else here, something on the trail." She studied the glare in the beam. "Looks like a flash of chrome about 100 feet in." She took her foot from the brake. "I'm having a look."

"Copy that. You're going to need backup."

A new voice responded, crackling from the radio. "Deuces to Dispatch!" It was Robert Zabek, the only other Windslow officer on duty. His car number was 222—*Deuces* for short. "I'm cross town. Be there in five."

"Copy, Deuces." Then, for the log, Becky gave the time. "6:02."

Sharo eased over the shoulder, gravel popping as she drove. She smelled the smoke now, sweet like burning tar.

Explosion . . . smoke . . . skids . . . debris on Cliff Mine . . . something in the woods. What's the connection?

She had learned to be wary of coincidences.

Connect . . . always connect.

"Two-Eleven. Confirming that glare of chrome. It's a sports car. Convertible." She saw the logo on the trunk, a snake with bared fangs. "Dodge Viper," she said. "Looks like Kirill Vorarov's car."

Kirill Vorarov was a Windslow big shot, a New York Russian who had become one of the prime backers of Lakeside Estates and Mountain Downs. He also owned a strip club out by the highway, a business venture that had not endeared him to the locals.

"Stand by for plates, Becky."

"Copy."

The car's condition became evident as Sharo pulled beside it: shattered windshield, blood-smeared trunk. "Looks like he drove down the trail, smashed into a tree." She turned her spotlight onto the reclining form behind the wheel. "Need EMS."

"EMS," Becky said. "The coal trail off Cliff Mine Run. Milepost Six."

A pause of barely a second, then the voice of EMS dispatch: "Copy, Windslow. Trail off Cliff Mine, Marker Six. ETA, seven."

"Copy. 6:03."

Sharo stopped the cruiser, set the brake. She was focused now, wide awake, her training kicking in as she climbed out, slammed the door, and switched on her portable radio. She keyed her mike, the one she wore clipped to her shoulder. "New York plates." She read the number, the world closing in, shrinking until it held only herself, the car, and the slouching figure behind the wheel. She called to him. "Mr. Vorarov?" The reds and blues of her cruiser's light bar pulsed around her as she rounded the bumper.

The driver wore a dark suit, cut in Vorarov's style, but his build was different, smaller. Sharo saw these details clearly enough as she came up behind the slumped shoulders. And then she saw something else . . . something that made her stop and step back.

The driver stirred, lifted his head, and looked at her.

Sharo gasped.

The head sneered. The teeth were sharp, bloody. Not a man's head. The man's head was gone. The thing looking back at her was a raccoon, standing on the man's lap, gripping his bloody lapels, peering over the stump of his neck.

"Get!" She drew her nightstick, rapped it on the car. "Go on! Scram!" She struck the car again, the forest ringing with the thump of wood on molded polymer.

The raccoon climbed onto the door and looked along the side of the car.

It seemed ready to jump, but then it recoiled, dropped onto the man's lap, went back to feeding on his blood.

And now the details clicked.

This wasn't merely an accident. The car may have struck a tree, but something else had killed the driver, shattered the windshield, smeared his brains across the trunk.

Sharo keyed the mike with her flashlight hand. "Two-Eleven to Dispatch." She drew her sidearm. "Apparent homicide, gunshot to the head." She looked back at the trunk, noting the way the flashlight beam played across the smears. "Recent . . . within the last few hours."

"Copy that, Two-One-One. 6:04."

Sharo turned in place, panning her beam along the trees. *Within the last few hours.* She studied the shadows. "No sign of the shooter."

"Copy that. Where's our backup? Deuces! What's your twenty?"

"Lower half of Old Coal Creek, coming up on Coals Hollow Park. ETA, three minutes."

"Anyone else in the area?"

"Cokesburg Thirty-Nine. Foster Plaza. Be there in seven."

"Copy, Coke Three-Nine. Anyone else?"

"Cokesburg Four-Oh. Bakers Run. ETA, ten."

"Copy, Coke Four-Oh. 6:05."

Something thumped beside Sharo, striking the ground near the front of the Viper. She turned, directing her beam in time to see a ringed tail racing into the forest. The raccoon was scooting away across a patch of flattened ferns. Like the back of the car, the ferns were smeared with blood.

What happened here?

"Dispatch to Two-One-One. Shooter could still be out there, Sharo. You'd best pull back to Cliff Mine. Await backup."

"Copy that." Sharo hurried toward the cruiser, opened the door, pausing again when she heard a sound coming from near the disabled Viper. It shrilled in the stillness, stopped, then shrilled again.

Cell phone!

She panned her light, swinging it low along the ferns, leaning on her open door. And there it was, a silver clamshell lying on a patch of bare ground near the bloody weeds, LCD screen glowing with the light of an incoming call. She noted the location, and then she saw something else, something that for a moment made her forget her training. In that instant, she was no longer a professional, not even a rookie, but a kid . . . a terrified kid staring at something that made her blood run cold.

A fter accelerating past the police cruiser, R.D. Ditwiter continued another mile and a half on Cliff Mine Run, coming at last to the rented house that his friend Vinny Donahue shared with a punk named Jason Herrington. Both Vinny and Jason worked the night shift at the Waynesburg Giant Eagle, stocking shelves, cleaning floors, and goofing off as much as possible.

Since R.D. worked a similar shift at the Windslow Mini Mart, he generally dropped by Vinny's for a beer before heading home. But this morning was going to be more than a one-beer drive-by. Today was Jason's anti-bachelor party, a bar-hopping road trip that Vinny had mapped out using the Internet. The purpose of the event was to get Jason's mind off his former fiancée, who had recently taken off with an interstate trucker.

Vinny's one-story house sat on a cutaway hillside, atop a steep gravel drive. R.D. liked the way his truck swerved when it hit the stones, fishtailing almost out of control before digging in and gaining traction.

Two cars sat parked by the back door. R.D. pulled behind them, got out, and crossed to the patio where Vinny and Jason sat drinking Iron City from aluminum bottles.

Jason's brother Benjie was there, too, but he was off by himself, a dozen feet from the patio, standing in a patch of weeds, hands in his pockets, looking at the ground. He wasn't drinking. There were two reasons for that. The first being that he was back on his meds. The second was because he had been drafted to serve as designated driver.

Vinny wore flip-flops, cutoffs, and a faded sports jersey. But he didn't look like a slob. He never did. And R.D., who always felt like a doofus no matter what he wore, envied him for that.

Jason was another matter. He wore sneakers, jeans, and an untucked flannel shirt that was supposed to hide his beer gut. Not that it improved his looks any. With the shirt tucked in, Jason would have just looked fat. With it out, he looked like a fat slob.

They sat in beach chairs, leaning back, legs stretching over the patio's cracked concrete. An old Panasonic TV sat on a stand beyond their feet. It was playing a DVD, some porn thing that they'd probably picked up at the Strip Mine Gentlemen's Club, but at the moment neither seemed to be paying it much attention.

Vinny turned as R.D. reached the patio. "Hey! My man! R.D. Ditwiter!" Vinny raised his fist, punching the air. "How's it hanging, Road?"

Road was one of R.D.'s nicknames, one of the good ones. Among the not-so-good were *Ditwit* and *Didiot*, but Vinny never called him either of those.

Jason slapped a cooler beside his chair. "Help yourself, *Ditwit*."

R.D. fished a cold one from under the ice. The aluminum chilled his hand as he looked toward the slope. "What's your brother doing in the weeds, Jason?"

"Ask him."

R.D. twisted the cap from his beer and tossed it toward Benjie. "Hey, Benjie! What's in the weeds?"

Benjie turned, squinting in the patio light. He didn't look at R.D., just in his general direction. "Not sure." Then he turned back around.

All things considered, Benjie wasn't a bad-looking kid. Unlike his older brother, he was lean and well proportioned, with clear skin and an angular face that in some light gave him a passing resemblance to Justin Timberlake. But the resemblance didn't reach his eyes, which always turned away when a person tried meeting them straight on.

"I mean," Benjie said, "there *was* something. It's gone now."

"He's not supposed to get like this," Jason said. "The pills are supposed to stop it."

"It isn't that!" Benjie spoke without looking back. "And don't be talking like I can't hear!"

"Sometimes he sees stuff," Jason said. "Hears stuff, too. It's like flash-backs without the backs."

"Don't talk about me!"

"What?" Jason called. "I didn't say anything."

R.D. took a drink, turned to Vinny. "Hey, man. Know what I just saw out on Cliff Mine Run?"

"Michael Jackson?" Jason said.

"I'm serious."

"Elvis?"

"I'm asking Vinny."

"So I'm answering for him." Jason opened a fresh beer. "What are friends for? Right, Vinny?"

"Let R.D. talk," Vinny said. "What'd you see, R.D.?"

"A freaking avalanche."

"Yeah, right!" Jason said.

"I saw it through the trees while I was driving."

Jason snorted.

"It was out at the old mine. The whole crater caved in."

"A crater can't *cave in*," Jason said. "It's, like, *already* caved in. That's what makes it a crater, *Ditwit*."

"I mean the high part caved in. You know, the wall around the crater? It roared like a freaking bastard."

"Told you!" Benjie said, standing up again, looking toward the patio. "I *told* you I felt an earthquake."

"Yeah, right," Jason said. "And then you saw a dinosaur in the weeds."

"I didn't say it was a dinosaur."

Jason took another drink, swallowed hard, belched loudly. It wasn't hard to see why a girl would leave him for a trucker.

"An avalanche at Windslow Mine?" Vinny said.

"God's truth. And I wasn't the only one who saw it. There was this other guy, a guy in a Jeep. He was parked sideways across the road, watching it."

"Just sitting there?" Jason asked.

"God's truth! I almost ran into him. Had to lay on my horn to make him move. And then there was a lady cop. I passed her another mile up the road. She was driving slow, watching the smoke."

"Smoke?" Jason said. "What smoke?"

"From the explosion!" R.D. turned back toward Vinny. He was easier to talk to than Jason. "That's what started the avalanche. First there was this explosion, then—"

"I've heard enough." Jason slapped the top of the cooler. "Sit down, *Didiot*. You're here to help me party, to get my mind off serious shit. Know what I'm saying?"

R.D. sat. "Anyway." He looked at Vinny. "It was an avalanche."

Benjie joined them, hunkering down beside the television, still looking toward the weeds.

"Vinny's got the itinerary all planned," Jason said. "He's the man. My man with the plan. My main homie!"

"I figured you could use some serious entertainment," Vinny said.

"Got that right. *Serious* entertainment. Totally *serious*!" Jason turned to R.D. "We're going to start at that strip club in Windslow."

"The Strip Mine?"

"Yeah. Some of the guys from the wedding party—the *ex*-wedding party—are meeting us for Amateur Lunch. You know what that is? Amateur Lunch?"

R.D. gave the kind of shrug that said he knew but wasn't impressed.

Amateur Lunch at the Strip Mine was supposed to feature local girls auditioning their pole and lap routines. R.D. had checked it out once, and he was pretty sure the girls were a long way from local. In fact, he was willing to bet they were Russian.

"That's where we'll start," Jason said. "At the Strip Mine! Then we'll head south. Vinny found this place in Morgantown. Tell him, Vinny."

"I got us some escorts."

"Hookers?"

"Better than hookers." Vinny leaned forward. "What would you say if I told you—"

"Another one!" Benjie stood up, bumping the television, nearly knocking it from the stand.

Jason grabbed the set. "Watch it, retard!"

Benjie leaped from the patio, pointing. "There it is! Coming this way!"

R.D. stood up.

A shadow curved out of the weeds, flowing like a tar-seam onto the grass, picking up speed as it pulled clear of the undergrowth.

"Snake," Benjie said. "A black racer. Big one!"

Jason stepped back from the set. "What's it doing?"

"Coming this way," R.D. said.

"No." Benjie stayed where he was, watching the snake. "They don't bother people. They keep to themselves." His voice was flat, matter-of-fact. "He'll turn around before he gets here."

"Yeah, right!" Jason said. "Don't look like he's turning."

"Black racer?" Vinny stepped up beside Jason. "They poisonous?"

"No," Benjie said. "They're, like, friendly snakes. They eat rats and mice. They—"

The snake was moving faster now.

"Definitely coming this way," Vinny said.

It weaved across the lawn.

"Not stopping."

"Big son of a bitch."

The snake veered right as it reached the patio, crawling parallel to it, heading toward the house. R.D. could hear it now, a smooth *sssshhhhh!* gliding through the grass.

Benjie followed it, stopping as the racer raised its head, flicked its tongue, and slithered up onto the patio.

"Benjie!" Jason said. "Get away from it, man."

"It's OK. He's just looking around. He'll—"

The snake picked up speed again, heading toward the kitchen door.

"Stop it!" Vinny said. "Get it!"

The storm door had a hole in it, a little flap where the screen pulled free of the frame. The snake reared up, turned toward the opening, and pushed its head inside. The rest of its body followed, picking up speed as it spilled along the kitchen floor.

R.D. lunged. He wasn't thinking. He just knew he was the closest, the only one in a position to do something. His fingers closed on the tail. "Got it!" He pulled, surprised at the feel of the thing, the dryness of the scales, the ropy tension in the muscles as the tail flexed against his grip.

Benjie came up beside him. "Don't hurt it."

R.D. pulled, tearing the screen as he yanked the snake out through the widening hole.

"The door, *Ditwit*! Don't tear the freaking—"

The snake flexed back on itself, shooting toward them.

Jason leaped back. Too late. The snake grabbed his hand, clamped hard. "Goddamnit!" He bumped the TV. "Get it!" He spun around. "Get it off!" The set slipped from the stand.

WHOMPF!

The tube shattered, spewing glass, and all the while Benjie kept shouting. "Not poisonous! Friendly!"

R.D. leaped toward Jason, grabbed the snake's head, yanked hard.

The snake let go of Jason's hand.

Jason fell backward, landing on his ass.

"It's friendly! Don't hurt it!"

Vinny grabbed the snake from R.D., held it by the tail, and swung its head against the concrete.

Crack!

"But they're friendly!"

Crack . . . crack . . . CRACK!

"Friendly snakes!"

"Goddamn retard!" Jason waved a bloody hand. "You say that one more time and I'll freaking nail you. I mean it!"

"But they are!"

Vinny stopped swinging the snake. Its head hung limp. "I think it's dead." He dropped it.

"Make sure," Jason said.

Vinny stepped on the head, trying to crush it with the heel of his flip-flop. The body twitched.

"Not dead," Jason said.

Vinny bore down harder. The body rose, twisting in the air, falling back down again to slither in place through the broken glass until the head popped like a nut.

Benjie moaned, biting his lip.

"Don't!" Jason roared. "Don't fucking say it, Benjie!"

Benjie covered his mouth.

Jason turned toward R.D. "And you, *Ditwit*!" He balled his bloody fist. "You goddamn son of a bitch!"

R.D. figured it was just bluster. Jason was always threatening to punch people out. But this time the hand shot forward, cracking R.D. on the jaw.

The world spun. R.D. fell, banging the fallen TV.

"Enough!" Vinny grabbed Jason, pulling him back, sitting him down beside the cooler. "Let me see that snake bite."

"Fuck it!" Jason raised the cooler's lid and shoved his bleeding hand into the ice.

R.D.'s jaw felt wet. He touched it. His fingers came away red. "I'm bleeding!"

"That's *my* blood!" Jason raised his hand. There were two deep gashes along the back. "That snake had his teeth in me, and you fucking pulled him!"

"Was just trying to help!"

The cuts kept bleeding, forcing Jason to push the hand back into the ice.

"I can take you to emergency," Vinny said.

"Screw that! If Benjie says they're not poisonous—"

"They're not!"

"That's good enough for me," Jason said. "He doesn't know shit about shit, but he knows animals."

"They're friendly snakes."

"Besides," Jason said. "I'm not going to the hospital, not this morning. We've got plans!"

"All right," Vinny said. "Keep it in the ice. The bleeding'll stop. Then we'll wrap it up. We still got bandages, right?"

"The hell if I know."

"I'll look." Vinny stood up. "How about you, R.D.? How's that jaw?"

"Bleeding."

"That's my blood, *Ditwit*!"

Vinny stepped closer. "Let me see." He turned R.D.'s face into the light. "Just smeared, is all. How's it feel?"

R.D. shrugged. "All right, I guess."

"So you two are cool?" Vinny looked at them both.

Neither spoke.

"I need to hear it," he said. "I don't want to go into the house looking for bandages and then come back and find we need an ambulance."

Jason moved his hand, sloshing it through the ice before bringing it out. "Yeah." He offered it to R.D. "I'm cool if you are."

R.D. shook his hand. It felt like raw meat.

"That snake just freaked me out is all." Jason put his hand back in the ice and looked over at Benjie. "What the hell you think it was doing, Benjie? What'd make a snake act like that?"

Benjie didn't answer. He just stood on the edge of the patio, staring into space.

"What's he looking at?" Vinny asked.

Everyone turned, following the direction of Benjie's stare.

To the southeast, visible against the spreading dawn, a column of smoke rose into the twilight sky.

3

Kirill Vorarov stood alone in his office. In his hand was a Soviet-era machine pistol fitted with a detachable shoulder stock and silencer. The room reeked of spent propellant. But as he looked at the bullet-riddled mass on the far side of the room, he knew that discharging the gun had been worth it.

After seeing his dreams turn to crap in a single night, he'd had every right to blast the room's centerpiece, the plaster rendering of the Mountain Downs Project. And so he'd blasted it. Twice. Once with an old magazine of vintage ammunition that he had been saving to sell to a gun collector. Then again with twenty rounds of new stuff. Forty rounds in all.

He set the gun on the desk beside his open bottles of aspirin and vodka—the combination of which had yet to touch the pain in his head and shoulders—and crossed to a window in the back of the room.

One of only two in the entire building, the window overlooked a strip of narrow pavement where he had parked a Jeep Wrangler after driving it back from the clearing above Windslow Mine. The Jeep now sat beside his car, a Dodge Viper, just like the one he had left at the end of an old haul road off Cliff Mine Run.

"Messy business."

He studied the cars: the Viper a sleek shadow in the dimness, the Jeep a dented mess with a shattered windshield and broken taillight. The left rear tire looked like it was going flat.

"Fucking mess."

Fortunately, the Wrangler wasn't his.

Unfortunately, it belonged to Sam Calder.

She'd be angry when she saw the damage. That was why he'd parked it out back, to keep her from seeing it right away when she came to meet him. He needed to talk to her first, let her know how everything had gone wrong, how he'd been lucky to get out of the woods alive. Once he established those things, he would show her the Jeep. Then he'd pay her for services rendered, promise to cover the repairs, and send her back to her cabin in the West Virginia hills. And then. . . .

Then what?

He stared out at the near-vertical face of the sheared-off hill behind his office. Layers of stratified rock shimmered in the light from the window: sandstone, shale, siltstone, fireclay—and pressed among them, so dark that they might have been gaps between the layers, coal veins ran in horizontal lines, swallowing his shadow as it moved across them.

He grabbed the window sill, feeling momentarily dizzy—a side-effect of the heavy dose of vodka and aspirin. The stuff always made him a little punchy, but there was nothing like it for a sprained neck. If that was all he had.

Behind him, his office phone started ringing.

He looked around. His neck popped. Then, for a moment, through the haze of gesso dust and gun propellant, he saw himself sitting at his desk, leaning forward to answer the phone.

He blinked.

The image lingered, the ghost of himself from eight hours earlier. The ghost's suit was clean. No rips. No stains. No dirt from the mine.

It's not really there.

He blinked again.

The ghost vanished.

The phone kept ringing.

I'm losing my mind.

He considered answering the phone. What if it was Sam? But calling wasn't Sam's style. She was too much of a loner for that: cold, calculating, self-reliant. She wouldn't telephone. The call had to be from someone else. Uncle Ilya? Arnold Gusky? The gaming commission in Harrisburg? Probably not. Such calls were certain to come, but not until after the Mountain Downs attorney failed to show up for the hearing in Harrisburg. Calls would pour in like crazy then. But not now. Not yet.

The phone stopped ringing.

Kirill checked the number, saw that it belonged to Janice Peterson, and realized that things were already closing in. Janice had probably tried calling Peterson's cell phone. Now, growing concerned, she was widening her net. Maybe the best thing was to call her back, tell her lies, keep her from calling the police. But doing that would complicate things later. For now, silence was the best bet.

He walked away from the desk, moving stiffly as he returned the gun to its mount inside the case in the corner of his office. The pistol would need to be cleaned, but that could wait until he returned. Right now he needed to go into hiding and contact Uncle Ilya. The old man would not be happy that their attorney was sitting dead in a Viper above Windslow Mine, but a nephew in trouble trumped concerns about a dead *mudak*. Ilya could be counted on to do the right thing, but only if Kirill stayed clear of the law.

The gun case held a dozen of his favorite pistols. He'd need to take one with him, something concealable but with enough force to keep him safe. He settled on the Smith & Wesson 640-1, a five-shot revolver with an enclosed hammer. He took it from its mount. It felt smooth and natural in his hand. Loaded with 110-grain rounds, the mini-magnum would provide good stopping power without the recoil of the standard 158-grain bullets. He loaded four of the chambers, rolled the empty one into line with the barrel, and slipped the gun into a Galco protector. Then he fastened the protector to his waistband, securing it against the small of his back.

An envelope in his desk drawer held Sam's payment. He stuffed it into his pocket and headed toward the door beyond the bullet-riddled model of Mountain Downs.

He saw the mess that the Stetchkin's 9mm rounds had made of the paneled wall. Some of the shots had gone clear through, possibly into the adjacent room, maybe even through the outer wall and into the face of the cutaway hill beyond. No matter. There'd been no danger of anyone getting hurt. The place was empty. At least, it should have been.

But it wasn't.

Kirill heard movement downstairs as he left his office. Someone was walking through the club, heading toward the bar. A moment later, he heard voices, two people talking, maybe more. He stepped onto the mezzanine that overhung the main room. The voices sounded official. One person asking questions. Another answering.

Taking the revolver from his waistband and moving it to the pocket of his jacket, Kirill started toward the stairs.

4

Sharo Jenkins leaned against her cruiser's open door and stared as a twisting mass came spilling into the clearing. It was snakes, dozens of them racing through the weeds, bodies undulating in the predawn light.

"Coke Three-Nine!" Becky's voice crackled from Sharo's radio. "What's your twenty, Three-Nine?"

The voice brought Sharo back to the moment.

"Windslow Mini Mart. ETA, five minutes."

"Copy, Coke Three-Nine. 6:06."

Help was on its way.

Sharo leaped into the car, slammed the door, shivered.

Snakes?

She closed her eyes, composing herself. She'd been bitten as a child, still had the scar on her leg. After all these years, the fear remained fresh. "Get it together, for chrisake!"

A siren wailed in the distance. Probably Zabek, almost here.

She settled back, reached for her shoulder harness, and then froze when she felt something moving on the floor between her boots.

She held her breath.

A triangular head rose between her knees, turned, and slid onto the armrest. Its tongue flicked, tasting the air. Then it turned again, setting its neck against her arm, coming toward her face.

"Two-One-One?" Becky's voice remained calm, professional. And why not? She was safe in the station, no sense of what was happening here. "What's your twenty, Two-One-One. Have you pulled back to Cliff Mine?"

Sharo dared not answer. The snake was now less than a foot from her face, back propped against the steering wheel, striking a pose like the emblem on the Dodge Viper. But there was nothing emblematic about this snake: lidless eyes, darting tongue, dark pits on the end of its snout. She knew about those pits. She had read about them as a child, back in the days when she had hoped that filling her head with facts might dispel her fears. Those indentations were like a second set of eyes, but they didn't see light. Instead, they sensed heat. That's how they found prey in the dark, by following beacons of heat.

Sharo stared at those dark holes. What must she look like to the snake? A spotlight in the darkened car? A neon sign?

She felt her temperature rising.

It sees my fear.

"Two-One-One?"

The snake studied her a moment longer, then turned, curving around the steering wheel to set its head on the dash. It was crawling away now, pulling itself from the floor, rising between her knees. How big was it? Three foot? Four? Its body kept coming, uncoiling from beneath the seat.

She drew her Glock. No safety. Racked and ready. She'd never shot a snake before, and she had no idea what might happen if she tried such a thing in the close confines of her cruiser.

Headshot. Got to be a headshot. Shoot it when it's against the glass.

She gripped the gun, watching the snake. Tiny head. Tough target.

Her hand trembled.

"Come in, Two-One-One. You copy?"

The snake stopped climbing, turned, looked back at her. Its head was against the dashboard now, barely visible in the dimness. It seemed to be reacting to the sound of the radio. Not that it could hear, of course. Sharo knew about that too. Snakes couldn't hear, but they sensed vibrations, and some frequencies could really set them off.

"Two-One-One?"

Sharo moved slowly, careful not to close her knees on the snake's body. She took the handset from the dash. Then she sat back and keyed the mike, realizing instantly that she'd forgotten to switch off her personal radio. It was a basic error, the sort of thing that a rookie might pull. But Sharo wasn't a rookie. She knew what happened when a car mike went live in the presence of an activated personal receiver.

Feedback!

She froze, gripping the mike, holding the button even as the electronic squeal filled the cab.

The snake reacted, head blurring, rushing toward her.

She dropped the mike.

The snake struck, piercing her shirt a few inches below the shoulder. Then it recoiled, leaning against the dash, watching.

"Two-One-One!" Becky's voice rose in pitch. "Come in! Sharo!"

Sharo couldn't answer without turning off her personal radio.

The snake kept watching, waiting for its venom to kick in.

"Two-One-One!"

Sharo's pulse raced. But it wasn't from the venom, which was now dispersing through the fabric of her shirt and the underlying layer of nylon that covered her body armor. The snake had bitten Kevlar.

"Two-One-One! Come in, Sharo!"

Something else shifted behind her. A second snake. It brushed her neck, the dry rasp of scales on skin. And now she lost control, recoiling, bringing her knees together. In that instant, everything blurred. The snakes shot toward her: one from the dash, the other from behind.

She screamed. The first snake struck her cheek. The other clamped her shoulder.

"Two-One-One! Reply if you copy."

The first snake held on, pulsing against her cheek, forcing her to grab it just behind the jaws. She wrenched it free. Her cheek spasmed.

"Deuces!" Becky said. "What's your twenty?"

"Cliff Mine Run. Milepost five. Almost there."

The snake struggled in Sharo's hand, mouth open, fangs extended as she slammed it against the side window. She couldn't shoot it in the head now, not with its jaws inches from her clenched fist. And she couldn't let it go.

"Copy, Deuces. Any sign of Sharo?"

"Negative."

"Copy that. 6:09."

Sharo jammed her gun against the snake's body, squeezed the trigger. The barrel flashed, illuminating a Rorschach of blood and glass as the report filled the cab. The sound slammed her ears like a hammer. After that, she heard nothing, only the muffled ring of temporary deafness as the snake recoiled, headless body whipping between her legs while its not-yet-dead eyes leered from her clenched fist. Its jaws gaped. She dared not let go. Detached from its body, the head could still bite her. So she held on. And all the while the second snake gripped her shoulder. She felt the fangs wiggling inside her, but the real pain—the agony of spreading venom—was still to come. That was the thing with a snake bite. The real pain took its time.

She shoved the snake's head down against the seat next to her, pushing it back to where the cushions came together, wedging it in deep before letting go. Then she pressed her gun against its head and fired again.

The muzzle flashed.

She felt the concussion. Heard nothing.

She reached for the second snake, but it had already let go. She felt it crawling behind her, slipping between door and seat as Zabek's lights dawned through the trees. He was on the edge of the trail. She couldn't wait, couldn't stay in the car. She threw herself against the door, grabbed the handle, tumbled out and keyed her mike. "This is Two-Eleven," she said, or tried to. Pain was spreading through her face, radiating from the bite on her cheek, filling her mouth. "I've been snake bit. Bit bad!" She gripped the side of the cruiser, the emergency lights strobing in her eyes as the pain in her shoulder spread to her chest. Her arm cramped. And now . . . on the edge of the forest . . . out where her light bar rained blue and red against the trees, something new was approaching. She tried bringing it into focus, watching it advance, realizing what it was as it stepped into the glare of Zabek's approaching lights.

I'm hallucinating.

She closed her eyes, opened them again.

The thing was still there.

It looked like a snake. But it wasn't. It didn't slither on the ground. It carried itself like a man. Arms swinging free. Legs striding. It was covered with scales . . . and it was running . . . racing out of the trees . . . coming right at her.

5

Paxton Scanlon liked mornings best.

He seldom slept nights, preferring to spend his time playing with Pacific Rim gamers, cyber opponents who apparently enjoyed kicking his butt at *World of Warcraft*, *Ridge Racer V*, and *Burnout*. But he was getting better, especially at *Burnout*.

On a good night, he gamed full-throttle from 1:00 a.m. until just before dawn, usually reentering the offline world when he felt the rumble of the garage door beneath his feet, the sound of his stepfather leaving for work.

By then Pax was wired, sweaty, and ripe with the smell of play. He removed his earbuds and opened the window beside his desk to retrieve the T-shirt, cutoffs, and beach towel that he always hung out there to dry. The practice had created a trail of wet slime that ran all the way down the side of the house. His parents would be pissed if they saw it, not that there was much chance of that. They never spent much time on the grounds around the home. His early-rising stepfather had his investments in town to keep him busy. And his mother, who usually slept until noon, had more than enough gin and lemons to keep her busy through the summer. They seldom bothered with him. Sometimes he liked that. Other times he wished they'd chew him out for something. If nothing else, it would prove that he really existed, that he wasn't just a ghost who left ectoplasmic skids on the north wall of the house.

After changing into his T-shirt and cutoffs, Pax grabbed his gear from the pile of stuff beside his desk and placed it on the bed. The snorkel, still holding a few ounces of lake water, dribbled over the blanket. The mask, flippers, and water-proof flashlight were dry. He placed everything but the flashlight in the center of his beach towel and gathered the ends together to form an improvised sack. Then he slung the sack over his shoulder and started down the hall.

He paused beside the master bedroom, glancing in to see his mother asleep on her back, mouth open, foot poking from the sheet that covered her like a tarp. He hit her with his flashlight beam, checking to see if she was alive enough to roll over and ask what he was doing.

She just lay there.

He turned off the flashlight and continued on.

In the kitchen, he took three granola bars from the snack drawer, a water bottle from the fridge, and a can of vegetable spray from the cabinet above the sink. He added these to his beach-towel sack and went out through the side door.

The house was one of the older ones, occupying a lot on the lake's west shore. It was also one of the few occupied homes in what the brochures touted as a "vibrant lakeside community." At the moment, that community, curving away to Pax's right as he stepped down onto the cobbled walk, looked about as vibrant as a cemetery.

He walked to the front of the house and shined his flashlight over the lattice skirt that ran along the base of the porch. One section stood at a slight angle from the others. He pulled it free, setting it on the ground and looking in at a flat oblong container that lay beneath the steps. It was made of plastic, open at the narrow ends, stenciled with a red warning:

DO NOT TOUCH

Despite the warning, the container had a plastic handle that made it look like a briefcase. He grabbed the handle, pulled the container toward him, and peered in through one of the open ends.

The thing inside stared back at him.

"You're mine now," Pax said.

The thing didn't answer.

Pax set the case on the ground and replaced the lattice. Then he picked up everything and headed across the development to a large oak growing 50 feet from the shore. Here he sat down and ate one of the granola bars.

The air smelled strange, like burning oil and rubber. To the east, past the earthen dam that sealed the southern edge of the man-made lake, a band of fog hovered between him and the first bluing of the dawn. Or was it smoke? He studied it, realizing it was rising from the future site of the Mountain Downs Casino. His stepfather was involved in that project through one of his subsidiary companies, which was how Mr. Arnold Gusky, C.F.A., liked getting involved in everything.

Pax took a deep breath, mouth open, tasting the air's burny sweetness. Something was definitely on fire down at the crater. Not that it mattered to Pax. Where he was going, fire couldn't touch him.

He pulled on his flippers, strapped the mask to his face, picked up his flashlight, and frog walked between a pair of unsold houses until he reached the water's edge.

The lake was much higher than it had been earlier in the month, bloated by the unregulated release of waters from an upstream dam. Pax had heard his stepfather going on about the benefits of the added water, talking about it on his Bluetooth headset, which seemed to be the only way Arnold Gusky ever talked to anyone. That Bluetooth could be unnerving. Sometimes Pax would think Gusky was asking him a question, but when Pax tried answering, Gusky would get this pissy look and turn away, cup his ear, and talk louder.

According to one of those cupped-ear conversations, Stepdad Gusky had arranged for the upstream release of extra water to improve the look of Lakeside Estates. More water in the lake would make for better pictures when the ad agency photographer returned to take some new shots. The previous photo session had occurred after a band of storms had raised the water higher than usual. But Gusky didn't like the way the lake looked in those shots. "It needs to be higher!" he said, pacing, cupping his ear. "The lake needs to look big. Bigger is better. Size matters! Know what I'm saying?"

So now the lake was even higher than it had been after the storms, a detail that, if widely known, would have aroused concerns among the people in Windslow, particularly those who lived along Bottom's Creek, where periodic flooding had already closed a string of under-insured businesses.

The last Pax had heard, Gusky was negotiating to purchase much of that flood-damaged property at a fraction of its price, all in anticipation of it rising in value once the casino project went through. That way everyone would have a place to live: expensive lakeside housing for investors and players, affordable floodplain apartments for casino employees. As Mr. Gusky liked to say: "Everybody wins! Know what I'm saying?"

Pax thought about these things as he stepped into the lake, bracing as the bottom fell away and the cold waters swallowed him. He gulped a lungful of air and dove, swimming down along a series of bench cuts, scars from the days when Silver Lake had been a limestone quarry.

He snapped on his flashlight. The beam danced across the jagged slope as he continued his descent. The weight of the water built up quickly. He pinched his nose, normalizing the pressure in his ears as an old culvert came into view below him, extending from the sloping base of the earthen dam. The culvert was no longer used to control water level. Instead, a spillway had been cut in a rock wall along the east shore, a temporary measure that the developers claimed would serve until the dam's as-yet unscheduled renovation began.

Paxton swam along the culvert, feeling the pressure build still more as he neared the deepest portion of the lake. He liked the feel of all that water encircling him, embracing him, bearing down on him. Sometimes, lying beside the culvert, he wondered what would happen if he breathed out all his air and filled himself with water. He had heard that drowning was a good way to die. He only lacked the courage to try it.

Maybe this time.

He rolled onto his back and shined his beam up through the dark waters. He breathed out. Not a lot. Just enough to send a few bubbles upward through the beam. They expanded as they rose, spreading out as the pressure decreased, bursting as they reached the surface.

His lungs ached.

He released another string of bubbles, watching them as his diaphragm clenched with the reflexive urge to breathe.

Do it!

He watched the bubbles.

Do it now! Right now!

The thought didn't seem to come from inside. It surrounded him, as dark and primal as the weight of the lake on his empty chest.

Breathe in! Do it now!

Forty feet above him, his last breath broke the surface, vanishing into the light of a smoky dawn. He thought about the rising sun and how it would look through that bank of low-lying smoke. He thought about the large black container emblazoned with the words: DO NOT TOUCH. And slowly, as he thought about these things, he started to swim—kicking upward through diminishing pressure while his lungs screamed for him to breathe.

And he would breathe . . . soon . . . as soon as he reached the surface. This morning was no time to die. Out on the shore, on the ground beneath a spreading oak, there was work to do.

6

Keeping his hand on the gun in his pocket, Kirill paused beside the mezzanine rail and looked down at a splash of early morning sunlight spreading across the tables and chairs of the main barroom. He felt disoriented, partly from the combined effects of pain and vodka, but also because there were no windows down there, only a front door, back door, and some emergency exits, none of which were positioned by the bar. Yet that was where the light was coming from.

And there were voices, too. Kirill listened to them as he started down the stairs, realizing as he cleared the edge of the mezzanine that both voices and light were coming from the same place. It made sense now. He took the gun from his pocket, returned it to his waistband, and continued down to the main level.

Pavel Danilov, the day manager, was sitting at the bar, eating a Sausage McMuffin and watching one of the four 60-inch plasma televisions that Arnold Gusky had purchased for the club. Gusky had insisted the TVs would be good for displaying close-ups of the dancers, a suggestion that at first hadn't made sense to Kirill. Why would guys look at a screen when they could see the real thing right across the room? It wasn't as if the club was ever so crowded that a guy couldn't get a decent view of the stage. But Gusky had been right. The past few weeks had seen more men sitting at the bar, watching plasma while live girls danced behind them.

But the girls weren't dancing now, and the woman on the 60-inch screen was fully clothed and standing before a map of Pennsylvania.

The manager turned, chewing as he looked at Kirill.

"You just get here, Danny?" Kirill said, calling the manager by his preferred name.

Somewhere between Brighton Beach and Windslow, Pavel Danilov had become Danny Love. Kirill thought it was a ridiculous name, but there was no reasoning with young people.

Danny swallowed. "Yeah. Got here just now."

Kirill wondered if Danny had been on the scene long enough to hear the muffled gunshots coming from the second-floor office. "Isn't it early for you to be here?"

"Yeah," Danny said. "What about you? Been here all night?"

"Yeah."

Danny glanced toward the mezzanine. "Is Bird still here?"

"No."

"Peterson?"

"No. Neither made it." That sounded ominous, but Kirill let it go. The kid was staring at him now. "Something wrong?" Kirill said.

"What's on your face?"

"What?"

"That gash."

Kirill touched his temple. There was something there, a scabby ridge that extended from temple to jaw. He had no idea how it had gotten there.

"Looks like it hurts." Danny lowered his gaze, frowning at Kirill's clothes. "What's that dust?"

Kirill's sleeves were covered with gesso from the blasted model in his office. "It's plaster, Danny."

"From what?"

"Never mind." Kirill looked at the television. "What's going on?"

"Weather." Danny took another bite of sandwich, talking as he chewed. "Weather report."

"Since when do you care about weather?"

"I don't. But something's going on. I thought maybe they'd be talking about it. But it's just weather and sports."

"That's why you came in early, to watch TV?"

Danny shrugged. "And the Amateur Lunch. That's always work, especially with that new girl, Duscha. She's a pain in the—"

"Duscha?"

"The one with the really bad teeth."

"What's her American name?"

"Sally Wilson."

Kirill nodded. "Sally with the teeth." He looked at the television. "Tell her to smile with her mouth closed. Maybe it'll look seductive."

Danny chewed. "Maybe."

The weather ended. A commercial came on. So far, it seemed like a slow day for news. Kirill figured he still had time to get out of town. "Listen, Danny." He dug in his pocket, pulling out the keys to the Jeep and the envelope of cash. "Sam's coming by. Give her these, OK?" He set the keys on the bar. "Tell her the Jeep's out back. Tell her I'll be in touch." He set the envelope beside the keys. "Tell her I'll take care of everything."

"Everything?"

"Her Jeep's a little roughed up. Tell her I'll cover it." Kirill wanted to leave, but he held back, trying to get his bearings beneath the weight of all that had gone wrong in the past eight hours. It had all been one mistake after another, and having Danny see him like this might complicate things.

"Something else?" Danny asked.

"Yeah, listen." He tried sounding nonchalant, just two guys talking, just business. "If anyone asks, you haven't seen me. OK?"

"Including Sam?"

"No. You're giving her this stuff. She'll know you've seen me. But if it's anyone else, I haven't been here. As far as you know, I'm in Harrisburg with—" He reconsidered. "I'm in Harrisburg *waiting* to meet with Paul Peterson. All right?"

"That true?"

"True enough." He glanced at the television. The commercial ended. Sports came on.

"Crazy, isn't it?" Danny said. "I heard this explosion. Rattled my windows. Woke me up. When I looked outside I saw smoke over the mine. But there's nothing on the news."

"Maybe it was nothing," Kirill said. "But even if it was, this is Windslow, Danny. Nobody cares what happens in Windslow."

"But that's going to change, right? You're going to change it."

Kirill felt a pain in his gut. What the hell was the kid talking about?

"With Mountain Downs." Danny said. "Once the casino opens, everyone will—"

Kirill's cell phone rang.

Danny crumpled his muffin wrapper. "You need to take that call?" He talked as he chewed.

Kirill checked the number. It was Arnold Gusky. Everyone was up early.

"I can go in the back," Danny said. "Let you talk in private."

"No. It's OK." Kirill turned off the phone. "It's nothing." He walked away from the bar. "Remember what I said. Tell Sam I'll be in touch. Anyone else, you haven't seen me."

"Got it."

Kirill pushed out through the front door and into the first light of dawn.

Smoke rose to the north. He pondered the size of the cloud. So much smoke. It looked as if the entire crater were burning.

Until the dust settled, Kirill needed to vanish.

7

She awoke on a bed of rock, lying on her back, staring at a twilight sky. *Which twilight? Morning or evening?*

The sky looked strange. The familiar stars were there, as was the deep blue-black hue of early dusk or dawn. But there were other things: drifting smoke, swirling sparks, flickering light.

She tried getting up. Her back protested. She rolled, lying on her side now, looking low across a barren landscape: rocks, scree, sandy clay. She knew the place.

Windslow Surface Mine. I'm lying in the crater.

She pushed against the ground, noticing the condition of her hands as she eased into a sitting position. One hand bled from the wrist and knuckles, the other had been gashed deep across the palm. The gash was dark, crusty, swollen. She had been using that hand to claw at the crater's wall, trying to grab hold as the rock face gave way.

After that, she remembered falling.

How did I survive?

She hugged her knees, looked down at the dust on her khakis. She was dressed for sniper duty: camouflage, utility belt, combat boots—all the things she had been wearing when she had first come to the mine. Kirill Vorarov had been with her then, but he was gone now. The last time she had seen him had been in a clearing a quarter mile back from the top of the crater. If he had kept to the plan, he was now a few miles south, safe in his office above the strip club, awaiting her arrival. She wondered how it would go when she got there, when she gave him the good news (the people who had killed Peterson were all dead) and the bad news (Peterson's body was still in the woods).

But she was alive. How had that happened? The last thing she remembered was losing consciousness amid the falling rock. And she remembered screaming. And praying.

"No, God. Please!"

But the prayer hadn't saved her. It couldn't have. God had no place in her world. Religion was her mother's fantasy, and her mother had been insane: a seer of visions, hearer of voices.

I'm not like that. I'm nothing like her.

Now, at last, she mustered the courage for a look back at the rockslide behind her. Her back twinged as she turned, but the pain was all in the soft tissue. Nothing broken. Her frame moved as it should.

Luck . . . conditioning . . . not a miracle.

Heaps of rock lay behind her, a serrated slope in place of a vertical wall. And beside that mass, rising from beyond a line of boulders, was something straight out of the Book of Exodus: a crackling pillar of flame.

Her mother's voice spoke to her, more vivid than memory, the consonants reverberating with the sound of something burning behind the rocks:

"And the Lord went before them in a pillar of fire."

Her back tightened as she got up. The ground seemed to tilt. She steadied herself on the rocks as she moved around them, advancing until the flame lay before her, rising from the charred remains of a metal chassis.

The Mustang?

But the chassis itself wasn't burning. Indeed, what she could see of it through the flames resembled a burnt cinder. The fire came from beneath it, rising from the ground, shooting skyward.

"You will know him as a pillar of light!"

The wind changed as she approached the Mustang. Smoke struck her face. She held her breath and passed through, rounding the car to look along its side to where something protruded from the wreck. It wasn't rock. Wasn't metal.

Bone!

The smoke wafted toward her again. She snorted, trying to clear the stink from her nose. But the smell hung on, stinging her eyes. She blinked. The world shifted. When she looked again, the car was gone, replaced by a smoking campfire on an open plain.

I'm not seeing this. I'm not here.

And yet it felt real.

I know this place. I was here . . . once . . . long ago. This isn't a vision. It's a memory!

She remembered.

She was in Colorado.

She had spent the night alone on the plains as part of a test, a rite of passage orchestrated by her mentor—a one-eyed survivalist named Incendiary Ray.

She had enrolled at Ray's camp after reading his book, *The Survivalist's Mission: Independence in a Dependant World*, and now, after a week of training, she was proving herself in the wilderness.

And so far she was doing fine.

She had gathered sticks and grass for a fire and had rubbed her palms raw using a hand drill to ignite the kindling. But now, with the fire going, there was little to do but tend the flames and contemplate the gigantic sky. In a way, the challenge seemed too easy. But then, as she took a stick from the woodpile, something lunged. It was there in an instant, flashing in the light, a brown twig with an open mouth. It struck her hand. She felt a pinch, nothing severe at first, mostly pressure.

A knothole popped.

Sparks flashed, illuminating her arm as she recoiled from the woodpile. The twig clung to her hand: long, dark, and cracking like a whip as she tried flinging it away. That's when its eyes caught the light, staring at her, cold and lidless.

"Goddamnit!"

She jerked her hand again, harder—and this time the thing let go, flying into darkness.

What just happened?

She held her hand to the fire. Still no pain, but there was blood—two dots where the fangs had gone in: one a perfect circle, the other spreading out, running toward her wrist.

She looked toward the grass beside her, the place where the snake had landed.

Rattler. It had to be a rattler.

Rattlesnakes were rare back home, but she'd come across more than a few of their copperhead cousins. Rattlers and coppers were both pit-vipers, and she had learned a few things about them over the years. Not much, just three rules, maybe enough to keep her alive.

Her mind raced.

She removed her belt and slung it over the back of her neck, making a sling.

Rule 1: Keep the bite below the heart, but don't let it dangle. Dangling concentrates the venom.

Her hand spasmed as she cradled it in the improvised sling.

Rule 2: Move slowly. Don't panic. Panic and exertion increase blood flow. Blood flow spreads the poison.

She resisted the urge to pull the sling from her neck and cinch the belt like a tourniquet around her wrist. Doing that would trap the venom in her hand. Tissue would break down faster if she did that. Better to let the toxins disperse while she worked on the most important step.

Rule 3: Seek help.

How was she going to do that?

She stood up, looked around.

The serrated line of the Rocky Mountains lay to the west. To the east, dawn rose above barren plains.

No one for miles.

Her pulse quickened.

I'm going to die here.

Then, from the fire, a command: "Sit!"

The voice came from an empty spot near the woodpile, the place where she had been sitting a moment before.

"Sit! *Now!*"

A man crouched near the flames, outlined in firelight.

"It's not like you have a choice." The man looked at her, eyes catching the light. "Sit down or fall down. Those are the options."

She felt the strength leave her knees.

"Slowly." The man reached for her. "Nice and easy." He took her good hand, holding her steady as she landed beside him. His fingers were long and delicate.

She wanted to ask who he was, where he'd come from. But her throat was swelling. She couldn't speak.

He stared at her, apparently reading her thoughts. "I didn't come from *anywhere.*" He held a stick in one hand, turning it over the flames. "This is where I *am.*"

She shook her head. "I didn't—" The words got lost in the swelling. She forced them out. "I didn't see you here."

"You didn't see the rattler either, but that doesn't mean it wasn't right beside you the whole time. And there's a lot more where that came from . . . a lot more you're not seeing." He lowered the stick into the flames, making it sputter.

The smoke struck her face. The stink of it got inside her. She coughed.

"You're breathing better now," he said. "It's the smoke. Smell the grease? That's what's doing it. But breathing it isn't enough. You need to get closer to the cure."

She didn't understand.

"The venom's still inside you," he said. "It's still spreading, killing nerves, digesting tissue. That's how venom works, you know. Vipers don't break down their food by chewing. One bite is all they get. Then they wait, let the venom digest the prey from within before they come back to swallow it whole."

She understood. The venomous snakes back east were much the same.

She'd once seen a copperhead bite a chipmunk, back away to watch it die, then advance again to gulp it down.

"Of course, you aren't exactly *prey*," the man said. "That rattler wasn't out to eat you. She was just protecting her claim, is all. Given the choice, most snakes will keep to themselves, but the world's more crowded than it use to be. Doesn't look that way from here, but it is."

His stick crackled in the fire.

She breathed the smoke, holding it a moment before letting it out. With each breath, her throat's tightness eased a little more.

"Take those mountains." He raised the stick, pointing west. "They look primeval, but get in close and you'll find them crosshatched with roads, fences, and mines. Wilderness is displaced every day, and displacement leads to aggression." He looked at her. "You follow?"

"I thought we were talking about snakes."

"We are." He lowered the stick back into the fire. "It's all connected." He looked over his shoulder, toward the rising dawn. "You're from back that way, aren't you? From back east—West Virginia, southwest Pennsylvania— that area?"

"How'd you know?"

"I could say it's in your manner. In your speech. Would you be comfortable with that answer?"

"I suppose."

"And I guess you suppose that none of this would be happening if you were safe at home, asleep in your bed. In that case, you wouldn't be here at all unless . . . perhaps . . . you were dreaming." He seemed about to say more, but he paused, leaning back, giving her time to ponder his words.

Dreaming? Am I dreaming?

The wind shifted. The smoke came toward her, but now it smelled of coal, burning rock, charred metal.

Windslow Mine! That's where I really am . . . beside the Mustang. This place is a dream.

"But it's not that simple," the man said.

"What's not?"

"What you're thinking."

"You know what I'm thinking?"

"Sometimes." His eyes flashed. "When the wind is right."

The wind shifted.

"Listen," he said. "You can rationalize all you want, but none of it will change what's in front of you . . . what you see . . . what you smell . . . what your senses tell you is real. Dream or memory, you'll die here if you don't do something about that snake bite."

The stick sputtered again.

She looked at it, noting a diamond pattern within the char. "That stick?" She leaned closer, finally seeing it for what it was: a rattlesnake impaled on a branch.

"It's yours," the man said.

"Mine?"

"*Your* snake. The one that bit you." He turned toward her, pivoting enough for her to glimpse the tip of something behind his shoulder—a feathered nub that might have been the joint of a folded wing.

"What are you?" she asked.

He straightened up, hiding the wing. "Lots of things," he said. "Depends."

"On what?"

"The situation. At the moment, I'm your guardian." He raised the stick, setting its end on the ground between his feet. "Take this." He pinched the snake's ribs, peeling a strand of cooked muscle. "Eat it." The flesh dangled, dripping in the light. "Eat it now, before your throat swells shut again, before you can't swallow." He pushed the meat past her lips. It was greasy, hot, salty with char. "Close!"

She did as he said.

The flesh slid along her tongue, leaving a greasy trail as it moved toward her throat. Then it was gone. Had she swallowed it? Or had it crawled into her?

"Here." He tilted the stick, pushing it toward her good hand. "It'll go faster if you feed yourself."

She reached out, touched the snake, then recoiled. The flesh was moving, cooked but still alive.

"Snakes are like that," he said. "Takes them a while to die. But this one can't hurt you."

The snake leered at her: one eye still living, the other an empty socket.

"Go on. It's your turn to bite!"

She touched it again. The flesh quivered. She held on, peeling a strip that flexed like a hooked worm.

"Quickly now!"

She brought the flesh to her mouth. Again, the stuff slithered into her, along her tongue, down her throat.

The cooked snake watched, its good eye pulsing in the firelight, charred jaws gnawing at the stick.

"Go on. Keep eating, Samuelle."

She flinched. "What'd you call me?"

"*Samuelle.*"

She tensed.

"That's your name, isn't it?" His eyes widened, brimming with reflected flame. "*Samuelle Calder?*"

"No one's called me that in a long time."

"Not since the crazy woman died."

"Crazy woman? My mother?"

"Was she crazy?"

"More or less."

"Then, yes . . . your mother."

"How do you know about her?"

He gestured toward the snake. "Keep eating."

She pinched another piece.

"Your mother had religion."

"That's what she called it."

"But you called it—"

"What you said. What you called her before. *Crazy.* She was insane."

"Why? Because she gave her children angel names?"

"It's not only the names. There's a whole lot more to it than what she called us."

"And she called you *Samuelle,* derived from *Samael, the Earth regent, the angel of death.*"

"She didn't know the name meant that."

"No. She wasn't a scholar of Hebrew texts. Wasn't a scholar at all. But you were, for a while, after she died. You read books she would have whipped you for touching."

"I needed to learn who I was."

"*Samuelle,*" he said, face barely moving. "*Sam-el, the venom of God.*"

"She didn't know that meaning either."

"No?"

"She thought the name meant 'one who hears God.'"

"Really?"

"She got it from a baby book."

"Simple woman, simple beliefs."

"I don't like talking about her," she said.

"But it's good for you, Sam. May I call you that?"

"It's better than the other."

"Talking about the past is good for you. The most important truths are the ones you avoid."

"What about you?"

"Me?"

"Who are you?"

He pulled the stick away from her, moving it to the far side of the fire. "I think you've had enough."

She looked at her hand, still dark and swollen, cradled within the sling.

"It'll look that way for a while, but it's healing. You'll recover."

She flexed the hand. Pain lingered. "Who are you?"

"You shouldn't ask such questions."

"What kind?"

"Ones you know the answers to."

"But I don't know the answer."

"You do," he said. "I told you. I'm your guardian."

"Guardian angel?"

"I didn't say that."

"But are you?"

"Your mother would have thought so. She would have called me *Kasdeja*."

"*Kasdeja*?"

"You know the name."

"I don't."

"You do, otherwise I wouldn't have said it. Your mother gave you more than you want to remember. The things I'm saying are already inside you, but it doesn't matter. I've been called many things. The first people had names for me, too—the Pawnee, Comanche, Ute. The names they gave me are older than the ones your mother knew, but none of them matter. Naming is a human thing. I'm older than human things."

"So what are you?"

"I told you."

"Kasdeja?"

"If you like, but I've already given you a better answer. Think on it. You'll get it sooner or later."

"Why don't you just tell me?"

"Because you haven't realized it yet. I can't tell you things you haven't realized. I can only suggest things you want to remember, and confirm those you do."

Her head ached. "I don't like riddles."

"No?" He touched her. "Then you'd better lie down." He pulled her hand from the sling, resting it beside her as he eased her onto her back. "Try resting. Save your strength. Clear your mind. The things you call *riddles* are just beginning."

She felt suddenly tired.

"That's better. Lie still. I'm not going far." He walked away, feet crunching on dry earth.

She waited. A car engine rumbled, idling behind her. Then something creaked, a metallic sound, like the opening of a hood.

She looked toward it, but the sun was up now, streaking the eastern plains with blinding light. She squinted and looked away.

A moment later someone knelt beside her, his face awash with morning glare. He wore a leather patch over one eye.

"Ray?" She tried getting up.

"Lie still," Ray said.

"Where is he?"

Ray pushed a hand against her chest, holding her down. "Take it easy, Sam. You've been snake bit. You need to lie still."

"Where's Kasdeja?"

"Who?"

"He was here."

"No. It's just you. You and that snake." He pointed toward the fire. "You clubbed him good."

"Me?"

"That's him over there, dead as a stick."

"I didn't club him."

"You did. I watched you do it." He opened a metal box and took out a pair of alligator clamps, the ends of jumper cables. "I was bivouacked half a mile back, watching you through a good set of NV binoculars."

"Watching me?"

"I never let students out of my sight. Good thing, too." He raised the clamps, each trailing a cable that connected to the box.

"What's that?"

"Venom zapper. Neutralizes neurotoxins with electric current." He touched the side of her face, tilting her head. "Don't look. It'll be easier if you don't look."

But she looked anyway, seeing a pair of standard jumper cables running from the metal box to the open hood of the Jeep.

"They use this cure in Mexico," he said. "Not approved in the States. Goddamn AMA."

"Cure?"

"Like I said, for snakebites." He turned a switch. The box hummed.

"I don't need it."

"Like hell you don't." He set one of the clamps on her hand, just below the bite. The other he placed above her wrist. The pressure was firm, not uncomfortable.

"He already cured me."

"Who?"

"The angel."

"You're delirious, Sam."

"He was here!"

Ray reached inside the box, turned something, then snapped a switch.

Her hand clenched. Pain leaped along her arm, into her shoulder. She contorted, seeing stars.

He gave the switch another flick. The current stopped.

Her hand unclenched, twitching like a gaffed crab.

"Hold on." He looked into the box, squinting as if reading a gauge or a dial. "One more."

"No, please—"

He threw the switch.

This time she blacked out, though only for a second. When she came to, he was removing the clamps, talking as he worked. "Effective treatment," he said. "Better than antivenin." He looked inside the box, frowned, and then put the clamps on the ground. "Only problem is the transformer." He touched the side of the box, pulling his hand away quickly as if it were hot. "Assembled in China. We could make this stuff in the States, make it a hell of a lot better, too. Don't get me started." He slid his arms under her. "I'm going to put you in the Jeep, drive you back to Camp Survival. No snakes to bother you there." He grunted as he took her weight. "No angels, neither. Maybe, if you're feeling better later, we can have a little celebration."

"Celebration?"

"You survived the night. You're a Camp Survival graduate."

She didn't care about that.

She looked around as he placed her in the back. Something dark and twisted lay on the ground beside the woodpile. It looked like a snake impaled on a stick. "He *was* here," she muttered.

Ray covered her with a sleeping bag, then turned. "Just got to disconnect the transformer," he said. "Then we'll go." He closed the door, shutting her inside. "One second." Stones crunched as he rounded the Jeep, leaned in the driver's side, shut off the engine.

Sam shivered.

Something bad's going to happen.

It wasn't a premonition. Premonitions were her mother's domain, not hers. Still, she had to get up, climb from the Jeep, stop Ray before he touched that box again.

"Ray!"

"Quiet, Sam. Rest." He was now at the front of the Jeep, disconnecting the cables, slamming the hood.

She gripped the door, pulling herself up, looking out to see him standing over the cables. "Ray!"

He looked back. "Lie down, Sam."

The cables shifted at his feet, twitching with residual current. One of them drew back into a coil, raised its clamp, opened its jaws.

"Ray!"

He didn't see it. He was looking at her, waiting for her to lie down. "That's an order, Sam. Lie—" The clamp struck, latching on to his left leg below the knee. He grabbed it, tried pulling it away. The other cable rose up, sparks flying from its jaws. It clamped his right ankle. They both had him now, holding tight as he struggled.

She opened the door, climbed out.

"No!" He waved her away. "I'll handle this, Sam!"

And that's when the transformer exploded.

Thwack-OOOM!

She fell back against the Jeep. Only it wasn't a Jeep anymore. It was a slab of rock beside a burning Mustang.

She stared at the charred chassis.

A shaft of bone extended from the wreckage. An arm bone. Maybe a leg bone. Blackened like a campfire log.

"Christ!" She put her head in her hands. The right hand was no longer swollen from the snakebite. That wound had healed long ago. She had other wounds now, fresh ones along her wrist and knuckles. And the left hand was even worse, the palm slashed almost to the bone.

"Jesus Christ!"

She wasn't praying. She never prayed. And she never had visions. She had been remembering. Dreaming. That was all. Dreaming of things that had happened back in Colorado.

But those things didn't happen that way!

She sat back, steadying herself against the slab of rock.

The cables. They didn't attack. None of that really happened.

The burning car shifted, its contorting frame groaning with the cadence of Ray's voice.

"I'll handle this, Sam!"

She got up. Her head throbbed. She felt dizzy.

Concussion. That's all it is. Just a concussion.

A new sound rose in the distance, engines approaching the mine.

She turned and hurried away, stumbling when she saw what lay on the ground behind her. It had been there all along, but so covered with dust and soot that it had blended in with the rocks. But now she saw it for what it was: a twisted corpse dressed in black jeans and a long-sleeve jersey. She remembered him. He had gone over the cliff with the Mustang, leaping free at the last moment, but falling nonetheless. His back was broken, twisted so that his ass was now in front. His eyes gaped, staring skyward, mouth wide as if he had just seen something wondrous.

She pushed past him, hurrying away from the pile of newly fallen rock and the sound of approaching engines, heading toward an older mass of rubble that sloped from the west corner of the highwall. There were trees there, heavy undergrowth, plenty of cover. She moved toward them, plunging in as the lights of the first fire truck rounded the turn into the crater.

8

Benjie stayed outside, sitting on the patio, watching the wooded slope change colors in the rising light. Occasionally things moved through the undergrowth, small things mostly, though once he saw what looked like a rat, maybe a raccoon. It advanced to the tree line, peered out, then darted away.

The other guys were inside, spinning the dial on a clock radio while Vinny bandaged Jason's snake-bitten hand. They were listening for news to confirm R.D.'s story about the exploding crater, but so far all they'd found were call-in shows about sports and politics. Now and then Jason and R.D. broke into an argument, usually instigated by Jason.

"There's no news about an explosion because there wasn't no freaking explosion."

"You saw the smoke!" R.D. said.

"Smoke don't prove it was an explosion."

"But that's what I saw."

"Yeah, right, *Ditiot.*"

"Don't call me that."

"*Ditwit!*"

"That's enough," Vinny said.

"We ought to drive out there," R.D. said. "Then you'd see."

A shadow passed overhead, descending into the trees. Benjie saw it for an instant. Then it was gone, landing with a thump at the top of the rise. Silence followed. For a moment nothing moved. Then leaves shifted. A branch snapped. The thing was moving, coming down the slope.

"There!" R.D.'s voice roared from the kitchen. "There it is! Turn it up!"

The radio blasted. Benjie caught the words *Green County* and *Richter scale.* Then Jason started shouting again. "Turn it down, *Ditwit!*"

"I want you to hear."

The thing in the woods stopped moving, but Benjie felt it looking at him. Not in a threatening or frightened way. But in a caring way. It wanted to get closer. It just wasn't sure about the voices coming from the house. Benjie sensed these things as clearly as if the animal had spoken them aloud.

"It's all right," Benjie said. He got up, moved to the base of the slope. "If you don't want to come down here, I'll come to you." He stepped through the tree line, onto the rising ground, and climbed until he heard the creature advancing toward him once again.

It sounded large, but big animals didn't frighten Benjie, who'd once stood within petting distance of a black bear at his uncle's cabin in Cook's Forest. He might have actually touched the bear, too, if Jason hadn't come running out of the cabin screaming at him to get away. The bear had reacted by chasing Jason back inside, where the big kid promptly shit himself, dumping a big one into the only pair of gutchies he'd brought along for the weekend.

But the thing at the top of the slope wasn't a bear. Benjie figured it was probably a wild turkey, possibly a pheasant. Either way, it was moving again, coming toward him faster now, wending through the trees and undergrowth.

Benjie averted his eyes, not wanting to scare it away with a direct look.

Inside the house, R.D. started yelling again.

"Hear that? They're calling it a *seismic event*!"

"What the hell's a seismic event?"

"Earthquake," Vinny said.

"Yeah, right!"

"I want to go," Vinny said. "I want to see it!"

Benjie tried tuning out the voices. They didn't matter. What mattered was the thing on the slope. It was close now, the weight of its gaze almost a physical presence on the side of his face.

Look at me, the weight said. *Lift your head. See what I am.*

Benjie hesitated.

Are you afraid?

Benjie shook his head.

What then?

"I don't like doing that."

Doing what?

"Looking at people."

You think that's what I am? A person?

"No."

Then look at me. Tell me what you see.

Twenty feet away, at the bottom of the slope, the screen door banged open. Footsteps scuffled across the patio.

"Hey, Benjie!"

"Where'd he go?"

"Woods, I bet."

"Hey, Benjie!"

"Retard! Come on! We're heading out."

Benjie turned toward them.

The creature crept closer. *Don't go, Benjie. Stay here. A minute longer. I need you to stay a minute longer.*

"He'll get mad."

Who?

"My brother."

You can handle him.

"Damnit, Benjie! The hell you at?"

Look at me, Benjie.

Benjie turned until he saw a dark foot on the ground beside him. The toes were long, like roots.

"Benjie! Get your sorry butt down here now!"

"You sure he's in the woods?"

"I *know* he's in the woods. He's *always* in the woods."

"Should we go looking for him?"

"No way! Freaking snakes, man!"

"I'll go."

"Yeah, you do that, *Ditwit*. One retard after another."

Benjie turned his gaze a little more, moving it along the tree-like leg. The knee looked strange, too, like the crook of a branch.

"Are you real?" Benjie asked.

The creature didn't answer.

"You aren't real, are you? I'm just making you up."

The creature sighed. "I'm real enough." This time it spoke the words aloud, close to Benjie's ear. Then Benjie heard another sound, a skitter of tiny paws on dry leaves. It came from behind the creature, moving away.

"Are you why the animals are afraid?"

"No. It's not me. It's the earth. The ground is changing. Crawling animals are feeling it first, snakes and rodents. Soon the larger ones will sense it, too."

"And people?" Benjie asked.

"Eventually. People will be the last to feel it. They always are. But you're different, aren't you?"

Benjie wanted to look at the creature. But still he hesitated. "How can the ground change?"

"How does any living thing change?"

"But the ground isn't alive."

"It is. It's the mother of everything. Think on it. You'll understand."

"Hey, Benjie!" R.D. called from the base of the slope. "Where you at?"

The creature touched Benjie's chin, raising his face until he found himself looking up at an impossible mass of foliage, rock, and flesh. It was shaped like a man . . . a winged man . . . a winged man with a long face and glowing eyes.

Benjie flinched and looked away. It wasn't real. It couldn't be. His mind was pretending.

R.D.'s voice drew nearer. "Benjie!"

Dead leaves shifted at Benjie's feet. Wind swirled, seeming to rise from the ground. And then. . . .

Vhooooomph!

The wind pushed him back, and suddenly he was looking up at something remarkable: a winged shape rocketing through the trees.

"You *are* real!" Benjie said. "I see you. You're real!"

The creature vanished as he spoke, sailing beyond the branches.

The wind died.

"Hey, Benjie!" R.D. came up behind him. "The hell you doing, Benjie?"

Benjie glanced at R.D., then looked away.

R.D. called toward the house. "I got him!"

"Did you see it?" Benjie said.

"See what?"

"It flew."

"All I see is you, Benjie." R.D. took his keys from his pocket. "We're heading out." He pushed the keys into Benjie's hand. "You're driving."

Benjie looked at the keys. "Now?"

"Vinny wants to see the earthquake."

"But it's over."

"Right, but he wants to see what's left."

Benjie turned for one more look at the high branches. Nothing there. The thing was gone.

9

Crouching in the trees, Sam watched the fire trucks steer toward the spreading flames. By now there was little left of the Mustang. The tires, paint, and upholstery were gone, and the fuel had certainly been consumed in the initial blast. All that remained was blackened metal and cremated bone.

The lead truck rocked to a stop. A firefighter climbed down, carried a nozzle toward the car, and loosed a jet of foam over the fire. Steam billowed, climbing skyward.

But it's not the car. The car isn't burning.

The firefighter loosed another spray of foam, lower this time, covering the base of the wreck as he moved around it. Any second now and he'd see the broke-back body lying just beyond the ring of flames. Soon the place would be crawling with cops.

She turned and hurried away, moving through the sloping forest, coming to a narrow pass that seemed to have been carved by intermittent runoff. Here the ground ran level until it connected with a wider ravine. It was water-carved as well, as evidenced by the smooth rocks that lay strewn along its center.

It was surprising how much the area's waterways had been transformed by dams, mines, and roads. Over the last hundred years, mountains had become valleys, valleys lakes, and lakes reservoirs that spilled into creeks that eventually found their way into the beds of vanished rivers. The space she was in appeared to be a drainage ditch, a hollow that would fill with water when runoff spewed from a huge spillway in the wall above her. When that happened, a raging river would course through the channel and wash over the Mustang. But that wasn't likely to happen any time soon. Aside from the smoke, the sky was clear, cloudless. No rain predicted for days.

Ahead of her, to the west, another slope rose toward a glacial curve that appeared to be the remnant of a natural hillside. The trees up there looked older, the undergrowth less dense. If she continued that way she would eventually come to Cliff Mine Run.

She hurried on, over the rounded boulders and into the old-growth trees that dotted the contours of the upper hill. Soon the ground leveled, running flat before descending again, this time into an older river bed. Water still flowed here, meandering south toward Windslow.

She paused, kneeling on mossy rocks to wash her hands in the creek. Then she froze.

Someone's watching.

She looked around. But there was no one in the tight little valley. Only herself and her wounded hands.

Get on with it. Treat the wounds and clear out.

She pushed her hands into the water, wincing as the cool currents washed them. Crusted blood dissolved, flowing away in scarlet ribbons.

The wounds on her wrist and knuckles didn't look so bad once she'd cleaned them, but the slash across her palm looked worse than ever, deep and jagged. She could stitch it closed once she got home. But right now she needed something to ease the pain, staunch the bleeding, inhibit infection.

Across the stream, a clump of invasive weeds grew in a shaded pool: pink flowers, red stems, blade-shaped leaves. She knew the plants. Her mother had called them angelweeds. Tea from their stems cured sore throats. Salve from their leaves promoted healing.

She crossed the creek to the cluster, remembering how her mother had made ointment by boiling the plants to sludgy paste. She picked some leaves and pressed them over the gashed hand, forming a green bandage that ran from trigger finger to wrist. But the leaves wouldn't stay in place for long. She needed something to cover the wound. Some kind of bandage.

She unlaced a boot, kicked it off, and removed her sock. She cut finger holes in the toe with her pocket knife and then pulled the sock over her hand. The leaves would remain in place now, and the wound would stay relatively clean.

The other hand wasn't so bad, but she dressed it as well, applying angel-weed and covering it with the sock from her other foot. The pain in both hands subsided, although she wasn't sure if the cause was medicinal or psychological. More than likely it was simply the result of having the wounds hidden. In any event, she could now turn her attention to other things: leaving the mine, collecting the money Kirill owed her, and heading home.

She stood, started walking, then hesitated again. The sense of being watched was stronger than ever. She looked around, and this time she saw them: not people, but a gaze of raccoons looking out at her from beneath a sandstone ledge. It wasn't normal for coons to be out in daylight, not healthy ones, anyway. But sick raccoons didn't stay in groups, and these didn't look rabid or diseased, just frightened—caught between the light of the rising sun and something equally troubling in their lair. Could it be that the fire beneath the car was spreading? Were coal seams burning underground, heating the raccoons' den?

Not my problem.

She kept her distance and pushed on, out of the valley, up the slope, pausing when she heard a siren wailing to the south, apparently approaching along Cliff Mine Run. Its northbound direction could mean that someone had found Peterson's body in the clearing above the mine. If that were the case, the roads around Windslow would soon be crawling with cops. She needed to be on her way by then, over the border, heading toward her cabin in the West Virginia hills.

The siren changed pitch, getting louder as it neared the top of the rise. And then, as she hunkered down and waited for it to pass, she heard a gunshot in the woods above the mine.

The siren raced by, so close that she felt the wind of the passing cruiser. She started climbing again, hearing another shot as she grabbed the guardrail and pulled herself over into the uphill lane. By now another vehicle was approaching, coming around a bend to the north.

She raced across the double-yellow and raised her bandaged hands, preparing to signal the car, determined to do whatever it took to keep the driver from leaving her stranded anywhere near the carnage in and around the mine.

10

Officer Zabek saw Sharo Jenkins standing outside her vehicle, leaning on the door, face pulsing in the light bar: red-blue-red-blue.

But someone else saw her too—a figure on the clearing's edge, 50 feet away, racing toward her.

Zabek hit him with the spot, took one look, and slammed the brakes.

The man kept advancing, eyes glowing, teeth flashing.

Zabek leaped out, getting a better look now: shaved head, ragged loin-cloth, torn sneakers, scale-covered skin.

Like snake skin. A fucking snake man!

"Stop!" Zabek drew down, ready to fire.

But the snake man had already leaped behind Sharo, grabbing her waist as she slid down along the door.

"Stop! Get on the ground! Now!"

The snake man hefted Sharo, slinging her over his shoulder.

"Goddamnit! *Stop or I'll shoot!*" But he couldn't. The risk of hitting Sharo was too great.

The snake man leered at the gun, then turned, stumbling as he adjusted to Sharo's weight, picking up speed as he lumbered back toward the edge of the clearing.

Zabek snapped on his personal transmitter, keying the mike as he gave chase. "Deuces! Officer abducted! I'm heading east. In pursuit of—" He tried to make sense of what he saw. There were no scales on the man's back. His shoulders and buttocks were dark, apparently tanned, but completely lacking the patterns that covered the front of his body. Snake scales in front. Skin behind.

"A man . . . six foot . . . muscular. Two hundred pounds. Caucasian, I think . . . tattooed . . . possibly painted . . . markings resemble—" The ground angled down, plunging toward a bank of low-lying fog and the sound of flowing water. Zabek followed it, trying not to slip on the tilting grade. "Markings like a snake, like scales."

"Copy, Deuces. 6:12." Good old Becky, calm as ever. You could tell her the Taliban had driven into town, and she'd ask for the license number, make and model.

A siren wailed in the distance, one of the Cokesburg officers approaching Cliff Mine Run. Zabek was panting now, breathing hard as he crashed through a thicket to see the snake man stumbling away, disappearing into a wall of mist. Then came the sound of splashing.

Zabek keyed the mike. "This is Deuces. Suspect is crossing a stream. I'm in pursuit!" Then he raced forward, into the fog, toward the sound of splashing water.

11

Jason was standing in the back of the truck when Benjie hit the brakes. The jolt threw Jason forward, onto his knees and against the truck's rear window. His beer went flying, over the roof to land on the downhill shoulder of Cliff Mine Run. "Freaking retard!" He looked through the window, banging his fist on the glass. "The hell you doing, Benjie?"

Benjie wouldn't look back. He just gripped the wheel, staring through the windshield, looking at someone standing on the road. It was a little guy in camouflage and combat boots.

Vinny, who had been riding beside Jason, pulled himself up on the roof. "Hey!" he said. "It's a girl."

Sirens wailed to the south. One of them was close, getting louder, racing toward them.

The girl stepped around to the driver's window, pulled herself up on the sideview, and tried talking to Benjie. "Take me to Windslow?"

Benjie wouldn't look at her.

"Sure!" R.D. said. "That's where we're going."

Jason set his foot on the cooler, leaning over the side, looking down at the girl. "You in the army?"

"No."

"AWOL?"

"I just need a ride to Windslow."

"Come on, then." Jason offered his hand.

The girl didn't take it. Instead, she pulled herself up on the side of the truck, climbing in on her own. She wore white, fingerless gloves. One of them had rusty stains along the palm. Was it dirt? Blood?

The wailing siren raced nearer.

Jason took a fresh beer from the cooler. "Want one?"

She looked toward the siren. "We'll want to get off the road." She ran her hand across her forehead, wiping her brow. "Tell your driver to pull onto the shoulder, stay in gear."

Jason cocked his head toward the rising smoke. "You see that?"

"Hard to miss it."

"Know what happened?"

The siren grew louder.

Jason took a drink.

The girl frowned at the beer. "What I know is that your beer's a violation. Open container law. That cop sees it, we could all be in a world of crap."

"She's right, Jason," Vinny said.

Jason slapped the rear window. "Hey, Benjie! Pull over. Keep it running." He hunkered down, holding the beer out of sight.

"Hiding it won't be good enough if they decide to stop," she said.

"What're you saying?"

"Ditch the beer."

"I just opened it!"

The siren was just around the bend.

The girl gripped the side of the truck, ready to bolt.

"All right!" Jason raised the aluminum bottle, chugged it down, then he tossed it into the weeds as a flashing cruiser cleared the bend. The cop glanced at them, racing by as Benjie eased to the shoulder.

The second siren was farther off, perhaps a mile away.

"Let's roll!" the girl said.

Jason slapped the rear window. "Drive, Benjie. To Windslow!"

The girl's bangs blew back as the truck accelerated. There was a cut on her forehead, a deep gash near the hairline.

"What happened to you?" Vinny asked.

"None of your business," she said.

Jason smirked. "We're giving you a ride."

"Then let's just ride, OK?"

The three of them were sitting now, hunkering down on the truck-bed floor, leaning back against the sides: Jason on the driver's side, Vinny and the girl opposite him.

Jason looked around as they cleared the next bend, glimpsing a veil of haze through a break in the trees. Something was burning in the mine, smoke pulsing with the flashing lights of fire trucks.

R.D. called from the passenger seat. "Should we stop?"

"No!" the girl shouted. "Keep moving!"

Jason stared at the girl. "I knew someone like you once."

"I don't think so."

"Yeah." Jason said. "That's the sort of thing she used to say."

"What? Keep moving?"

"No. Not that. What you said before, to Vinny."

The girl looked at Vinny. "Is that your name? Vinny?"

"Yeah."

She nodded. Didn't offer her name in return.

"I'm Jason." He offered his hand.

"I know," she said. "I heard. That's what Vinny called you."

"Right," Jason said. "And you are?"

She looked toward the siren. "Going to Windslow."

"Evasive," Jason said. "She was like that too, this other girl. The one I used to know. She was a lot like you."

The truck took the next bend tight and fast.

Vinny tilted, going off balance. He put out his hand, grazing the front of the girl's shirt before grabbing the tailgate.

The girl stiffened.

"Sorry," Vinny pushed back. "Accident."

She stared at him.

Vinny scooted back a little more. "No shit," he said. "I wasn't messing with you."

The girl kept staring.

Vinny looked away.

"All right," the girl said. "An accident." She looked at Jason.

Unlike Vinny, Jason didn't look away.

"I don't like people touching me," she said.

"That so?"

The girl had two buttons missing from her shirt. The sides hung open, revealing a hint of cleavage.

The siren wailed.

Benjie slowed, pulling over.

"Hey, Vinny!" R.D. called from the passenger window, his voice barely audible above the wail. "Ask her where in Windslow! Where's she going?"

Jason looked at the girl, waiting for her answer.

She folded her arms as if she knew he'd been scoping her chest.

The cruiser raced past, siren becoming a deafening scream before falling away.

"Any place in particular?" Jason asked.

She hesitated, seemed to consider her options, then answered matter-of-factly. "The Strip Mine."

"Say what?"

"The club," she said. "By the interstate."

"You shitting me?"

"That's where I'm going."

Vinny turned toward the cab. "The club!" he shouted. "The Strip Mine!"

Benjie pulled back on to the road, picking up speed.

"Same as us," Jason told the girl. "That's where we're going. Meeting people for the Amateur Lunch."

"Kind of early, isn't it?"

"It is now, but we weren't planning on going straight there. We were going to look at the earthquake, but now—" He slapped the cooler. "Guess we'll have to tailgate till the club opens. Want to join us?"

"No."

"You work at the club?"

She didn't answer.

"Do you?"

"That's my business."

"So you do?"

"I didn't say that."

"You said it was your business. Are you an amateur?"

Something thumped under the truck, a two-beat *whump-umph*. A second later, a flattened groundhog appeared in the road behind them.

"Another one?" Vinny said. "That's, like, what? The third one this morning."

"Some kind of record," Jason said.

The truck took another turn.

Jason scooted over, coming around to lean against the tailgate, closer to the girl. "So are you?" he asked.

"Am I what?"

"An amateur?"

"An amateur what?"

"An amateur what-do-you-think?"

Up close, Jason saw that her eyes weren't completely blue. They were darker near the center, becoming almost red around the pupil: ice with hearts of fire.

"Listen," the girl said. "We're just riding here, OK? You're giving me a lift. You're going to drop me off. I'm going to say thank you, and that's it. That's all this is."

"Just a ride?"

"That's what I said."

"Right. That's what you *said*. But what do you *mean*?"

She swallowed, a sign that she wasn't nearly as disinterested as she pretended. "You're drunk," she said.

"So what?"

"So why don't you go back to your cooler."

"It's warmer over here."

The truck took another bend.

Jason eased closer.

She didn't move, didn't lean away. "Listen," she said. "Let me be clear. No ambiguity. No doubt." She lowered her voice, barely audible in the wind. "If you come closer . . . if you even *try* touching me—I'll throw you out of this truck."

"Really?"

She braced against the bed liner. The new pose opened her shirt more than before, revealing the lower curve of her right tit, almost all the way to the nipple.

"You know what you are?" Jason said.

"I know what I am. The thing is, do you—"

"A peach," Jason said. "That's what you are, a real peach."

The truck took a hard right onto Old Coal Creek Road.

Jason leaned with the turn, not aggressively, not fast, just a slow move in perfect sync with the swaying truck. His hand slid onto the girl's shoulder. Another moment, and they'd be together in the crook between wheel well and tailgate, continuing their verbal sparring with his arm around her shoulder.

She moved toward him, apparently giving in.

"A peach," he muttered again.

And then her feet were under him, kicking up, pushing hard. The truck came out of its turn, and Jason was flying. A blur of branches passed above him. And beneath him—

WHAM!

He landed on the shoulder, crashed through a thicket, somersaulted into weeds that hazed into darkness.

She met him there . . . in the darkness . . . smiling as he pulled her toward him.

"*A peach*?" she said. "No one's ever called me that before."

In the distance, beyond the limits of his dream, truck tires braked hard, squealing to a halt on Cliff Mine Run.

12

Named Alex by a father he had never known and renamed Akeo by the great-grandmother who had raised him, the man who now called himself *Axle* began the day hitching a ride in a battered Cadillac Escalade.

The driver was buck naked, skin squeaking against his leather seat as he steered along the mile-long drive of a mountain estate. His long hair, crimped from braids that had come undone during the night, hung in a tangled mane that shifted in the breeze from his open window.

But if the driver looked crazy, Axle figured he himself must look certifiably insane. He wore a windbreaker, though not in the usual fashion. It was tied upside down around his waist, serving as a pair of improvised pants. Otherwise, he was as naked as the driver.

"So we've changed," the driver said. His name was Maynard Frieburg, though he preferred being called *Bird*. "We're skyborn, right?"

"That's what my great-grandmother would have called it," Axle said.

"She was Okwe?"

"Half Okwe. So she claimed."

"She taught you the old ways?"

"Yeah." Axle looked out the window. "But I was never sure how much was from Native legends, how much was just made up."

"Guess you know now."

"Do I?" Axle turned toward the side window, looking through his reflection and onto the manicured grounds of the Frieburg estate. What must it have been like growing up with such wealth, with property and privilege acquired through the hard labor of miners like Axle's own father?

"What're you looking at, Axle?"

"Not sure." He shifted in the seat, looking back toward a garden wall 50 feet away. Something had been crouching in the shadows of those stones. It had resembled a winged man, a creature like the one that had saved him and Bird from Windslow Mine's collapsing highwall. Axle remembered the thing swooping down as the rocks gave way. And he remembered it taking off with them, carrying them . . . where? Axle couldn't remember. But the bigger mystery—the one that tugged hardest at Axle's soul—was the sense of a deeper connection between him and the creature, a connection of spirit, but also of blood.

"You remember falling?" Bird said.

Axle looked skyward. A few stars remained, dimmed against the blue-black sky.

"Do you, Axle? You remember that? Did that really happen?"

"You tell me."

"No idea. Might have dreamed it. That's why I'm asking."

"What do you remember?"

Bird thought a moment. When he spoke, his voice sounded distant, dreamy. "That winged man . . . he carried us into the sky. Then . . . the next thing I knew . . . I was falling. Must have been a mile up. I could see Pittsburgh . . . or maybe it was Waynesburg. Anyway—I saw you. You were falling, too."

"What about the winged man? What do you remember about him?"

"Freaking monster!" Bird said. "Like a winged devil. Came out of nowhere, grabbed us, carried us out of the mine. If it wasn't for him, we'd have died in the rockslide."

"We died before that." Axle shifted in the seat, shoulders sticking to the leather. "We died before the rockslide. I had a bullet in the brain. You took one in the chest. People don't walk away from stuff like that."

"Yeah, Axle. But we didn't *walk* away. We flew away. That thing carried us into the sky."

"You sure it was the sky? I remember being lifted into darkness. And then, after that, I remember falling through sunlight."

Bird let up on the gas, steering around a bend in the drive.

"So the thing is," Axle said. "What I want to know . . . is what happened in between? Between the darkness and the light. What happened? We must have gone somewhere. You remember anything about that?"

Bird thought a moment. "No." He toed the accelerator, coming out of the turn. "You neither?"

"Nothing clear. Just fragments. I remember having wings. The creature was gone and I was flying on my own, riding the spirit wind . . . the dream wind."

"You were Kwetis," Bird said. "Like in the Okwe legends. That's what you were, Kwetis—the nightflyer."

"But after that I was sitting with my great-grandmother in her trailer . . . only it wasn't really her trailer. It was that shack in the mine. And then I was with some kid, scaring the crap out of him, making him wake up screaming.

I think he was the son of your attorney."

"My attorney?" Bird looked at Axle. "You mean Peterson, the guy you killed?"

"I didn't kill him."

"Your friend did. The guy with the shotgun. He shot me. Then he shot Peterson."

"I told you last night, Bird. The guy with the shotgun wasn't my friend. None of those guys were. They hired me to drive, is all. I had no idea they planned on robbing you, that things would go like they did."

"You must have known something going in."

Axle shrugged. "I knew a few things. Suspected others. But I needed money. I don't suppose you'd understand."

They were nearing the end of the mile-long driveway, and now the north wing of Bird's mansion was emerging from a line of trees, coming into view with the steady inevitability of an ocean liner sailing into port.

"But you knew about my attorney," Bird said.

"I didn't, but I do now. It's hard to explain. It doesn't all make sense yet, but I think it will." He squinted as the rising sun streamed through the side window. "But don't go blaming me for what happened to your attorney, especially since I know it was you that put that bullet in my head last night. The kid with the shotgun might've shot you in the chest, but that wasn't until after you opened fire on us."

"I just wanted my briefcase back," Bird said. "When people steal a man's shit, they got to expect shit with interest."

"Yeah," Axle said. He had his head against the window, remembering how it had all gone down, how he had driven the crooks to a dark section of Windslow Road and waited for Bird to drive by in his Escalade. Then they had stopped him, robbed him, and pushed the Escalade into the woods. And that might have been the end of it, too, if Paul Peterson hadn't come speeding along to find Bird lying on the shoulder. Within minutes, Bird was in the passenger seat of Peterson's Viper, chasing Axle's Mustang into the hills above Windslow Mine.

"Guess we all wanted something," Axle said. "Guess we all got something, too." He closed his eyes. He was tired of talking. Tired of thinking. His head ached, though the pain was nothing like he remembered from the night before, when the bullet from Bird's gun had gotten lodged in his skull. But that was over now. They had both been skyborn, given new bodies that were better than the originals. And Axle had been given something else, too. He sensed its presence when he closed his eyes. It was inside him, a power waiting to rise the next time he dreamed, a dream persona named Kwetis. His great-grandmother had told him all about it. Half man, half spirit—Kwetis could shape the world by infiltrating dreams. But even now, Axle was beginning to wonder what all that really meant. He sensed there was more to it than Great-Grandmother had ever suspected, a bigger reality that the old stories and legends only hinted at, a truth beyond human understanding.

"I hope the servants aren't up," Bird said. "They already tell enough stories about me. They see me coming home naked with a kid in windbreaker pants, and it'll be all over."

Axle kept his eyes closed, said nothing.

"You all right?"

"Tired," Axle said. "I need to sleep."

"Ride the dream wind?"

"Something like that. I feel like there's something I need to know about, a new development we need to take care of. If I sleep, I'll know what it is."

"You can sleep in the house," Bird said. "Got plenty of bedrooms."

"Only need one." Axle sat back as the driveway swung behind the mansion.

A new structure came into view: brick walls, peaked roof. It looked like a stable that had been converted into an upscale garage, a suspicion that was confirmed when Bird stopped in front of it and thumbed a remote, opening the door.

Lights came on inside, shining over a row of cloth-covered Vipers, a Mark LT pickup, and a bright red Firebird.

"You got enough cars?" Axle asked.

"The Vipers aren't mine." Bird eased inside, pulling beside the Firebird. "I'm holding them for a friend, a business associate." He turned off the engine, got out, and wrapped a flannel cover from one of the Vipers around his shoulders. It hung like a robe, covering his body.

Axle stared at the uncovered Viper, pondering it until Bird came around to the Escalade's passenger side and opened the door.

"Getting out?" Bird said.

Axle glanced back at the uncovered car. "That Viper," he said. "Looks like your attorney's car."

"Right. Same model. My business associate got a mess of them when his uncle foreclosed on an upscale rental company. Sometimes he gives them away, for favors, to buy influence. Want one?"

"No thanks." Axle tried climbing down from the passenger seat, then stopped.

"Need help?" Bird asked.

"Feeling dizzy."

Bird reached for him. "No." Axle waved him away. "I can do this."

"You sure?"

"Yeah." His skin squeaked against the seat. He felt cold, vulnerable. "You got one of those car-covers for me?"

"I can get you one."

"I'd appreciate it."

Bird turned, heading toward another Viper.

Axle tried standing. The garage seemed to tilt. He steadied himself on the open door, getting his balance before taking a step.

Twenty feet away, Bird lifted the cover off a bright red Viper, snapped it in the air to shake off the dust, then turned toward Axle. "Hey! Hold on, Axle. Wait for me."

Axle felt the ground pitch again. This time he lost balance.

"Axle!"

He fell, face first toward the concrete floor.

Crack!

Axle heard the sound but felt nothing. No pain. No loss of consciousness. He rolled onto his back, looking up at Bird.

"Christ, Axle!"

"I'm OK."

Bird draped him with the flannel cover.

"I'm just tired, is all." He closed his eyes. "It's like . . . like all the dreams in the world are inside me, waiting for me."

"You cracked your head."

"It's nothing." He felt Bird's fingers on his forehead, probing for damage that wasn't there.

"Bone on concrete," Bird said. "No contest. You should have cracked your—"

Axle forced his eyes open, focusing on Bird who was now looking at the garage floor, the spot where Axle's head had made contact.

"Damn," Bird said.

"What?"

"The concrete," Bird said. "You cracked the freaking concrete!"

"Whatever."

"Goddamn concrete, Axle!"

Axle closed his eyes. "I'm tired, Bird. Just want to sleep . . . OK?" His voice seeming to come from someplace far away, from a realm beyond the world. "Leave me here. I'll be . . . all right. Just—" He heard wind blowing, not through the garage, but through his mind . . . through his spirit. And then he was flying, soaring with the wings of a hawk, still conscious of his earthly body that was even now being lifted from the floor, out of the garage, and across the courtyard that led to the rear of Bird's mansion.

obert Zabek snapped off his flashlight and returned it to his belt as he advanced to the creek. Dawn had already broken beyond the trees, and although twilight lingered in this forest valley, it was still bright enough for him to see his immediate surroundings. Twenty feet away, things started to dim, becoming outlines in the mist. A little beyond that, fog thickened to a wall of haze.

The snake man was maybe 20 yards ahead, slogging through the water.

Zabek's radio crackled. "Cokesburg Three-Nine. On scene."

"Copy Three-Nine. 6:14. Deuces. Recommend?"

Zabek didn't like doing the chase alone, but he couldn't risk getting his backup officer lost in the fog. He keyed the mike. "Stand by, Three-Nine."

"Copy that." The cop sounded relieved, probably getting his first look at the death car. "This is some mess here."

Zabek stepped down from the shore, into the fast water. It was cold. Numbingly cold. He pushed on. The stream rose, reaching his knees as the sound of more splashing came from up ahead. Then came a thump followed by rustling grass, sounds of the snake man reaching the shore. Someone moaned. Sharo? Zabek called out, voice ringing flat against the fog. A moment later, he heard the snap of breaking twigs, footsteps receding along the bank, getting away.

Fighting the current, Zabek splashed onward until a shape appeared to his left, one end submerged, the other angling toward the shore. It was a fallen tree, rotted along the bottom, covered with warty growths. *Fungus*, he thought. *Tree mushrooms.* Except that the growths were moving. *Distortions in the air?*

The creek bed rose as he approached the tree. The mist thinned, giving a better view. The growths weren't mushrooms. They were rats, dozens of them. Their noses twitched, catching his scent, sizing him up as he drew nearer.

A voice rose from his radio, the second backup officer approaching the scene: "Cokesburg Four-Oh. Milepost five."

"Copy, Four-Oh," Becky said. "Hold up at the turnoff. Deuces reports debris on the road. Secure that scene."

"Roger that."

"6:17."

Another rat scrambled onto the tree, moving along the trunk, pushing in among the others near the water line. The rats weren't acting right, massing inches from the creek, scrambling to get as far from shore as possible. One of them lost its footing, plunking down into the water. It paddled, turning in a half-circle before being swept away between algae-covered stones.

Zabek kept moving, coming to an overhanging ledge of ragged grass. He pulled himself up, out of the water, onto the shore. His feet were numb. He stumbled, heading north now, following the snake man, and finally catching sight of him around a bend in the valley. The bastard had climbed the slope with Sharo still on his back. He was on his knees near the top of the rise, catching his breath, adjusting his grip on Sharo's waist.

"Police!" Zabek raised his Glock, taking aim at the man's back. "Stop!"

The snake man stood up, muscles flexing. He had to be in incredible shape, lugging all that weight down one slope and up another. Sharo was a small woman, barely 110 pounds on her own. But her extra gear—duty belt, shoes, Kevlar vest—all of that easily added another 20. And she was unconscious, essentially dead weight.

This guy was strong.

"I said stop! Stop now!"

The snake man lumbered away from the slope and out of sight beyond the grassy fringe.

Zabek followed, struggling up the valley wall, out of the low-lying mist and into sight of a wood-and-brick structure that waited 30 feet back from the top of the rise. It was a house, tilting at an angle, weather-beaten and roofless. Not a home, only the suggestion of one. He pushed on, off the slope and onto the edge of a level field.

And then he saw them.

He stumbled to a stop, trying to comprehend.

Two rows of devils stood between the edge of the slope and the front of the house: feet anchored to the ground, bodies slanted forward, wings spread to catch the morning breeze. They had been constructed of junk. Their eyes, fashioned from broken glass, glowed in the first light of dawn.

The snake man staggered among them, laboring under Sharo's weight, making for the house.

"Stop!" Zabek took aim, but still he didn't fire. "Police! Put her down or I'll shoot! Do it *now!*"

The snake man climbed the stairs to the front porch. Then he turned, almost falling. "Can't," he gasped. His voice was thin, breathy: the hiss of a snake. Was that his real voice, or was he simply out of breath, gasping for air?

"Down!" Zabek advanced, scurrying fast and low between the junk devils, leading with his weapon. "Put her down!"

The snake man turned away. Sharo's head hung limp against his back. She looked dead, face swollen, eyes rolled back.

"Put her down now, motherfucker!"

"Told you. Can't." The snake man looked back at the gun, seemed to detect the bluff, then ducked through the house's cloth-covered entrance.

Zabek raced up the stairs, stopping when he saw what awaited him on the porch.

Copperheads!

"Christ!" He leaped back.

Unlike the devils in the yard, the snakes were real.

Zabek keyed his mike. "This is Deuces. I'm—"

"Hey!" The snake man stepped back out through the curtained doorway, returning to the porch. He didn't seem to mind the copperheads, and they didn't bother with him. He just stood among them, empty-handed. Sharo was somewhere in the house.

Zabek released the mike, steadied his aim.

"Listen," the snake man said. "I—"

"On the ground! *Now!*"

The radio crackled. "Deuces. Come in, Deuces."

"Listen!" the snake man said. "I can—"

"On the fucking ground!" Zabek sighted along the barrel, aiming at the man's chest. "Now! Face down!"

"Come in, Deuces."

The snake man glanced at the radio mike. "You better turn that off."

"I said *down!* On the *ground!*" He was screaming now, throat raw, face burning. Part of him wanted to just shoot the bastard, take him down and run into the house.

The snake man's eyes narrowed, staring at Zabek, taking his measure. "All right," the snake man said. "OK." He descended the steps, dropped to his knees, and eased facedown among the tufts of shin-high grass.

Zabek stepped around him, noticing his skin, how the stream had washed the painted markings from the legs. One shin was pale and hairless, the other dark and ribbed with scars. And there were more scars on his arms, the damage clearly visible now that carrying Sharo had smeared the paint. But it wasn't really paint. Zabek saw that now. Up close, its texture was clear. The guy had decorated himself with colored dirt.

"Hands on your back."

The snake man did as he was told.

Zabek cuffed the right hand, cinching it tight.

"You got a name?"

"Dalton," the man said. "Dalton Davies."

Zabek grabbed Dalton's other hand. The skin felt cold and leathery. The thumb had withered, curling like a dried tuber, lying close to the palm.

Becky's voice called from the radio. "Deuces. Twenty?"

"You need to turn that off," Dalton said. "These snakes are sensitive to sounds like that. Makes them buggy, and they're already riled up about something."

Zabek cinched the cuff tight below the withered thumb.

"There's still a few of them in this grass, heading for the steps," Dalton said. "You and me, we're in the way. And your radio—"

"Shut up!" Zabek keyed his mike, getting ready to make his report.

Dalton turned, looking back along the ground.

"Lie still!" Zabek said.

Becky's voice came again, just the time stamp: "6:32."

Something slapped Zabek's leg, striking from behind. It didn't feel like much. Just a slap, then a pinch, then it was gone.

"Damn!" Dalton winced. "Told you."

Zabek looked back to see a copperhead recoiling in the grass. Behind it, another was slithering up the steps, body zigzagging over the risers and treads.

"He got you good," Dalton said. "Right through the pants. They can do that, you know. Three-inch fangs, needle sharp."

Zabek felt a tingle in his leg. No pain. Just a quiver, like a muscle going to sleep.

"Right now you're thinking maybe it didn't really bite you. You're thinking that it didn't hurt enough to be a snake bite."

Zabek moved away from the snake. He wanted to roll up his pants, check the leg, see if Dalton was bluffing.

"You don't feel the real pain right off," Dalton said. "But you will. Best thing to do is—"

The radio crackled. "Deuces! Twenty?"

Zabek felt a slap on his other leg. "Christ!"

This time the snake held on.

"*Motherfucker!*" He kicked.

The snake let go. It was bigger than the first, fat around the middle, thumping loudly as it hit the ground. Then it slithered away, wound itself into a coil, and looked back at Zabek. The first bite was burning now, the leg cramping. He keyed his mike. "This is Deuces!" His voice cracked. "I've been—" The leg spasmed. He went down hard, dropping the mike.

"I know what you're feeling," Dalton said. "I've been there. Wish I could tell you it doesn't get worse. But it does. A lot worse. These coppers pack nasty venom. It's something about this place, makes them wicked." He got up, hands still cuffed behind him, looking down at Zabek who was fumbling for the mike in the tall grass. "Best thing to do is lie still. Wait for help." Dalton flexed his arms, pulling at the cuffs until a hand slid free. It was the deformed hand, the one with the shriveled thumb.

Zabek picked up the mike, keyed it. "Deuces! I'm—"

Dalton lunged, grabbing Zabek's gun in his good hand, hooking the mike cord with the other. "You don't need these." He tossed the gun toward the side of the house, but Zabek kept his grip on the mike, pulling it back, pressing the key. "Deuces! I'm down!"

Dalton lunged again.

"Officer down! *Two* down! Me and Jenkins! We're—"

Dalton grabbed the mike cord with both hands, pulled hard, yanking the wire from the receiver. Then he took Zabek's shoulders, pushed him face down, and straddled his back.

"Listen," Dalton said. "Listen! Lie still and listen!"

The pain kept spreading.

"You need to know—"

Zabek struggled.

"*Listen!*" Dalton roared.

Zabek coughed. "Can't breathe."

"Right. That's the venom. It comes on like a freight train, just a rumble at first, then a roar. And there's no stopping it. No matter what we do here, it's going to run its course." He spoke close to Zabek's ear. "One bite and you might've had a chance. But two? From these critters? At your age? In your condition? Shit, man. You're probably dying."

Zabek thought about the house. There was another radio in there, Sharo's radio. He tried getting up.

"Easy." Dalton tightened his grip. "If you don't fight me, I'll help you. Help you inside." He got off Zabek's back, then turned him around, easing him into a sitting position. "All right? " He kept his grip on Zabek's shoulders. "I'm going to take you inside. OK?"

Zabek tried answering, couldn't find his voice.

"Here." Dalton took Zabek's arm, slung it around his shoulder. "Try standing. On three. One . . . two . . . *up!*"

The next thing Zabek knew he was on his feet, arm around Dalton, legs burning beneath him.

"Can you walk?"

A shadow passed in front of them, cutting the low-angled sun, slipping up along the front of the house.

Dalton looked skyward. "The devil's coming," he said. "We need to hurry."

14

Fearing a roadblock on Cliff Mine Run, Kirill drove home on the inter-state, heading north and getting off at the Blaston exit. From there it was a long drive before he reached the turn that brought him down onto Old River Trail.

The pain in his sprained back worsened as he drove, shooting along his neck and into his head, spreading like lightning along his shoulders and down his arms. The seat's cushions gave some relief, especially when he braced his arms against the wheel and pushed back against the headrest, but the cracked and broken pavement was killing him, streaking his vision with sparks of pain each time the car struck a pothole.

By the time he reached Silver Lake Dam, the pain had become a crushing weight. He needed more aspirin, more vodka, a hot shower. He also needed food and sleep, and there would be plenty of time for those once he had left town.

But first he had to get home.

He drove faster as he came to the old bridge that ran parallel to the down-stream slope of the Silver Lake Dam. A few hundred feet later, he reached an upper stretch of Cliff Mine Run, a quarter mile north of the coal-hauling road that led to Paul Peterson's body. He didn't doubt that the corpse was still there. Hidden in the woods, it might sit for days before someone hap-pened upon it, plenty of time for Uncle Ilya to get things under control.

Kirill's residence sat on a rise just beyond the entrance to Lakeside Estates. He pulled around the side to where a two-car garage stood across from the wooden deck that cantilevered out from the second floor of the house. He hit the remote in his glove compartment and nosed in beside a second Viper, an orange SRT10. Then he reversed out again, cutting the wheels until his silver Viper pointed toward the front of the property. Then he got out, went into the garage, and got some traveling money from the stash that he kept there.

He never hid money in the house. It was an old superstition, but there was always an element of truth in such things.

Since he didn't expect to be away for long, he settled on a single brick of bills, 20 straps of banded Jacksons, shrink-wrapped into two packs and then wrapped again into a bundle of $40,000: five pounds of cash, enough for a few weeks of hiding, more than enough time for Uncle Ilya and the *mudaks* to get a handle on things.

He closed the garage and hobbled up the deck stairs that led to the rear entrance of his house. He needed to be quick. Twenty minutes, max: long enough to shower, change clothes, and kill his pain.

He put the brick of money on his bed and entered the bathroom. His reflection in the mirror looked terrible, with the abrasion on the side of his face running in a raw streak from temple to jaw. He still had no idea how it had gotten there. But it had been a hell of a night. So much had happened. It was impossible to remember it all.

Pressing his hand against the glass, he slid the mirror along its track, uncovering a sparse medicine cabinet: salve, bandages, vodka, and a large bottle of aspirin—extra-strength, 500 milligrams. He shook out a dozen tablets. He had a name for them back home: little wheels—*kolesa*. He lined them up on the counter beside the sink, muttering to himself. "*Prokatitsia na kolesah.*" Time to get on his little wheels, drive away from the pain.

The house phone rang. He let it go, listening as he crushed the aspirin beneath a twelve-ounce tumbler.

The answering machine clicked on after four rings: "Hello! Please leave a message."

Kirill swept the 6,000 milligrams of crushed aspirin into the glass.

"Hey, Kirill! *Pree-vyet n'at!*"

Kirill winced. It was Arnold Gusky. The jerk couldn't speak Russian to save his life, or maybe he just buggered the accents to be annoying. *Pree-vyet*, when pronounced correctly, was the Russian equivalent of *hello*. *N'at* wasn't Russian at all. It was Pittsburgh slang for *and all that*. The combination had the effect of nails on slate. *Hey, Kirill! Hello and all that!*

"Listen," Gusky said, speaking to the machine. "I already tried your cell, left a message there, too. My next call's to the club. If you're not there, I'm going to start worrying. There's some kind of crap going down, and I need to hear from you that it's all copasetic . . . nothing to worry about, n'at. OK? Call me back, *chuvak!*"

Kirill scowled at the phone. *Chuvak!* He took a bottle of Stolichnaya from the cabinet and poured it into the glass. Then he swirled the glass to dissolve the aspirin, thinking about the things he would like to do to Arnold Gusky. As epithets went, *chuvak—meathead—*wasn't so bad. It was just that Gusky's use of it implied that he and Kirill were the kind of guys who could call each other names and still be chums. Buddies *n'at*.

The answering machine shut off.

Kirill drank his medicine. It left a chalky taste, so he took another drink to wash it away. Then he peeled off his clothes, got in the shower, and waited for the aspirin to kick in.

There'd been a time in his life when pain hadn't mattered. He'd taken a bullet in the thigh once, chased the shooter five blocks, then beat the crap out of him with his bare hands. Now, after a few minor smash-ups in Sam's Jeep, he felt like a cripple.

The shower helped a little, driving the pain back to a persistent ache. He let the water run against his shoulders for a good ten minutes, then climbed out, toweled off, and returned to his bedroom.

The phone rang again, but this time the caller clicked off when the automatic voice answered. He considered checking the caller ID, but it was all he could do to concentrate on dressing: easing his arms into the sleeves, working the buttons, stepping into fresh trousers. The pain may have subsided, but his head still felt wrong. Not drunk, but addled. Perhaps it was a delayed reaction to last night's accidents: crashing broadside against a tree, sideswiping a guardrail, spinning out on flooded pavement. He had heard about the delayed effects of whiplash, how people sometimes sustained serious damage without realizing it. Was that the case here? He flexed his shoulders, turned his neck, and stopped when pain flared anew at the base of his skull.

Sooka!

He sat on the bed, bracing his hands against his knees until the pain subsided. He had to remember not to turn like that. Maybe, if he let it rest, it'd get better on its own.

He stood again, taking it slower now. He set an overnight bag on his bed, put the brick of cash in the bottom, and returned to the bathroom for the aspirin and vodka. He swallowed a few more tablets just in case, washing them down with a drink straight from the bottle. Then he went back to the bedroom where he put the vodka, aspirin, and some extra clothes atop the brick in the overnight bag.

The phone rang again as he zipped the bag and hobbled down to the waiting Viper. Or was the ringing in his head? In his ears? He crossed the deck and paused at the top of the stairs.

The ringing stopped.

He pushed on, gripping the rail, taking it slow, assuring himself that all would be better once he got behind the wheel. Then he would drive south, cross the border, and park at the Morgantown Airport. From there he'd take a taxi to a hotel where he could hole up until he was rested, until the pain subsided, until he was able to think.

He put the overnight bag in the Viper's trunk and climbed behind the wheel. His head felt worse than ever after the walk from the bedroom. His hand trembled as he put his keys in the ignition. Something was definitely wrong with his head. Maybe the best thing to do was go back inside, eat something, lie down. *One hour*, he thought. *I'll be better in an hour.* Was there time for that? He closed his eyes, thinking. There was food in the fridge, ready-to-eat meals prepared by that girl with the bad teeth, the one that smiled too much and pole danced like a monkey on a stick. She was a piece of work, but she made terrific *pelmeny*.

His stomach throbbed in time with his aching head. A little food would probably take care of that, wake him up a little, give him the energy he needed for the short drive south.

I'll be quick.

He got out of the car.

Again, he heard bells, but this time they stopped when he slammed the door. *Keys in the ignition?* He looked down at his empty hand. *This is bad. I'm not thinking straight.*

He looked back at the car, turning with his neck instead of pivoting on his feet. Fresh pain flared at the base of his skull. It sparked behind his eyes, bright red like the strobe of a light bar. *Sooka!* He lost balance, stumbled, and put out his hand to catch himself on the car. His fingers slapped the door. He kept falling.

The ground came up hard.

The red pain went dark.

For a while, Kirill slept.

15

The sun broke through the eastern haze as Pax Scanlon made his way back to the tree. He dried off, spread his beach towel over the ground, and retrieved a band-aid box from a hole beneath the tree's roots. Inside the box was a butane lighter, a wire spool, and three tightly rolled joints that he had purchased from a groundskeeper. He took out the lighter, flicked it, and pressed a joint between his lips. This was his favorite part of the day. Exhausted from the night's games and his swim in the lake, he could lie back and catch a buzz while the rising sun went from red to gold through the pines.

After finishing the smoke, he ate another granola bar, stretched out on the blanket, and fell into the empty hole that always came after a deep swim. He seldom slept long, usually awaking after forty minutes or so, but this morning he roused sooner, his sleep broken by the familiar growl of his stepfather's van. He saw the vehicle first in his dream, a black juggernaut emerging out of the void, coming toward him, forcing him to choose between being run over or waking up. And when he did wake up, the van was there, 100 feet away, gliding past the front of the stone house that belonged to Mr. Kirill Vorarov.

Pax eased against the tree, peering around it, watching the van's windows as if he could see his stepfather's eyes peering through the tinted glass. Then the van vanished, pulling out of sight between Vorarov's house and garage, where it stayed for barely five minutes before backing out and speeding back the way it had come.

"The Russian got a short meeting," Pax said, not so much talking to himself as he was taunting the contents of the long black container he had brought with him from beneath the house. "That's a *power* meeting!" He tilted the container, looking into the open end.

Lidless eyes stared out.

"Our meeting will take longer."

The snake in the container was a copperhead, coiled on a bed of glue, caught in a trap set by the animal-control service that had been contracted to deal with the neighborhood's pest problem.

All summer, the control workers had planted traps, sprinkled poisons and repellents, and worked with the grounds crew to clear nesting sites and erect a two-foot high fence along the development's northwest perimeter. But the snakes and rats remained. The control workers said it was because of the location. Copperheads had lived in these hills far longer than people. Their nests were deep, and the abundance of prey—made even more abundant with the proliferation of dumpsters—had only increased their numbers.

Pax flicked his lighter. The butane flame leaped up, reflecting in the snake's eyes. The pupils contracted, becoming dark slits. But Pax was more interested in the openings below the eyes, thermal pits that detected heat rather than light. Snakes felt sound and saw temperature. How different the world must seem to them.

"You know things I don't know." Pax took his thumb from the lighter, snuffing the flame. "You see things I can't see."

The snake flexed its jaws.

"You want to bite me?"

The mouth twitched, revealing the nubs of retracted fangs.

"You have poison in your mouth, but I have fire in my hand." He flicked the lighter again. "Which is stronger?"

The snake twitched on its bed of glue.

Pax put the trap down, slid the lighter into his pocket, and walked back to the forest on the edge of the property. He returned a few minutes later, carrying sticks and leaves. One of the sticks was green, freshly ripped from a young cedar. The others were dry, ripe for burning. He shaped the dry ones into a cone between his feet. Then, carefully, he upended the trap and slid the glue bed onto the ground.

The snake was a big one, its body looping like a snarled chord. The head had gone into the trap first. Then the body had followed, trying to free the head by leveraging against the glue. Now its entire length was locked in place, waiting for one of the animal-control workers to transport it out into the wild. Pax had heard that they took the snakes deep into the mountains and freed them by dissolving the glue with cooking oil. Hearing about the cooking oil had given Pax his own ideas.

He picked up the piece of green cedar and jabbed the end at the snake's mouth.

The mouth snapped.

Pax withdrew the stick, waited a moment, and jabbed again.

One of the animal-control people had told Pax that snakes had no memory. They lived only in the moment. For that reason, once they were transported and released into the mountains, they went on with their lives as if nothing had changed. No post-traumatic stress for snakes. But Pax figured there was also a downside to having no memory. A person stuck on a bed of glue would eventually become resigned to his fate, but a snake never would. For a snake, each moment of lingering entrapment would be a moment of terrible discovery. *Hey!! What's this? I'm trapped! What am I going to do? Maybe if I just rest a moment. . . . Hey!! What's this? I'm trapped! What am I going to do? Maybe if I just rest a moment. . . .*

Pax poked the snake again. "Remember me?"

The snake snapped.

"That didn't work! Don't you remember?" He poked again.

The snake snapped.

"Let's try something new."

The snake stared.

"But it's *all* new to you, isn't it?" Pax took the spool of metal wire from the band-aid box and, working carefully—not wanting to get his fingers stuck in the glue, and certainly not wanting to get bitten—he lashed the snake to the stick. By the time he finished, the snake's jaws were open wide, fangs extended.

He set the snake aside, giving it a moment to forget and rediscover its new predicament.

Then, as the snake watched, Pax built a fire.

tupid!

Sam ran along Old Coal Creek Road until she reached a bridge. She jumped the side, landed on a slope, and bounded down to a foul-smelling stream. Debris littered the banks: tires, bottles, appliances. . . .

The kids in the truck yelled at her to stop. But they wouldn't come after her until they'd retrieved Jason.

Stupid! I should have just backed away. What was I thinking?

If Jason went to the cops, or worse if he went to the hospital and the cops came to him, she might find herself in a world of crap, especially since all four boys had gotten a good look at her. And yet she laughed as she ran, remembering the look on Jason's face as he went over the side, his expression faltering between desire and disbelief.

She leaped over an old truck tire. Mosquitoes swarmed. She ran faster, climbing now, up the opposite slope, through a stretch of woods, toward the sound of interstate traffic.

A sign appeared high atop a metal pole:

STRIP MINE!
GENTLEMEN'S CLUB

She and Kirill had things to talk about, protection to negotiate, cover stories to plan. And they needed to plan quickly. She did not want to linger on the edge of Windslow any longer than she had to.

The lot held only a blue Nissan, the day manager's car. Neither Sam's Jeep nor Kirill's Viper were anywhere in sight.

The club's door was locked.

She pressed the buzzer.

Danny Love answered. He looked her over, his gaze snagging on her muddy boots, dirty clothes, sock-covered hands. "Rough night?"

"Where's Kirill?"

Danny took an envelope and set of keys from his pocket. "He said to give you these."

She put the envelope in a thigh pocket, buttoned the flap. "Where's the Jeep?"

"Out back."

"Kirill?"

"Harrisburg."

"Don't bullshit me, Danny."

"What the fuck, Sam?"

"Where's Kirill?"

"Where do you think?"

"The lake?"

"I didn't say that."

"But it stands to reason." She looked back at Danny's car. "Early for you to be here, isn't it?"

"Yeah."

"Been here more than an hour?"

"No." He glanced at her hands again. "Looks like you had some trouble, you and Kirill both. He looked like crap, too."

"Thanks, Danny." She turned and started away.

He called after her. "He said he'd take care of everything."

"I'll remind him of that when I see him."

"You want to come in, use the bathroom, wash up?"

She had to pee, but she'd rather go in the weeds than set foot in the club. "I'm fine, Danny." She kept walking.

Danny remained in the doorway.

When she looked back, he was watching the smoke on the horizon.

17

Benjie waited in the truck, leaning forward against the wheel, sucking nervously at his arm until he heard voices coming from the side of the road. He sat back, adjusted the rearview, and saw the three of them walking toward the passenger door.

Jason didn't want to ride in the back. Vinny and R.D. helped him into the cab, where he sat a moment with his feet on the running board. He had a big skid mark on his back, grit and grass stains mostly, but there was a nasty scrape on his arm, running from elbow to hand.

"We need to head back," R.D. said.

"No," Jason's voice was flat and drawn, like there was something broken inside him.

"The hospital?" Vinny said. "Emergency?"

"No." Jason turned, facing the windshield.

Benjie glanced at his face, then turned away, watching from the corner of his eye.

Jason's expression was like his voice, dull and empty.

"Where, then?" R.D. said. "What do you want to do?"

Jason raised his battered arms, grabbed the seat's shoulder restraint and pulled the buckle down across his chest. "The club." He tried clicking the buckle but couldn't get it to work. The belt kept slipping from his hand, sliding up along his chest.

Vinny helped him, grabbing the buckle, locking it down. "You need to put something on that arm, Jason."

"I'll wash it at the club."

"Club's not open yet," R.D. said.

"We'll wait then." Jason seemed to come alive, turning to R.D., looking him straight on. "*She* was going there, remember? That's what *she* said." His voice did something strange each time it hit the word *she*. It seemed to hesitate then rush forward, like hitting a snag. "We need to find out who *she* is, talk to the manager."

"You want to press charges?" Vinny asked.

Jason turned back around, voice going flat again. "I want to find out who *she* is." Then he just sat there, a lump on the seat, refusing to say anything more until Vinny and R.D. slammed the door and climbed into the back. Then Jason turned to Benjie. "This isn't funny."

Benjie put the truck in gear.

"You laugh, I'll kill you."

Benjie just drove.

"I mean it. I'll freaking kill you, retard."

Benjie drove, right on Windslow Road, then right again when they reached Strip Mine Drive.

The club's front door was open. A man stood within it, looking out, watching the horizon.

Benjie pulled into a space in front of the door, a few slots away from a blue Nissan. He glanced at Jason. "Want help getting out?"

"Kill you," Jason said. "Laugh and I'll kill you."

The passenger door opened. Vinny and R.D. took Jason's arms, helping him down.

"Club's not open yet," the man said.

Vinny turned toward him. "You the manager?"

"That's right."

"We need to talk to you."

The manager glanced at Jason. "What happened to him?"

"That's what we need to talk about," Vinny said.

Benjie climbed out.

The parking lot was big, empty, and full of noise from an interstate overpass that curved beyond its eastern end. Cars and trucks raced by, cutting the morning air. *Whooosh! Whoooooooosh!*

"It's about one of your girls," Vinny said. "We gave her a ride. She threw our friend from the truck."

"Really?" the manager said.

"*She* was one of your amateurs," Jason said. "A bitch in khakis."

The manager grinned. "Really?" He said it different this time. "Khakis?" He stepped aside, letting them into the club.

"Camouflage," Vinny said.

The manager seemed amused.

"*She* told us *she* worked here," Jason said, still snagging on the *she*s. "*She* told us—"

"Let's get something on that arm," the manager said. "There's a sink." He put his hand on Jason's shoulder. "We'll fix you up." He looked at the others. "Fix you guys up, too." He gestured to the bar. "Have a seat. We'll be right back." He led Jason away, down a hall toward a back room near a glowing exit sign.

Vinny and R.D. headed for the bar.

"Hey, Vinny," R.D. said. "Hear that? Fix us up."

"This might work out OK," Vinny said.

"He's gonna fix us up!" R.D. slid onto a stool beneath a high-def monitor.

"When he comes back," Vinny said, "you let me do the talking."

The news was on the TV, something about the economy, nothing about Windslow.

"This place doesn't have a liquor license," R.D. said. "Should I get the cooler?"

"No." Vinny leaned over the bar, grabbed a bag of chips from the display. "They've got drinks. Complimentary stuff. For VIPs." He ripped open the bag, offered the open end to R.D. "Today, we're VIPs."

R.D. took a chip. "Freakin' A!"

"But we have to play it right." Vinny set the bag on the counter. "I do the talking. Remember that."

Benjie took a stool at the end of the bar, looked around, frowned. There was something in the air, a sharp stink like dust and fire. "This place smells funny."

"It's poontang," R.D. said.

Benjie looked up along the stairs, toward the mezzanine. The smell was coming from up there, like someone had been setting off caps or fireworks.

"*Amateur* poontang," Vinny said.

"Except they aren't amateurs," R.D. said. "They're, like, immigrants."

"That girl in the truck wasn't an immigrant."

"I guess you'd know. You rode with her." R.D. looked toward the door. "How long you think it'll take her to walk here?"

"Hard to say. She might be hiding, afraid we're looking for her. And if she's keeping off the roads—" Vinny shrugged. "She might be lost in the woods. She was all screwed up. Did you see her hands? She had socks on them. Tube socks, clear up both arms, like she was covering needle marks."

"Junkie?"

"That's how I figure. How else could a bitty thing like that throw Jason over the side?" He grinned. "She was hepped on something. And the manager, he knows. Probably gives her the stuff, which means he's going to do whatever he can to keep us quiet, make us happy."

"You mean—"

"Whatever we want, Mr. Road! This is our—"

The manager reappeared from the back hall. "Your buddy's fine. Just scratches. Nothing broken. I showed him the sink, gave him some bandages.

He wanted to do it himself." The manager stepped behind the bar, saw Benjie sitting alone, turned toward him. "You the boss?"

Benjie turned away.

"Designated driver," Vinny said.

"So no drinks for him?" The manager opened a cabinet beneath the bar, took out a bottle of Ikon. "Jason tells a good story." He produced two glasses, poured—two shots each. "Not too early, right? Jason says you're here to party."

Benjie stared at them now. It was safe. No one was looking. He could study them all he wanted. Vinny was looking confident, in control, the way he usually did. Benjie wondered what it must be like to be that way around people, to look them in the eye, make them listen. And the manager was listening, leaning forward, looking like he really wanted to be Vinny's friend. As for R.D., he wasn't doing much of anything, just sitting there, staring, not touching his vodka glass, waiting for Vinny to drink first.

"We're waiting for your girl," Vinny said.

The manager grinned, looking amused. "My girl?" He tugged his face. The grin went flat. "Jason told me. But she isn't my girl. She doesn't dance here. Doesn't work for me. She works for the owner. And you're too late if you want to see her. She's already been here. Took her Jeep and left."

"Left?" Vinny glanced at R.D. "Did we pass a Jeep?"

"No."

"She would've left the back way," the manager said. "Down the back ramp, out toward Route 19."

"You sure? Khakis? Short hair? Same girl?"

"She wouldn't like you calling her a *girl*," the manager said. "She's more like a soldier."

"Soldier?"

"A tough little piece of work," the manager said. "And that's about all I know." He pushed the shot glass toward Vinny. "She comes here now and then. Does stuff for the big boss. Sometimes he leaves envelopes for her. She takes them and goes."

"Envelopes of what?" Vinny asked.

"Don't know. Don't want to know. No one wants to know." He grinned. "Listen. This is your day. We have nice girls coming in. You'll like them, and maybe . . . if you and your friends forget about this soldier business . . . the girls will like you. Know what I mean? OK?"

Vinny said something after that, but Benjie didn't catch it. Something new had his attention. Footsteps coming down the hall, moving closer, getting louder. The others were too busy talking to notice, but Benjie looked toward the sound, watching until Jason stepped into the light of one of the hi-def monitors. He looked no better than before, worse actually. His pants were unbuttoned, zipper partway down. A couple of fresh scratches ran along his cheek. His eyes were more distant than ever.

He took a seat beside R.D.

R.D. turned. "What the hell?"

Jason braced against the bar. His arm wasn't bandaged, and the gauze on his wounded hand was coming off in dirty clumps. He looked at the manager. "You were wrong."

"Wrong?"

"What you said, what you told me. You were wrong."

"What I told you?"

"You said *she* left. But *she* was still there. Still out back."

The manager looked at Vinny, back at Jason.

"I went out the back door," Jason said. "*She* was changing a tire."

The manager said something, a snorting word that seemed to catch in the back of his throat. It sounded angry, like cussing in another language.

"Damn, Jason!" Vinny leaned toward him. "What'd she do to you this time?"

"*She* was changing the tire," Jason said. "*She* had her back to the door, tools on the ground. One of them was a crowbar . . . you know, for hub-caps." He saw the untouched drinks on the bar, took the one in front of R.D., knocked it down.

"Those scratches on your cheek," the manager said. "She did that? She fucked you up again?" He turned to Vinny, spread his hands, a gesture that seemed to say: *What can I do if he keeps messing with a soldier?*

Jason put down the shot glass, rapped it hard against the bar. "*She* didn't," he said. "*She* didn't fuck me up." He reached for the other glass, Vinny's glass.

Vinny grabbed his wrist, stopping him. "Slow down, Jason. Tell us what happened."

The manager glanced toward the hall, acting as if he expected the soldier to reappear any second.

"What happened?" Jason frowned. "I *did* her, that's what happened." He forced his hand from Vinny's grip, took the glass, pulled it toward him. "I hit her with the crowbar. Then I *did* her. *Did* her good."

"*Did* her?" Vinny asked.

"You know. The deed. *Did* the deed."

"You *fucked* her?"

The manager blanched.

"Yeah." Jason downed the second glass. "She's out there," he said. "Lying in the weeds. Maybe dead. I don't know. She wasn't moving."

The manager cussed again, hard and angry. He glanced toward the hall, then grabbed the glasses from the bar and threw them in the sink. Benjie understood his movements. He had seen animals do the same thing. He was preening, taking care of little business to avoid the big stuff.

"So she's still there?" R.D. asked.

"Yeah," Jason said. "If she's dead, she is. And if she isn't—"

"You better hope she is." The manager took Vinny's potato-chip bag, crumpled it up, chips and all, threw it away. "You better hope she is dead. Because if she isn't—"

"I'm going out there," Vinny said.

"Hell with that." R.D. got up. "Let's just leave."

"Can't do that," Vinny said. "Not now! Jesus Christ! This is a goddamn train wreck."

Benjie got up. No one looked at him. He'd become invisible, so far removed from the scene that no one would notice him as long as he moved slowly, quietly. He stepped away from the bar, moving toward the hall until he saw the exit sign beyond the restrooms. The big steel door hadn't closed all the way. Daylight rimmed its edge. He reached it before the others realized he was gone, and by then he had his hand on the door, pushing it open, stepping out.

"Benjie! Where's Benjie? "

Footsteps raced into the hall behind him.

"Goddamnit, Benjie!"

But Benjie was already through the open door, standing on the edge of a narrow strip of bare asphalt that ended at the base of a vertical wall of rock.

There was nothing else there: no tools, no Jeep, and no soldier girl in forest-green khakis.

After putting Axle to bed, Bird went to his own room where he pulled on a pair of cotton briefs and faded jeans. The fabric felt strange against his skin, pinching in places it never had before. He seemed to sense each seam, each fiber, each shifting point of contact with his skin—so much so that he almost pulled the clothes off again. But he figured he'd adjust. Besides, the servants were up now, starting the cleaning and maintenance routines that kept the big country home functioning. He was bound to cross someone's path sooner or later, and it would be best not to be naked when that happened.

He entered his walk-in closet, considered putting on one of the leather vests that he had been wearing since becoming interested in the Okwe of southwestern Pennsylvania, but he opted for a blue work shirt instead. The cuffs felt tight against his wrists, but the sleeves covered his arms, hiding the lack of tattoos on his new skyborn body. The fewer questions he raised about his looks and behavior, the better.

Sun streamed through the windows of the central hall, gliding over him as he descended the stairs and headed for the terrace behind the north wing. The light beams felt like physical things, resisting slightly as he passed through them. And they had a fragrance, too—a warm, clear scent that he had never noticed before.

I'm different. Not the person I was yesterday. Perhaps not a person at all.

The thought troubled him, not greatly, but persistently—like the fibers of his clothes. It had been chaffing at him ever since he had awakened in the forest, lying on his back beside his Escalade, his mind fresh with memories of falling from the sky.

Or had the sky fall been a dream?

The notion tugged at him, leading to more questions. If the falling had been a dream, then everything before it may have been a dream as well. In which case, where did that leave him now?

He continued toward the terrace, stopping at the wet bar inside the French doors. He poured a few fingers of single malt into a crystal glass, raised it to the light, and pondered its colors—shades and hues that he had never noticed before: blue sparks flashing amid the amber swirls. The smell was new too, so overwhelming that it nearly knocked him down as he brought it to his lips. The sensation was akin to vertigo, a realization of smells between smells that deepened with each whiff. He set his hand on the bar, bracing himself.

I can't drink this.

It wasn't the alcohol that he couldn't handle. He sensed he could drink all he wanted and never get drunk. Instead, it was the taste and smell of the drink that made him back away. With his senses fully dilated, a single sip might overwhelm him, fill his head with scents, textures, and flavors that he had never realized existed before.

He lowered the glass, turned, and walked outside onto a garden ledge. The air sang to him, the smell of flowers in the rising sun. The world was waking up, his senses becoming more aware of it with each passing moment.

I have to sit down.

A heavy chair waited beside him, its legs singing as they drank heat from the low-angled sun. It wasn't a conventional piece of outdoor furniture. He had never liked sitting in those. Instead, it was a heavy antique, an heirloom taken from his father's study. He eased into it, feeling the slow wisdom of its weight, the purity of its construction. He set his hands on the armrests. The wood and leather spoke to him. *We are brothers and sisters, plant and animal, children of the earth.* And beneath those whispers, the deeper voice of brass accents and iron nails. *We are the fathers and mothers. Iron and alloy. Ancient as the stars. Eternal.*

But those voices were barely a whisper compared to the voices of chanting sunlight, humming grass, singing flowers. They spoke to his vision. Their colors and movements overwhelming him until he had to close his eyes. But when he did, the song continued in the smell of the garden, grass, and trees. Could he shut those things out, too? Of course he could. All he had to do was stop inhaling, and when he did, he discovered that he no longer needed to breathe.

Shutting out his other senses was more difficult, but each seemed to disconnect on its own after a few minutes of sitting quietly, at which point he found himself floating in the heart of something vast—a wordless void where all time was one time, all things one thing . . . or perhaps nothing at all. He lingered there in the empty oneness, drifting until he felt something pull at him. He tried shutting it out, but it held on.

We're not alone!

He opened his eyes.

The voice came again, calling from a second floor window. "We're not alone!"

Bird stood, turned, looked up.

Axle's room was above the garden: one floor up, twenty feet to the left. The window stood open, the drapes closed. "Axle?" Bird walked along the terrace, the flagstones humming beneath his feet. "Axle!"

A face peered around the side of the house. It was Jim Dooley, one of the estate's caretakers, with a pair of shears. "Mr. Frieburg? I didn't know you was there."

"Did you hear something?"

"Something?" Jim forced a smile. "Only you, Mr. Frieburg."

Bird looked again at the window, then hurried inside.

The central hall had changed. It was darker now, as if clouds had rolled in, blocking the window light, chilling the air.

Upstairs, something stirred: gusting wind, snapping curtains. And the closed door to Axle's room shivered in its frame, rattling the latch and hinges, vibrating with the cadence of speech.

We're not alone! The rattling said. *Not alone!*

"Axle!" He turned the knob, but the door wouldn't open. Something held it closed. He pushed harder. The door swung inward, freeing an out-rushing blast of rain-scented wind.

The room stretched before him, filled with howling darkness that seemed to exist somewhere apart from the house. Indeed, even with the drapes closed, the room could not have been as dark as it seemed. And the wind didn't come from the window. It came from within the room, from the bed on which Axle lay sleeping.

"Axle?" He stepped toward the bed. "Hey, Axle!"

The wind gusted, slamming the door, sealing the room, shutting the darkness in. And yet Bird could see. Not colors, but outlines: the nylon windbreaker on the floor, the rumpled bedclothes, the dented pillow where Axle's head should have been.

We're not alone! The wind said. *Not alone! Alone!*

As before, when Bird had been sitting outside, the words came from somewhere above him. Not from a window this time, but from the ceiling.

Bird stepped back, looking up, squinting as dark wind spilled across his face. At first he saw only the vaults of the carved ceiling, the arched curves reminiscent of cathedral stone. But two of the arches were closer than the others, hanging lower, suspended like sails on the wind that still swirled through the room. A body lay between the sails: flared hips, narrow waist, muscular chest, angular head. The thing hovered, rocking like a tethered kite. It was Kwetis, the nightflyer.

His great eyes were closed, twitching behind dark lids.

Bird tried making sense of it.

Kwetis was a dream spirit. His existence required a human host. In this case, that host was Axle. But where was Axle now? Why was his bed empty? And how could Kwetis be here if Axle was gone?

Bird felt dizzy, and yet he continued gazing up into the wind, pondering the most perplexing detail of all: Kwetis's eyes, closed and twitching with the movement of dreams. What did it mean? Was the dream spirit dreaming? And if so, what was the nature of those dreams?

Dreams within dreams, questions within questions—it was too much for Bird. He had wandered into something he couldn't handle. And now he needed to leave, get out of the room before he lost his mind.

He took a step back, then another, reaching for a door that no longer seemed to be there. And then, just as Bird was ready to turn and get his bearings, Kwetis opened his eyes.

19

Benjie stood on the narrow lot behind the back door of the sex club, watching as Vinny and R.D. argued with the manager.

Jason didn't say much. He just stared at a patch of flattened weeds, squinting as if he still saw something lying there.

"So what are you saying?" Vinny asked the manager. "You're going to call the cops?"

"The cops?" The manager spit toward the wall of cutaway rock. "No way! This isn't for cops."

"So we're even, then?"

"Even?" the manager said. "Even how?"

"Your girl messes with Jason, so Jason messes with your girl. Both walk away. Even."

"She is not *my* girl," the manager said.

"Whatever."

"No, not whatever. She is not *mine*, and she is not a *girl*. I told you—"

"A soldier."

"That's right."

"Whatever that means."

"What it means," the manager said, "is that you have no idea the shit you're in."

"Why?" R.D. said. "If she's not out here, that means she drove away. And if she drove away, she can't be hurt too bad."

"Look," Vinny said, talking louder—as if volume would make it all come together. "She threw Jason out of our truck. He could have been killed!"

"But he wasn't," the manager said.

"That's the point. And neither was she. Jason just roughed her up, is all."

"He did more than *rough* her."

"Knocked her out," Jason muttered, talking to the flattened weeds. "Then I *did* her. Did her good."

"Doing her is not *even*," the manager said. "It's not even close to *even*."

"Feels like *even*," Jason said.

"You guys don't get it." The manager looked around, up along the wall of rock, scanning the cliff as if he expected to see someone looking down from a ledge. "Things like this never get *even*. We're wasting time even talking here. You guys have all got to go. Now!"

"But we've got people meeting us!"

"Then you should call them. Tell them to stay away."

"All right!" Vinny looked at the others. "We're out of here." He turned, looked as if he was about to reenter the rear door and cut through the club, but then he backed away, spit on the pavement, and took off along the side of the building.

R.D. looked at Benjie. "You got the keys?"

Benjie slapped his pockets. "Yeah."

"Give." R.D. put out his hand. "I'm driving now."

"You've been drinking," Benjie said.

"Half a beer back at the house." He snapped his fingers. "My keys!"

Benjie handed them over.

Then R.D. started walking, hurrying after Vinny.

Jason stayed where he was, staring at the weeds. "Hey, Benjie."

"Huh?"

Jason glanced up. His eyes were wide and dark. Like animal eyes.

Benjie looked away.

For a moment they just stood, a heavy silence between them.

"We should go, Jason."

"That's right," the manager said. "Both of you. Now."

Benjie and Jason started walking.

The manager followed.

Jason leaned close to Benjie. Too close. Benjie tried stepping away, but Jason just sidestepped, closing the gap. "I didn't really," he whispered. "I can tell you that. But the others . . . the others can't know."

"Know what?"

"I didn't really do her. Not really. Not all the way, just almost."

"I don't care," Benjie said.

"But I need to say it."

Benjie just kept walking.

"I hit her on the leg." Jason spoke slowly, not looking at Benjie. "I knocked her down. Then I jumped her. I put the crowbar on her throat, but she kept moving . . . moving under me. It felt good. Then she stopped moving."

"No," Benjie said. "I don't think so. I don't think I want to listen. I don't like it."

"But I have to tell someone, Benjie." Jason raised his hands, pressed them to his face. He seemed to be crying, but he wasn't. He was smelling his fingers. "I touched her," he said. "When she stopped moving, I took off her pants. Then she coughed."

"She was still breathing?"

"Not *still*," Jason said. "She stopped for a while. Then she started again."

"So she was OK? You knew that. When you came inside, when you told us what you did, you already knew—"

"No. I didn't. See . . . I hit her some more." He raised his bandaged fist. "That's when my hand started bleeding again." They neared the front of the building, heading toward the whoosh of freeway traffic. "I hit her on the head until she stopped moving. I didn't check to see if she was breathing after that. I just left her there, pants around her knees."

Benjie walked faster. He wasn't in a hurry to reach the truck. He just wanted to get away from Jason.

But Jason sped up, keeping pace as they rounded the front of the building. "And something else, Benjie. There's something else—"

"Goddamnit!" R.D. shouted. "You've got to be kidding me!"

R.D. and Vinny stood beside the truck's open door.

"Benjie!" R.D. said. "What the hell'd you do to my truck?"

"Me?"

R.D. slammed the door. "Won't freaking start."

"Had trouble like this before?" the manager asked.

"No," R.D. said. "Never." He raised the hood. "I just had it tuned." He looked inside, doing a double take as he glanced down along the front of the engine. "What the hell? Jesus Christ! Someone's messed with it!"

The manager backed away. "Tell you what," he said. "I know a guy . . . an engine guy." He looked at Vinny. "Let me give him a call." He turned and started toward the club.

Benjie watched him go, noting something odd about his movements, his voice, the way he abruptly slipped through the door when he reached it— opening it just wide enough to pass through, then closing it fast behind him.

He doesn't know an engine guy.

Benjie shivered.

He knows something else . . . something bad's going to happen.

The sex club's door gave a muffled click, the sound of a latch falling home, sealing the entrance from within.

R.D. backed away from the hood. "The wires are cut!" He looked at Vinny. "She did it, huh? Jason did her, so she did my truck." He turned toward Jason, glaring at him. One of R.D.'s eyes was still swelling from the sucker punch Jason had landed back at the house, and now R.D. looked ready to give Jason one of his own. But before he could, the strangest thing happened—something so random that Benjie wasn't sure he really saw it.

Behind R.D., mid-way between him and the back of the truck, a piece of asphalt broke away from the surface of the lot, leaped into the air, and landed again with a skidding thump.

Vinny turned toward the sound, looking down while a car backfired on the freeway. At least, it sounded like backfiring—a concussive burst followed by an echoing *THWAACK-kakk!*

R.D. seemed to hear it too. He looked toward the freeway, then stumbled. "Uh!" He coughed, the air rushing out of him as if someone had just punched him hard. But there was no one near him.

Vinny frowned. "R.D.?"

R.D. pivoted, going off balance, catching himself on the side of the truck, gasping for breath.

The popping sound repeated, coming from the freeway.

THWAACK-kakk!

R.D.'s shoulder darkened, blood oozing through his shirt, dripping down his arm. He stared at it, mouth open, gasping for air.

Vinny looked toward the freeway. He seemed to see something. Or maybe he had just put everything together: the leaping pavement, bloody shoulder, echoing report. "Shit." He backed away from the truck, toward the club. "Inside! Everybody get inside!"

The truck's rear window shattered, spraying fragments over the dash.

"Inside now!" Vinny turned, running, heading for the sex club's door as the distant report reached them once again.

THWAACK-kakk!

This time Benjie thought he saw the glint of something beyond the freeway overpass. And then, a split second later, a silent flash.

Vinny stopped running, the sound of his footsteps giving way to the hiss of his body skidding along the pavement. And then, once again, the delayed report.

THWAACK-kakk!

Now Jason was running. His bowels giving way with an explosive fart that would have been funny if it weren't for the piece of pavement that leaped up behind him.

And still R.D. stood by the truck, looking at his arm, clinging to the fender. His face blanched, zits standing out like gray pebbles on bleached sand.

THWAACK-kakk!

Jason reached the door. It wouldn't open. "Hey!" He slapped the metal, making bloody smears with his wounded hand. "Open up! Let me in!"

Something struck the pavement beside the truck. It was R.D., his left side soaked with blood. He wasn't breathing anymore, wasn't doing anything, just sitting, staring.

Jason pounded harder. "Someone's shooting at us! Someone's—"

He stiffened as part of his head broke away. Then he slumped, slid to his knees, toppled sideways to land on his face.

Now, at last, Benjie screamed, the sound coming not just from his mouth, but from his eyes, ears, fingers, and soul. "*Jasaaaaaaaahhhhhhhhhhhn!*"

The thunder from the hill beyond the interstate echoed one final time: *THWAACK-kakk!*

One of Jason's legs was smeared with poo. He'd really crapped himself this time.

This isn't funny, Benjie!

Benjie scuttled backward.

I mean it, retard!

Benjie bit his lips.

Laugh and I'll kill you!

Benjie turned and ran.

You're next, Benjie. Get out of here!

A line of jaggers grew at the edge of the lot, thorny stems woven with clinging vines. He'd get scratched up bad if he went in there, but he had no place else to go.

Into the weeds, Benjie! That's where you always go. Where you always hide. Into the weeds, Benjie. Now!

Benjie leaped for the jaggers.

20

Parked on a hill above the interstate's northbound lanes, hidden from the traffic but not from the sex-club parking lot, Sam watched the boy running for cover. She reloaded and took the plugs from her ears. For now, she was done shooting. She had no more against the running boy than she had had against the other hapless shits who had gotten between her and her payback. She had been aiming at Jason, the prick who had raped her, the fat bastard who now lay like a lump on the shot-up pavement. The others had been collateral damage.

She would have done better with a rifle, but her case of supplies in the back of the Jeep had held only a .44 Magnum and a partial box of 240-grain rounds. Although effective at close range, the gun lost power and accuracy at distances over 50 yards. Hitting things beyond that point meant elevating the barrel and aiming high: two-to-three inches high at 100 yards, over half a foot at 150. Then there was the problem of drift. At such a distance, even a mild crosswind would cause a bullet to veer. And Sam had been lobbing her rounds over a freeway, contending with wind-patterns that would pose a significant handicap to even the best shooter.

But these things had not been her main concerns when she'd cut the wires on the Chevy truck and drove to the hill above the interstate. Sightlines were what mattered.

And something else.

A 240-grain round would blow through a man at 50 yards. But it lost power after that, yielding to the forces of wind and gravity. It could, if it struck home, still kill a man at distances of 100 or 150 yards, but the way it killed would be different, less surgical, messier.

But the hill that Sam stood on was not 100 to 150 yards from the parking lot. It was, by her calibrated eyes, a little over 200 yards—a distance at which hitting her target would require equal doses of marksmanship and intuition, and at which her rounds stood a better chance at maiming than killing.

For her first shot, she had rested the gun's grip against the Jeep's dented hood, elevated the barrel a foot above the distant dot that was Jason's chest, and swung her aim a few degrees to the left. The force of the first shot reopened the wound in her left hand. She didn't mind the pain, but wet blood on her palm would interfere with her grip. There was a first-aid kit in the back of the Jeep. But it was too late for that once she started shooting. Her first shot had landed short of Jason, hitting the pavement, knocking out a clump of asphalt.

The boys turned.

She raised the barrel a little more, braced herself on the fender, squeezed again.

The report thundered, echoing around her as the kid standing beside the truck took a shot in the back. He jerked, steadied himself, and looked east, squinting into the sun.

Her palm throbbed, bleeding through the sock. And her head was bleeding too, dripping from the fresh cuts above her eye. She didn't remember Jason hitting her face, didn't remember much of anything between the time he had thrown himself on top of her and the time when she had awakened to find her pants bunched down around her ankles. The revulsion of what he might have done to her was even greater than the pain in the leg that he had struck with the crowbar . . . greater than the throbbing pain from the head trauma he had inflected while she was down.

She wanted to wipe her brow, but if she moved her hands she'd lose her mark. So she tilted her head, hoping the blood would veer past her eye as she raised her aim a little more. Then, with gun raised and head tilted, she fired again, taking out the truck's rear window as the shot veered right.

Now the tall kid was running for the sex-club door. He was the one who had touched her by accident in the truck. She had no grudge against him, but his running carried him close to her target . . . too close. Her next shot hit him. He fell hard, sliding—knocked unconscious, maybe dead.

And now Jason was running.

Two more shots remained.

The first struck close to Jason's heels, kicking up a wedge of asphalt as he charged for the door. Was that door locked? Probably. She had seen the way Danny Love had reacted when the kid from the passenger seat looked under the hood, the way he had glanced around, hurried inside.

One more shot.

She raised the barrel, sighted through the blood dripping into her eye, and waited for Jason to reach the locked door.

THWAACK-kakk!

* * *

She cleared out fast, returning her earplugs and the reloaded magnum to the gun case and then speeding onto the dirt trail that led down to the foot of the hill. Here she pulled into the forest, reversing until the trees closed around her.

Working quickly, she removed the Jeep's roof panels and doors. She stowed them in the back and lowered the shattered windshield. Then she climbed under the front bumper and took a look at the radiator. Hot fluid dripped from a crimp beside the drain plug. A few more miles and that seepage would be high pressure steam. The car would never make it to West Virginia.

"Damn you, Kirill! How'd you manage this one?"

She remembered their last conversation, Kirill's frantic call to her cell phone while she tracked Paul Peterson's killers through Windslow Mine. Kirill had driven into a ravine, and she had made the mistake of suggesting he use the winch to haul himself out.

"And you used it, didn't you, Kirill? You crazy bastard!"

She slid out from under the radiator and leaned against the bumper. Kirill had evidently gotten the Jeep snagged on something after activating the winch, and, rather than killing the power and clearing the obstruction, he had kept the spool turning until something gave way. That something had been the radiator.

"No wonder you didn't stick around to meet me at the club!"

She stood, pulling herself up on the bumper, wincing at the pain in her leg, the point below her left hip where Jason had landed his blow with the crowbar. The swelling seemed to be getting worse. She touched it, smearing the pants with her bloody hand as she probed the growing lump.

"I'm a mess."

There wasn't much she could do about the leg, but the hand was another matter. She pulled off the sock. The palm was swollen, throbbing. The sensation was like holding a handful of pain, a physical weight that bore down on her as she inspected the damage. The angelweed hadn't done much. Indeed, the leaves seemed to have irritated the wound. So much for her mother's medicine. It was time to use some of her own.

She limped around to the tailgate where she retrieved her first-aid kit from beneath the stowed roof panels. Inside were the usual: bandages, adhesive, wet wipes, Neosporin, saline. But there were other things as well: clamps, needles, sutures, scalpels, disposable syringes, and two vials each of medical-grade morphine and methamphetamine. She kept these things apart from the others, in a slim plastic container held closed with a rubber band.

Using the wet wipes, she cleaned the wound. Then she poured saline over the slit, padded it dry, and covered it with Neosporin and bandages. It hurt worse now, her fingers throbbing as she unhitched her pants to inspect the damage to her leg.

A fist-sized lump had formed midway between hip and knee. Parts of it were already discolored, but bruising was the least of her concerns. She sat on the bumper and straightened her leg, flexed her foot. The pain intensified, but everything moved as it should.

She considered dropping her briefs, checking for semen. But finding none would prove nothing, and, if it were there, seeing it would be more than she could bear. Sometimes, ignorance was best.

"He's dead," she muttered. "He doesn't exist. If I forget it, it never happened."

She hitched her pants and carried the first-aid kit to the driver's side mirror. The wounds above her eye looked as if they had been left by a fist, not a crowbar.

"Big mistake," she said, talking to his memory. "You should never have let me live, you prick."

She bandaged her head. Then, to make herself look less like a walking casualty, she cut away her pant legs below the knees and knotted the pieces into a bandana. She checked the results in the mirror. "Not bad." Then she started the Jeep and drove out to the road that ran beneath the interstate, heading north toward Kirill's.

Cliff Mine Run was the most direct route, but that would take her past the turn-off where Peterson's body lay in his car. Cops would be there, possibly restricting traffic past the haul road. She couldn't risk being seen by them, not the way she looked. Her best bet would be to take Windslow Road past the base of the mine and toward what she hoped would be an off-road route to Old River Trail. The Jeep would probably get her most of the way. After that, she could ditch the thing and walk. Not an optimal plan, but it was the best she had.

She drove north.

The air thickened as she neared the mine, turning first into a sulfur glow, then to a gray haze that smelled of coal and tar. By then she had passed a surprising number of road kills: a raccoon, two groundhogs, and a furry skid that might have been a rat. Finally she nailed one of her own, a snake that thumped beneath the floorboards as she drove over it. Checking the sideview, she saw that she had smashed its head flat against the pavement, leaving its body to whip like a sputtering cable.

Her mother's voice came back to her, quoting Genesis, Yahweh to Satan: *"You will crawl on your belly and you will eat dust all the days of your life."*
The voice seemed to come from the wind.
"And I will put enmity between you and the woman."
"Shut up," Sam said. "You're not here. I'm not hearing you."
"She will crush your head!"

"You're dead, Mother. Gone! I'm not listening!"

Thump-thump!

Something else passed beneath her wheels. She didn't check the mirror this time, didn't even want to know what it was.

Lights flashed to her left, reds and blues dispersing in the fog as she passed the turnoff to Windslow Road Extension. The fire trucks were still down there. She looked for the smoking Mustang, but already the road had veered, carrying her away from the highwall and down a straightaway that coursed along the base of a hardscrabble slope. The ground here looked like mine debris, neither toxic nor fertile, indifferent to life. A few weeds had taken root, unfurled scraggly leaves, and died. Dirt-bike trails ran among them, coiling back on themselves, leading nowhere. Dead weeds and dead ends.

Sam pondered her location, northeast of the mine, heading toward Blaston Township. Silver Lake lay to the northwest, with Old River Trail running east-to-west past the face of the lake's earthen dam.

"It's got to be up there somewhere."

Her radiator was steaming now. She'd overheat soon. If she was going to try for Old River, it had to be now.

She steered left, engaged four-wheel drive, and hit the slope.

"Please, God. Let me find the trail. Let me—"

She stopped herself, biting her lips.

I wasn't praying. Just talking.

The temperature gauge held steady beneath the red.

"Please! Just a little farther."

She cleared the rise, and there it was: Old River Trail, snaking west through the trees. She disengaged four-wheel drive and hit the gas. Could she make it? She checked the gauge once more. The needle hadn't moved.

A miracle, her mother said.

"I don't believe in miracles."

You used to.

"That was another life."

No. The same life. You only get two, and you're still on the first.

"Leave me alone."

Can't! Can't never leave you. I'm part of you. Forever!

"No, you're gone. Dead. I watched you die! I buried you. Leave me alone. I wish to God you'd leave me alone!"

Sam bit her lips.

The wind howled, but it was only wind, whipping the bandana around her head as the road swept down toward a straightaway between the trees. She took the Jeep out of gear, coasting to save what remained of the engine.

When she looked at the dash again, the temperature was falling.

The road was longer than expected, turns gave way to more turns . . . on and on . . . an endless succession of unknown places.

Steam no longer billowed from the radiator. Either the fluid had boiled away or something had sealed the hole. She doubted the latter, and she kept looking at the temperature gauge, waiting for it to rise. Another mile passed. The needle remained as before, barely moving as she ascended a hill that brought her into sight of a slope overgrown with grass and weeds. A waterfall ran along its side, hissing from a spillway that opened beneath a bridge of painted wood and iron beams. The wood ran along the upper part, the portions visible to anyone driving or walking across it, while the iron, which looked like the remnants of a far older structure, made up the lower supports: rusty beams, some eaten clear through, dangling in empty air.

The slope beside the bridge was the downstream face of the Silver Lake Dam, the 600-foot-long embankment that had transformed an abandoned quarry into a scenic mountain lake. She drove parallel to its face, crossing a bridge much like the one that spanned the spillway. Far below her, a stone culvert extended from the base of the dam. Water trickled from its mouth, forming a rill that meandered through stones and weeds, eventually connecting with the swifter waters from the spillway. The resulting stream flowed south through the valley. She saw all these things in an instant, getting her bearings as the forest trail brought her back to Cliff Mine Run, safely above the haul road.

She turned right at the intersection, heading north until she came to the gates of Lakefront Drive. And now, with less than an eighth of a mile to go, the radiator erupted. Steam jetted beneath the car as Kirill's prefab McMansion swung into view, seeming to tilt out of the landscape. And then, with her engine losing power, she steered into the driveway, coasting around the bend to see Kirill's Viper sitting between the garage and house. He was home!

She stopped the Jeep, the coolant cloud rising around her as she climbed out. Her wounded leg cramped. But she limped on, out of the steam and toward the Omni-Stone walk that led to Kirill's front door. And it was there, as she neared the front of the house, that she saw something 100 feet from Kirill's property line, a figure sitting on the ground, tending a fire. He had a stick in one hand, holding it over the flames, turning it slowly.

She stumbled.

The figure looked up, nodded, and raised his stick. Charred scales shimmered in the morning light. The man (or was it a boy?) was roasting a snake.

Is it real? A vision?

She turned and hurried toward Kirill's front door.

When she looked back, the figure was still there, watching.

21

Even the copperheads on the porch and devil statues in the yard could not have prepared Robert Zabek for the interior of the snake-man's home. Snake skins dangled from the rafters, swaying in the breeze from the open roof, hissing as they rubbed together. A large bed lay near the entrance. At least, it resembled a bed. The headboard was a truck grill covered with braided plastic. Sharo lay on her back, unconscious, possibly dead.

A naked woman stood beside the bed. Zabek tried bringing her into focus. Her skin was cracked, dented in places.

Not a woman . . . a mannequin.

Zabek tried to speak as Dalton put him down beside Sharo. The words wouldn't come. His throat was closing.

The mattress felt stiff and uneven, as if constructed from cardboard lain atop bags of grass and leaves. Zabek tried getting up after Dalton let him go. He couldn't. It took all his strength to suck air through his swelling throat. He seemed to be having an allergic reaction, his entire body poisoned from the bites in his legs.

"I need your belt," Dalton said, removing it and setting it on an industrial spool beside the makeshift bed. "Need your keys." He went through the belt's compartments, found what he wanted, then removed the cuffs from his wrist and looped them through the headboard. "A precaution." Dalton closed the cuffs over Zabek's wrists. "For when—"

A gust descended from the open roof, spilling through the beams, stirring the snake skins. A moment later, the shadow was back, streaking fast and low beyond the open section of roof.

"He's coming," Dalton said.

The snake skins twirled.

"Circling. Be landing any second."

Zabek remembered what Dalton had said outside: *The devil's coming.*

The shadow came once more, slower this time. Then it stopped, grabbed the edge of a roofless gable, and came to rest with a groan of shifting brick, creaking timbers. Grit drifted down, through the rafters, onto the mannequin.

Zabek gasped, trying to scream.

"Don't," Dalton said. "Remember what I told you about spreading the venom. Better to lie still."

The thing peering through the rafters had black wings, a wolfish face, pointed horns—or were they ears?

"Hey!" Dalton said, looking at the thing, gesturing to the bed. "Look what I've got."

The devil folded its wings and leaped onto a second-floor beam. The house creaked: once as the devil landed, then again as it hopped in place, turning around, peering through the hanging snake skins.

"They're cops," Dalton said.

The devil stepped from its perch, dropped between the beams, and landed with a thump on the industrial spool. "Cops?" The devil's voice was low, gritty. "I can see that, Dalton." The spool rocked as the devil hunkered down. Its head was indeed like a wolf's, but with a human jaw, angled cheeks.

By now, Zabek's pain seemed to be overrunning his body, spilling into the room. Everything hurt: the bed, the rafters, the hanging snake skins, the mannequin, even Dalton and the devil. It occurred to Zabek that the pain might not be so bad if he closed his eyes. He tried that. No good. Closing his eyes only sealed in the pain, making it worse. But now he was trapped. The closed eyes wouldn't reopen.

The devil's voice rasped in the pained darkness. "And what do you want me to do with them, Dalton?"

"They've been snake bit."

"I can see that."

"You need to help them."

"I can't heal them."

"But you can keep them alive."

"Yes. I can do that, if you want them to be like you."

"No!" Zabek screamed.

But his voice, like his pain, remained locked in darkness.

22

Sam rang the doorbell and waited for Kirill to answer. A moment passed. She looked back to see if the strange figure was still sitting beside the lake. It was. Still tending a low fire, still holding a roasted snake, still staring at her.

I am so not in the mood for this.

She left the porch and walked to the side of the house, looking back as she went.

The figure kept watching.

She didn't know which bothered her more, the figure's staring or its resemblance to the snake-roasting angel in her Colorado dream. Either way, she felt relieved when it passed out of sight beyond the garage.

She rounded the parked Viper and looked along the sloping backyard that led to the water's edge. Kirill wasn't one to leave his car sitting out unless he was planning to go somewhere. If he wasn't in the house, perhaps he was down by the lake. The development's engineer had an office in the boathouse. Kirill sometimes met with him to go over plans for the dam. But the boathouse looked quiet and dark, no sign of Kirill. Except for the mysterious figure out front, the place seemed deserted.

She turned and started back the way she had come, and it was then that she noticed Kirill's keys dangling from the Viper's ignition.

All right. That settles it. He's got to be close.

She leaned on the Viper, resting her swelling leg and looking up at the sliding door at the end of the second-floor deck. With Kirill's keys, she could let herself into the house, wash up, maybe find some clothes. Considering what he'd done to her Jeep, he wasn't really in a position to mind if she did that.

"You owe me, you bastard."

She took the keys, climbed the back stairs, and let herself in.

"Kirill!" She peered inside, making sure he wasn't home. "Hey, Kirill!"

No answer.

She entered.

The air smelled of soap and shower steam.

"Hey, Kirill!" Louder this time. "It's Sam!"

Silence.

She entered the kitchen and opened the fridge. Kirill wasn't much of a housekeeper. He had a woman come in a few times a week to cook and clean, and thanks to her the fridge was full of single-serving meals. She took out a bowl. It looked like dumplings. Seeing it made her realize how famished she was. She took a spoon from a drawer and ate while leaning against the counter.

I've done this before.

The impression came on strong at first, then faded as she ate. There was a name for that feeling, for the sensation of remembering something that had never happened.

Little visions, her mother had called them, but there was another word. *Déjà vu.* And that word recalled another: *Kasdeja,* the name from her Colorado dream.

She tensed. This was no time for remembering things that hadn't happened. She moved away from the fridge and put the bowl in the sink, setting it atop a pile of dirty dishes.

An empty wine bottle sat nearby, upside down in a silver bucket. Had Kirill been entertaining, playing host to one of the women from his club? That wasn't the fat man's style. But either way, she didn't want to think about it.

She left the kitchen and started exploring, up the stairs and through a long hallway until she found the master bedroom. A suit lay on the floor beside the bed: Armani jacket, slacks, and white shirt with sweat-stained pits. Empty hangers lay on the bed. Beside them, imprinted on the spread, was the impression of an overnight bag. Unlike the dishes in the sink, these things looked fresh.

"So," she said, looking around. "You were just here."

She studied the floor between bed and bathroom. The carpet was damp, not to the eye, but to the touch when she knelt to press it with her hand.

"You left your car in the driveway," she said. "Then you came here to wash up."

She went to the bathroom and looked inside. A streak of white dusted the counter beside the sink. She dabbed it with a finger, tasted it.

"You took aspirin, changed clothes, packed a bag . . . and then what?" She turned away from the bathroom, walked to the window, and looked down at the Viper. Wherever he was, it couldn't be far. If not at the boathouse, perhaps he'd gone up the street to meet an investor who lived there.

One way or the other, when he returned, he'd see her Jeep, find his keys gone from the Viper, and know she'd let herself in. He wouldn't begrudge her that. Nor would he be in any position to complain if she used his bathroom and borrowed some clothes—although the latter might pose problems in the fit-and-style department.

"Let's see what you've got for me."

She went through his drawers, coming out with a plaid polo shirt and knee socks. The shirt would hang to the middle of her thighs, making a serviceable dress. The socks would cover the rest.

"It'll have to do."

She returned to the bathroom and locked the door, gasping when she turned to face the mirror. Her face looked worse than it had when she'd checked it in the Jeep's sideview. The bruises had darkened. The swelling had spread to the eye.

"What a mess."

She turned away, tugged off her shirt, and pushed back the glass on the shower stall. A few pubic hairs lay near the drain, curled like threadworms. She wrenched the spigot to hot. Steaming hot! The better to flush Kirill's leavings and scrub her body. Scalding hot to wash away the dirt and whatever filth that bastard Jason had left on her . . . *in* her.

She trembled.

Just thinking about that made her ill.

She turned the spigot a little more, realizing as she did that her condition wouldn't take the heat. Regardless of how much she wanted to scald herself clean, hot water would only serve to open the wounds, spread swelling, draw bruises.

"Cold! It has to be cold."

She wrenched the handle the other way.

The water changed pitch.

She removed her boots and trousers, looking down to see that the bruise on her thigh now extended to her hip and knee. There was a dent in her leg, a deep valley between ridges of swollen flesh. It was the imprint of the crowbar, a straight line of compacted muscle that felt numb and hard to the touch. Sitting on the toilet, she stretched the leg, testing the bone. The femur was the largest bone in the body. You could fracture it, and it would still take your weight. But a broken bone would radiate pain, upward into her pelvis, down into her knee. This pain remained centered in her thigh. Recovery would be long and painful. But for now she'd get by.

"Now for the hands."

Blood had soaked through the bandage, forming clots that clung to the fibers, breaking apart as she once again uncovered the gashed palm. The wound ran free, dribbling onto her fingers as she pulled the sock from the other hand. The raw knuckles and wrist looked worse than before. Both hands would probably need medical attention.

"I'm a stinking mess!"

And she still hadn't taken off her briefs.

The shower kept running, venting a chill breeze from the open stall.

"Take them off. Look inside. Just do it!"

She stood, grabbed the elastic band, and pulled the briefs down. Then she sat again, checking the crotch, looking for discharge. Nothing. No blood. No semen. She touched herself, probing, wanting to be sure. She was hardly an expert when it came to this region of her body. Her mother had made sure of that.

It's the Devil's crater. The wound that never heals.

She decided to leave it be. One way or the other, the bastard who had touched her was dead. No one knew what had happened. No one but God and the Devil, neither of which existed; and her mother's ghost, who lived only in memory.

She stepped into the shower, closed the partition, and eased down to squat within the cleansing rain.

Her leg cramped. She forced herself to stay put. Then, slowly, she opened her slashed hand beneath the flow, letting the water coarse along her arm, into her palm, over the wound. Bloodstains dissolved and flowed away, revealing older wounds: twin punctures near her thumb, scar tissue on her forearm—more remembrances of Colorado.

The snake bites proved that some of her Colorado memories were true. Dreams didn't leave physical scars. But the angel with the roasted snake was a different matter. She had no physical proof that he'd ever existed. Certainly she had dreamed him.

Kasdeja.

The name drummed with the sound of the cascading shower, the slugging drain.

Kassssssshhh-deja!

Where had that name come from? Why had she dreamed it?

She closed her eyes and listened to the water. In her Colorado dream, she had asked about the name, but the angel, if that was what he was, had refused to elaborate.

I can't tell you things you haven't realized.

Those words rang with the weight of memory. They didn't feel like something from a dream. And yet she knew that the only other presence in the desert that morning had been Incendiary Ray, spying on her from a distance, coming to her aid after the snake had bitten her. The other things—the angel by the fire and the snake on the spit—those had never happened. She had never seen those things, except. . . .

She felt a chill. Not the chill of the water. Something deeper.

Her mind flashed to the figure outside, how it had been sitting, leaning forward, gripping the spit, staring at her just like the figure from her dream. Had the dream predicted him?

Prophecy?

She didn't want to consider that.

Vision?

She flexed her hand, making it hurt. The pain was real. This moment was real. And the moment was all that mattered. Soon she would climb from the shower and into another moment. She would wait for Kirill and ask him to get her home. And then, once she was home, she would be back in her world, surrounded by the real, safe from doubt. That was how she would survive, by focusing on the real: *real* plans, *real* moments, *real* memories.

But there was a problem.

The real memories were as troubling as the dreams.

After zapping her with the cables, Ray had placed her in the back of his Jeep and shut off the engine. She drifted after that, edging toward sleep, half aware of his footsteps as he returned to the transformer box. Then came more dreams, more things that hadn't happened: her calling to him, looking over the seat, and seeing the electric cables of his transformer box come alive like vipers.

In truth, she had simply lain in the Jeep's backseat, awaking hours later to find her arm no longer swollen. The puncture wounds were there. So were the burns from the electric cables. But otherwise she was fine . . . or so she thought until she climbed from the Jeep and found Ray's body lying a few feet in front of the grill, dead beside the exploded transformer.

He wore a cell phone on his belt, but it was as dead as he was, evidently fried by the same blast that had killed him. There would be no calling for help, and she couldn't carry him into the Jeep alone. The best she could do was return to Camp Survival, tell the people there what had happened, and hope they could retrieve Ray's body before the bugs and animals got to him.

The Jeep's GPS system guided her back, but when she arrived she found the camp deserted. It was nearly noon. The staff should have been preparing lunch, but even the kitchen was dark, empty, silent. She went to the sink, ran water into her hands, splashed her face. Then she turned her head under the spigot and took a long, deep drink. But water wasn't enough. She was starving.

She entered a walk-in cooler, turned on the light, and pulled a metal tray from a sliding shelf. Inside lay an industrial-sized serving of chicken and dumplings, already cooked and ready for reheating. She took a handful, dropping gobs of it on the floor, eating straight from the tray.

Then she noticed the ice bucket.

It stood beside the door, off to the side, propped in the shadows. She licked her fingers as she approached it. A towel-draped bottle sat inside the bucket. There was no ice. That would be added later, when the wine was served. She picked up the bottle and read the label: *Chateau Ste. Michelle*. It meant nothing to her, but it looked expensive. Had Ray been planning a celebration?

She wiped her hands on the towel and left the cooler. She was trembling now, not from the residual effects of venom or electric shock, but from a dawning realization of what Ray might have had planned for her once he got her back to the camp.

A private dining area lay behind the mess hall. This was Ray's space, the captain's chamber. The table was set. Two wine glasses stood on the bar, one clean, the other dusty. She picked up the dusty one, looked inside. Not dust. Powder. She knocked the bottom against her palm. The powder shifted. It looked like crushed aspirin. She dabbed it with her finger, tasted it. It wasn't aspirin. It didn't taste like much of anything, which meant it wouldn't be noticed when mixed with a few ounces of *Chateau Ste. Michelle*.

The pieces fell together. She was getting the picture.

Ray's apartment was across from the mess hall, in a building that looked out over a mountain ridge. She'd never been inside, but, once she broke in, finding the bedroom was easy enough. And finding the webcam was even easier. It was directly above the bed, hidden in the hub of a ceiling fan. She stood on the bed and pulled the staring eye from its moorings. Then she threw it to the floor and crushed it with her heel.

Then she trashed the rest of the bedroom.

She left, but not before taking Ray's prize possession from the rack in his gunroom: the M40A1, custom built at Quantico, Virginia. It was hers now. And so was his Jeep. She loaded the back with provisions and gear, helped herself to what cash she could find after breaking open the lockers in the barracks. Then she hit the camp's infirmary, hunting through the shelves until she found a bottle of Adderall, 30 mgs. The stuff would keep her awake and alert until she was well out of the area. She downed two of them, then fled east, driving through the day and into the night, not stopping until she reached the center of Ohio eighteen hours later. She found a cheap motel off the interstate, paid in advance, unloaded her gear, and then drove the Jeep to a nearby shopping center. She left it there, parked along a cinderblock wall, midway between two mercury-vapor lamps, hidden in plain sight. She did not know how long it would take people back in Colorado to realize

Ray was missing. Perhaps, if she hadn't trashed the camp, his absence might have been dismissed as voluntary. But she couldn't undo that mistake. She could only watch her steps from here on, remain cautious, keep cool.

She returned to the motel, drew the drapes, and crashed.

When she awoke a day later, she had no idea where she was.

Water drummed on her back, thundered in her ears, coursed along her body. Her fingertips were shriveled, nails turning blue. She'd fallen asleep in the shower. Her back tingled, but it wasn't from the chill of the water. It was a different kind of tingle.

Someone's watching me.

She straightened up, looked beside her, and saw him standing outside the shower door, silhouetted against the beaded glass.

It wasn't Kirill. Kirill wasn't that tall.

And Kirill didn't have wings.

atan rode in the back of the cruiser, behind a metal screen that separated him from his best friend, Hamilton Township Officer Michael DeAngelis. The seats behind the screen had been taken out and replaced with a level floor. No cushions. No armrests. No floor mats. Satan didn't need such things. The grated openings in the back window were enough for him, and at the moment he had his nose to the holes, sniffing the morning breeze as DeAngelis sped north on Cliff Mine Run.

Becky's voice called from the radio. "Hamilton K-9. Location?"

DeAngelis keyed his mike. "Hamilton K-9. North on Cliff Mine, about—" He saw lights flashing up ahead. "I'm there."

"Roger that, K-9. 6:51."

DeAngelis slowed, pulled around the sputtering remnants of a 20-minute flare, and rolled down his window.

A Cokesburg officer approached.

"Straight on back." The officer waved toward the forest. "They're ready for you. One from Cokesburg, three from Blaston."

DeAngelis nodded. "And the staties are on their way?"

"That's right. Maybe you can start tracking before they get here."

DeAngelis raised his window, pulled off the pavement and onto the coal road that ran deep into the forest.

Satan whined as they entered the trees. DeAngelis understood the sound. He knew exactly what it meant. Indeed, he often understood Satan's sounds and movements better than he comprehended the words and gestures of his fellow officers, which was understandable given his relationship with the dog, the three-year-old Belgian Malinois that most people mistook for a small German shepherd.

DeAngelis and Satan worked together, lived together, ate together, and—as much as DeAngelis's wife of two years would allow—slept together, in the same room, if not side by side.

Satan whined louder as the clearing came into view. The other officers were there. So was the death car, the body still inside. EMS had been told not to hurry.

"You smell it, don't you, boy?"

Satan's whine changed pitch: *Yes. Bad smell. Dead man.*

The other officers approached.

DeAngelis stopped the car and climbed out. He opened the back door and attached the leash.

Satan hopped down, staring at the death car while DeAngelis sized up the Blaston cops.

The first officer was Rashod Fisher, a stocky black man whose hair had been shaved to an airbrushed shadow. He had shoulders like a Steelers linebacker, but his age—mid 40s—might slow him down once Satan started moving.

The second was Tiffany Rose: sloe eyes, almond skin, flat-line lips, late 20s. She looked stoic, well aware of her size (DeAngelis put her height at five-six, weight at a strong but wiry 120). She would have had to continually prove herself at the academy, contending with covert hazing and overt sexism. That one of the missing officers was a woman would only bolster her commitment. He would be able to count on her.

The third cop was trouble. Courtney Leroy, with the last name taking the accent on *roy*. He was sandy haired, hazel eyed, five-ten, early 20s. He had a reputation for being a pain-in-the-ass know-it-all.

These things registered in a flash as DeAngelis approached the officers. For better or worse, these were his fellow trackers.

The Cokesburg officer would remain on scene, and that was just as well. DeAngelis knew him: Toby Machesney, an old-school cop who was counting the months to retirement. He'd been a two-pack-a-day man in his prime, and just talking about following a track dog over hills and valleys would be enough to make him winded.

"The trail's over here," Fisher said, hurrying past the death car.

DeAngelis glanced at the body, then did a double take when he saw the passenger seat. "There's a snake in that car."

"Right," Machesney said. "And I saw another go up in the engine."

"And there's two more in the Windslow cruiser," Rose said. "Three if you count the pieces of the one that got shot in two."

"That's not normal," Leroy said.

No one commented.

"Trail starts here." Fisher paused at the edge of the clearing. "We've stayed off it, waiting for you."

"Should be good then."

"Just one thing." Fisher ran a beefy hand over his scalp. "There's water down there, a stream. Fairly wide, wading depth."

"We'll deal with it." DeAngelis glanced at the others. "We'll track to the water's edge, then cross. Satan can pick up the scent on the other side."

"All right," Fisher said. "Let's roll."

24

The shower door moved along its runner, rumbling back to reveal the tall figure from Sam's Colorado dream.

She glanced up at him, backlit by the lights above the mirror, the glare radiating around his head and shoulders, leaving his body in silhouette—or nearly so. She saw that he was naked, the curve of a huge phallus just visible in the shadows of his groin. She turned away, averting her eyes, covering herself with her hands. It was all she could do, trapped in the shower, weak, defenseless, nowhere to hide.

He reached toward her, fingers long and delicate, with four joints instead of three. "Samuelle." He touched her hand. The touch was warm, made almost hot by the chill of her skin.

She tried pulling away. There was nowhere to go.

"I need you to come with me, Samuelle." There was no threat in his voice, only kindness and warmth.

"Where?"

"A place that must be seen, not told." He tightened his grip, gently. "Come on."

"I need to get dressed."

"Why?"

"Why do you think?"

"Say it."

She felt like a kid—vulnerable, uncertain, ashamed. "Because I'm *naked!*"

"Really?" He pulled on her arm, forcing her to stand. "And why does that matter?"

Water dripped from her, chilling her as she stood. She lowered one hand, pressing it to her crotch, keeping the other over her breasts.

"Come here. Let me show you." He pulled her toward the mirror. "Look."

She couldn't.

He touched her chin, raising her head until she saw her reflection.

"Let go of yourself," he said. "Come on." He pulled her arm. "Let yourself go."

The arm slid from her chest. She started to put it back. But then she saw what lay beneath . . . or, rather, she saw what *didn't*.

"There," he said. "It's nothing."

She looked at her breasts. No nipples. No areolae.

"The other," Kasdeja said. "The other hand." He helped her, pulling it away to reveal the featureless, hairless dome of her mons pubis.

The tension left her arms. She stood, staring at her body. The wound that her mother had told her would never heal was gone.

She looked at him, furtively at first, then again, letting her gaze linger. He was as naked as she, and as sexless. His nearly featureless groin bore only the suggestion of a phallus. The shadow she had seen from the shower was merely a symmetrical ridge curving down between his thighs. Nothing else. Like her, he had a form more mannequin than human.

His face was much the same. Blemish free and perfectly angled, it might have been carved from stone.

"Walk with me." He took her hand, the one that had been slashed nearly to the bone. But that wound was gone, too, and her fingers closed easily around his as he led her from the bathroom, down the stairs, and out through the door in the back of the house. They didn't pause to open the sliding glass. They simply passed through it, feeling it yield like the taut surface of a waveless pool. Then they were outside, their skin glowing in the brightening day.

They descended the deck stairs and crossed a back lot bordered with flowers and hedgerows. It occurred to her that, like herself, the lakeside community had been reborn. It was now a modern-day Garden of Eden, but one where the fruit had never been eaten, where good had never lost to evil.

"How did this happen?" she asked.

"How did what happen?"

"These changes. When did the world become so beautiful?"

"It hasn't," he said. "Not yet. But it will. It's waiting to happen, waiting for you." He took her hand. "I'll show you how, but first we need to leave the dream, reenter the world." They took a sharp right at the back of the house. Once again she felt tension against her skin—the same pressure that she had felt when passing through the backdoor of Kirill's home. She leaned into the tension. It broke. The world dimmed.

Kasdeja walked faster, leading her to the edge of the lake where a two-lane road ran 600 feet along the top of the dam. She recognized the structure. This was the dam as it really was, a flawed design in need of serious renovation.

She looked out along the lake as they followed the road, noting how its banks widened before narrowing to a tree-lined channel. How far off was that? One mile? Two? And how much water lay beyond that channel? Sam couldn't tell. But one thing was sure. The lake was huge.

To the south, the dam's earthen embankment descended forty feet into a deep valley. A river had flowed there once, but now all that remained was a wide, fast stream carrying the runoff from the dam's spillway.

They followed the road until they reached the center of the dam, a point where lake water lapped dangerously close to pavement. She paused, looked back the way they had come, and realized that the dam had subsided in the middle.

"You see it, don't you?" Kasdeja said.

"The subsidence?"

"Yes. It's nothing new. It's been sinking for years. Your friend, Mr. Vorarov, has engineers working on it, but it's proving more troublesome than expected. That is, more troublesome than Vorarov expected, not the engineers. They've been warning him from the beginning. He bribed the ones he could, threatened others, got them to vouch for his plans. You were part of that, you know? You helped him make those threats."

"No," she said. "He's sent me after his competitors, not engineers."

"Don't be so sure, Samuelle. Your efficiency precedes you. People you've never met fear your reputation. We're alike in that respect. Kindred spirits." His voice seemed to smile, though his features remained as before. "Sometimes vague threats are as convincing as actions. Other times . . ."

They stood a moment, side by side, listening to the waves lapping close to their feet. Then he turned, faced the valley. "Let me show you something else." He climbed over the guardrail and onto the weedy slope that angled into the valley.

She followed, once again seeing the road that she had driven on the way to Kirill's. It curved out of the trees and onto a bridge that spanned the river valley. Beyond the bridge, the valley deepened, descending in the general direction of Windslow Mine.

A utility road curved from the east end of the bridge, winding toward the stone culvert at the base of the dam. This, too, she had noticed before. All of it was part of the mental snapshot she had taken while driving to Kirill's. Now, seeing it from this angle, she sensed the potential power of the scene: deep valley, subsiding dam, bloated lake.

"The dam was born from special interests," Kasdeja said. "Vorarov's plans for a lakeside resort may be the most audacious, but they are hardly the first."

"He told me about that," she said. "He liked that the infrastructure was all in place."

"Some of it was. But it's substandard, done on the cheap by people with short-term goals." He led her down the slope until they reached the culvert. It looked even larger now than it had from the bridge: high enough to walk through, wide enough to serve as a garage. Kasdeja's voice echoed as he stepped inside. "This conduit was designed to control lake levels. When it collapsed, the engineers cut the spillway along the east shore. It was only supposed to be a temporary fix. You saw that spillway driving in?"

"Yes."

He took her hand. "Let me show you things you haven't seen." He stepped forward, leading her into a dark tunnel beneath the dam.

"I thought you said this culvert was collapsed."

"It is." His voice echoed from the walls, filling her ears, resounding in her bones. "The damage is farther in, below the heaviest part of the dam."

Water trickled around her feet, chilling her. And soon she became aware of other currents, waves shifting beyond the stones, pressing down, yearning to flow free.

"There were drain pipes here," Kasdeja said. "The controls were in a tower that once stood in the center of the lake. Kirill had it dismantled. Now his engineers are working on alternative ways of draining the water to make repairs."

"They still plan to drain it?"

"The engineers do. Mr. Vorarov isn't thinking that far ahead. For now, his concern is getting good photographs for a new marketing campaign. That's why the water's so high. He'll get his pictures. Then he'll pressure the engineers to work a miracle. But I have another miracle in mind." He extended a hand, fingers glowing against a wall of broken rock and clay. "This is why I need you, Samuelle. I can't work the miracle alone. I need a hand in the physical world." He set her palm against the rocks. "You can feel the weight of the water . . . the weight of its desire . . . and you can feel the dam, too—submitting, yielding, sinking."

Something passed through her, the dam's pain aching in her bones.

"But what does all this mean to me?" she asked.

"Everything." He pulled her away from the wall. "I'll show you."

They pushed out of the culvert and down into the valley beneath the bridge. For a while they walked in silence, giving her time to study the landscape, get her bearings. The stream widened, fed by other streams meandering down from surrounding hills. At one point she glimpsed what looked like the top edge of a gable in a field above her. It looked weather-beaten, roofless. She saw it for an instant. Then it vanished, hidden beyond the top of the rise.

A short distance later, the valley forked: rising to the left, sinking to the right. They took the high road, moving along a dry spillway, heading southeast now, toward the mine.

The valley narrowed still more as they passed beneath the remnants of a bridge, a steel girder slung between walls of rock. A little farther on, the spillway angled down to a half-pipe that overhung the northern edge of the mine. They walked through it and into empty air, suspended above the western edge of the mine. To their right, beyond a glacial rise, lay the place where she had dressed her wounds with angelweed. To the east, beyond a slope of weedy trees, the air above the crater was thick with smoke and the pulse of emergency lights. Directly below them, a dry channel ran south for a few hundred feet before curving back toward the floor of the mine.

"Over here." Kasdeja held her hand now, guiding her downward, over the slope of weedy trees and into the pulsing haze. "This place is different from the last time you saw it."

She discerned a new light, dimmer than the strobing flashes of emergency vehicles. It came from the ground, from a glowing hole surrounded by emergency tape.

"Sinkhole," Kasdeja said. "It opened beneath the burning Mustang. Now it's spreading, deepening, growing hotter. The ground has ignited, Samuelle. Left untended, it will consume the world."

"And I made it happen," she said. "I started the fire that made the driver lose control. This is my doing, isn't it?"

"No," he said. "There were other forces at play. If it hadn't been you, it would have been someone else." He turned toward her. "But you can stop it. I know. I saw it long ago. It's the reason I saved you when I did."

"In Colorado?"

"Yes."

"So that wasn't a dream? It was real?"

"Dreams are real, Samuelle. They're another level, another strata. You need to trust that. And you need to stop this fire before it swallows everything."

"But how?"

"I've already answered that." He turned toward her, his face shifting with reflected light.

"The dam?"

He stared at her, letting her continue.

"The old river valley. It leads here. If I open the culvert—"

"The culvert is the key," he said. "But the opening needs to be bigger. Much bigger."

"You want me to destroy the dam."

"Not directly," he said. "Remember what I told you about actions. Actions beget actions. Consider what happened last night. You started a fire on the highwall. The fire caused the Mustang to fall. The Mustang exploded and ignited the ground. Now the ground is burning."

"I already know those things."

"And you already know a few things about bringing down dams. Trust me, Samuelle. Look to your past. The answer is inside you. The tools you need are there for the taking. Use them. Make it happen. Bring down the dam. Douse the fire. Save the world."

She closed her eyes.

Look to your past.

She felt wet and stiff, chilled to the core.

I'm still in the shower!

She opened her eyes, and suddenly she was staring at her feet, toes clenched against the cold, blue against the shower's white-tile floor.

25

Kirill awoke to find himself lying beneath a ceiling of hammered brass. He was on his back, stretched out on a leather couch, wearing a neck brace. He tried getting up.

"Hey!" A hand appeared, swinging down to thump his chest, holding him in place. "Don't move." The hand belonged to a big guy: bucket head, no neck, broad shoulders. Kirill knew him. He was Arnold Gusky's driver. What was his name?

"What the fuck?" Kirill said.

"You're not supposed to move."

"Who says?"

The driver turned away. He wore a hands-free communicator over one ear. "Hey, Doc," he said, speaking to someone not in the room. "He's awake."

Kirill tried turning his head. No dice. The brace stopped him, forcing him to turn his eyes to see the wall behind the driver. The wall was all glass. Beyond it, the lower bends of Cliff Mine Run serpentined north toward the future site of Mountain Downs. He knew this place. He was in Arnold Gusky's office in the fifth floor of a renovated department store. It had been a Woolworth's once. Then a Joe Workman's. After that it had lain fallow and boarded for seven years before Arnold Gusky transformed it into Gusky Tower, a pretentious name for a five-story building, but Gusky was a little man. The building probably looked like a tower to him.

Kirill had been to the fifth floor of Gusky Tower many times, but always as a guest, never a prisoner.

"How'd I get here?"

The driver pressed down harder on Kirill's chest, holding him in place.

"Get your hand off me," Kirill said.

"Can't. Doc says you could hurt yourself."

Kirill tried pushing the hand away. It was like trying to push a truck.

"You shouldn't do that," the driver said.

Kirill stopped struggling.

The office door opened. Footsteps crossed the room. A woman in a tight-fitting smock appeared. She had a wide face, full lips, professional smile—the kind that said, *I care about you because I'm paid to care.*

She approached the sofa, looked down at Kirill. "If Joe moves his hand, will you lie still?"

Kirill glanced at the driver. *Joe. That's his name. Joe Spotts. Why didn't I remember?*

"Will you?" the woman asked. "It's important. The X-rays show a slight cervical fracture. Not serious, but we want to play it safe."

Listening to her voice, Kirill realized that he knew her, too. She had a medical practice in the first floor of Gusky Tower. Kirill sometimes sent his girls to her. She was thorough, discreet, and expensive. She was also Gusky's personal physician. *Polidori with tits* Gusky called her. Kirill had no idea what that meant, but Gusky always seemed to think it was clever as hell. Her name was Dr. Something-Polish. Kirill tried remembering. *Wasuski, Waslewski, Wasiechowski? Whatever!*

Gusky just called her *Dr. Was.*

"Will you?" Dr. Was asked.

Kirill frowned. He'd forgotten the question. "Will I what?"

"Will you promise to lie still if Joe moves his hand?"

Joe's hand was hot and clammy. It felt like a big sweaty foot on his chest, bearing down, constricting his breathing. "Yes! I promise." He glanced at Joe. "Let go, *mudak!*"

Joe raised his hand and backed away.

Dr. Was moved closer. Like Joe, she wore an over-the-ear communicator. Gusky had a thing about staying in touch with his people. She looked at Kirill. "Can you tell me your name?"

"What?"

"Your name."

"You know who I am."

"Right, but do you?"

"Is this a brain test?"

"That's right. You've had quite a fall. And there're signs of other trauma, not to mention elevated blood-alcohol. You evidently had quite a night."

"Not enough to forget my name."

"So what is it?"

He hesitated. The name was there. It was all through him. He saw it, heard it, even felt it on his tongue. He just couldn't say it. "This is ridiculous," he said. "I'm fine. I was having some pain before, but it's gone now.

I feel better than ever."

"That's the painkiller," she said. "I gave you an injection for the pain. It'll be wearing off soon. When that happens—"

"Kirill!" he said. "My name's Kirill."

She nodded, tapped her earpiece, and turned away. "Arnold? He's awake. You might want to get up here."

"Tell Arnold he's in deep shit," Kirill said.

She turned toward Kirill again. "Mr. Gusky's on his way. You can tell him all about it when he gets here."

"And it's not just him," Kirill said. "It's all of you. You're all in deep shit."

"And why's that?"

"Kidnapping," he said. "Abducting me from my home. Breaking my neck."

"It's not broken. Only fractured. And Joe didn't do that intentionally."

"I couldn't leave you in the driveway," Joe said.

"What the hell were you doing in my driveway?"

"Mr. Gusky sent me to find you. He was worried because you weren't answering the phone."

"It was 6:00 in the goddamn morning! Maybe I was sleeping!"

Dr. Was smiled that professional smile again, like she was considering a new strain of virus. "Actually," she said, "you *were* sleeping, out cold on the driveway."

"That's how I found you," Joe said. "I pulled in and there you were, lying on the pavement."

Kirill didn't say anything. It was coming back to him now: getting out of the car, losing his balance, falling.

"I called Mr. Gusky," Joe said. "He told me not to call an ambulance. He said you wouldn't want that. He told me we needed to handle you in-house."

Kirill frowned. "That's what you call this? *Handling me in-house?*"

"Mr. Gusky told me to bring you back here. That wasn't easy. I had to drag you to the van. Then I had to heave you up."

"Heave me up?"

"You know, like prop you on the running board, get under you, heave you up."

Dr. Was smiled. "We figure that's how you got the fracture."

"Bastard!" Kirill turned his eyes, looking at Joe. "You broke my neck, you son of a bitch."

"Fracture," Dr. Was said. "But the real concern is head trauma. That and the pain. You came to when we carried you from the van. Started screaming. That's when I gave you the painkiller."

"I don't remember that."

"Right," Dr. Was said. "Like I said, head trauma's the real concern. If I had my way I'd put you in the hospital and order a series of—"

The office door opened. Someone walked in. The steps were small and quick, and Kirill knew even before the little bastard came into view that it was Arnold Gusky, the size-36 suit that walked like a man.

"Kirill!" He had a face like a weasel—long nose, little eyes, big teeth. "You had us scared, big guy."

"What the hell's going on, Arnold?"

"What's going on?" Gusky said. "Shouldn't I be asking you?"

"Me? I don't know what the fuck's going on."

"No?" Gusky frowned. "That's too bad. Because if you don't know, who does? I mean, does Joe? Should I maybe ask Joe?" He turned toward Joe. "Hey, Joe. What's going on? How come Kirill doesn't return my calls?"

"Don't know, Mr. Gusky."

"How come there's smoke rising from the Mountain Downs site?"

"Don't know that, neither."

"Then how about this. How come Paul Peterson's wife calls me at the crack-of-fucking dawn to tell me that her husband never got home last night?" Gusky didn't wait for Joe to answer. He just snapped his pointy face back around and stared at Kirill. "Joe don't know those things, Kirill. Joe don't know shit. That's why he's a goddamn driver."

Kirill frowned. "Peterson's wife called you?"

Gusky looked at Dr. Was. "You have patients waiting, I bet."

"One or two."

"Go ahead. I got this. And Joe, go wash the puke out of my van."

"Puke?" Kirill asked.

"Yours," Gusky said. "No chunks. Just milky vomit, some blood. My guess, it's mostly vodka and aspirin." He shook his head. "Damn, Kirill. I told you about that. Aspirin and alcohol. It's a bad combination. You could overdose."

"That's my business."

"Yeah? Well, your business left a mess in my van."

Joe and Dr. Was left the room.

"She called you?" Kirill asked, after Joe closed the door. "Peterson's wife called *you*?"

"Yeah, but not until after she called you and Maynard Frieburg. Said she couldn't get neither *yinz*."

Kirill winced. *Neither yinz*. Gusky was an intelligent man, a University of Pittsburgh communications major with an MBA from Robert Morris

University, but he had a disconcerting habit of slipping into Pittsburgh dialect when he got fired up. And he apparently didn't appreciate it when people failed to comprehend that *neither yinz* meant *neither of you*.

"She wanted my help," Gusky said. "Told me Peterson *needed found*!"

"What?" Kirill said.

"What? What do you mean *what*?"

"Peterson's wife," Kirill said. "What'd she tell you?"

"Peterson *needed found*!" Gusky spread his hands. "What the fuck, Kirill? You need me to talk Russian, or what?"

"Needs *to be* found," Kirill said. "Is that what she said? That someone needs to find Peterson?"

"What the hell did I just say?"

"Is that what this is about?" Kirill asked. "Peterson's wife calls you, so you come gunning for me?"

Gusky took a seat on a stool beside the sofa. "Here's what. Here's the problem, and it's not pretty. In fact, it—"

"I can't do this."

"Do what?"

Kirill tried sitting up.

"No, Kirill." Gusky set his hand on Kirill's shoulder, tried holding him down. "Dr. Was says you have to stay—"

"The hell with Dr. Was! I have to sit." He threw his arm over the back of the sofa, shifting his weight onto his hips, pulling himself into a slump. "I can't talk to you lying down. It's too much like you're screwing me." He pushed against the seat cushions. His neck stiffened. "*Sooka!*"

"Hurt?"

"Like a bastard." He turned his gaze toward the window. The smoke to the north was growing thicker, blacker.

"You see that smoke?" Gusky asked. "Because that's part of what we need to talk about." He spoke more slowly now, a little calmer. That was the thing with Gusky. He could be smooth sometimes. But the smoothness was like spring ice: thin, fragile, not to be trusted. "I know you're hurting, but you need to put that aside for a moment. Try to see my perspective. I'm not like you. I don't have backing from a New York uncle. It's just me on my own, and I'm mortgaged to the eyebrows. Maxed out. More than maxed." He lowered his voice, nearly whispering. "What I'm saying is, today matters."

"Today?"

"Gaming-commission day. Paul-Peterson-in-Harrisburg day. The day-we-were-supposed-to-get-approval-for-everything day."

"It's a big day for both of us."

"Bigger for me than you." Gusky sat back. "I couldn't sleep last night for thinking about it. I know you told me it was a done deal, that there was no way things could go wrong, but still, when a man's got everything riding on something—more than everything—well, it makes him a little squirrelly."

"Squirrelly?"

"Nervous," Gusky said. "It's make-or-break time, Kirill, and you know how I get. I'm high powered, maybe a little high strung."

"A little?"

"Just listen, OK? I need to get this out. So it's, like, 5:30 AM. I'm try-ing to sleep, but it's no good. I'm all knots. So I come in here, figure I can check the overseas markets, which are shit, by the way. But I'm checking them, and I'm thinking how much I need Mountain Downs to turn things around, and then I hear what sounds like thunder. It's not real loud, but it goes on too long. So I look out the window, and there's smoke rising from the crater. A goddamn pillar of smoke!"

Kirill thought of what he had seen while fleeing the mine, how the en-tire highwall on the north end of the crater had seemed to break apart, fall away. And then he thought about the thing that he had seen climbing through the rising dust: a flying monster with a man in each hand. Kirill decided not to mention that to Arnold Gusky. It would just confuse him.

"Smoke," Gusky said. "I didn't know what the hell it meant, but it didn't look good. So I went down to Joe's office. He's got a police scanner. I turned it on, and what do you think I heard the cops found sitting out in the woods near Windslow Mine?"

"You're asking me?"

"Asking you? I'm asking you shit, Kirill! It's a fucking rhetorical ques-tion. What they found was a goddamn Viper with a body in it! So I'm thinking, Oh, shit! It's Kirill."

"Wasn't me."

"Obviously," Gusky said. "You're here. But where's Peterson?"

"Harrisburg?"

"No, Kirill. Not according to his wife, he isn't. So I call you. First I call your cell, then your house. No answer either place. So I try the club. You're not there, either. But Danny Love answers and tries telling me he doesn't know shit. He doesn't sound too convincing, so I'm like, 'Danny! It's me, Arnold Gusky, the guy who bought those goddamn HD-TVs! I'm like Kirill's partner, ferchrisake!' And he's like, 'OK. He's up d'house.'"

"He said that?"

"Words to that effect." Gusky got up, walked to his desk, and picked up something from the blotter. Kirill couldn't see what it was. He had to wait for Gusky to walk back in front of him. Then he saw that it was a Smith & Wesson in a Galco holster. "This was in your pants," Gusky said. He crossed to the window, took out the gun, dropped the Galco on the floor. "I never was big on guns, Kirill. Not like you. Never saw the need." He pushed the barrel to the glass, pointing with it, gesturing toward a block of boarded storefronts across the street. "You see those buildings, Kirill?"

"No." Kirill couldn't turn his head that far. "But I know the ones."

"Then you know they're mine. And those ones, too." He raised the gun, pointing to a line of row houses that were fast becoming condominiums. "I own half this town, Kirill. And why not? The property's cheap, and my credit's good." He turned. "I'm a rich man, Kirill. On paper." He crossed to the stool, sat down, looked at the gun.

"You should put that pistol down," Kirill said.

"Why? Making you nervous?" Gusky raised the gun, studied its profile. "The hell kind of gun is this, Kirill? Where's the freaking hammer?"

"Inside the gun."

"Really? So it's not like a powerful gun, huh? Just like a big derringer, or some damn thing?"

"No," Kirill said. "It's powerful. The hammer's enclosed to keep it clean, but it's plenty strong. At 20 yards, it'll take your head off."

"Really?" He bounced the gun in his hand, feeling its weight. "Sort of like Dirty Harry without the *Dirty*." He raised it, aiming at Kirill. "So tell me, Kirill. Are you feeling lucky?"

"That's not funny, Arnold."

"No? So maybe I should stick to business, avoid comedy." He sighted across the barrel. "A man's got to know his limitations, right Kirill?"

Kirill would have gotten up if he could, would have leaped at Gusky, ripped the gun from his hand. But the neck pain was coming back now, hammering like a bastard. And there was pain in his gut, too—like he had to take a monster crap, except there was nothing there. No crap. Just pain.

"Tell you what, Kirill." Arnold got up and returned to the desk. "I think I'd better explain something." He picked up a remote.

A motor whirred. Curtains parted behind the desk, revealing a large plasma screen.

"I'll make it simple, Kirill." He set down the gun, picked up a digital pad. "I need to show you just how bad things are." He tapped the pad.

A line of icons appeared on the screen behind him.

"I'll show you," he said. "Then I'm going to make a proposition. If you go for it, we'll proceed as partners. If not—" He glanced back at the table. "If not, I'll pick up your gun and blow off your freaking head." He forced a grin, all teeth, no lips. "OK?"

"My neck hurts."

"Right. We all have issues." He tapped the stylus on the pad. "Now here's mine." He touched an icon.

'm still in the shower.

The cold had stiffened her muscles, hardened her joints. She reached for the shutoff, her hand was dark and shriveled, but at least the wounds had stopped bleeding. She turned the handle. The stream fell back to a trickle. Then she got up, stepped from the stall, and stood before the mirror. The angelic body from her dream was gone. She was herself again, flawed and naked: blue nipples, dripping hair, bruised leg.

She dried off, bandaged her hands, and donned the polo shirt from Kirill's dresser. As anticipated, it extended nearly to her knees. The plaid design and stitched logo over the left breast made it look like a private school uniform. She pulled on the knee socks, which extended nearly to her hips. Next came her combat boots. She laced them tightly and stood before the mirror. "Damn!" She frowned. "Prep-school chick from hell!"

She pushed her hair back, combing it with her fingers, pressing it against her head. Like her other wounds, the gashed brow had stopped bleeding. She covered it with Band-Aids and then returned to Kirill's bedroom where she found a golf cap. The brim drooped across her eyes. She turned it around, wearing it like a beret. It looked goofy, but it covered her wound.

She paused beside a bedroom window, looking past the dam, toward the smoke rising from the mine.

A voice spoke inside her.

Make it happen.

She steadied herself against the window, feeling dizzy, holding on.

Bring down the dam.

She set her head against the glass.

Douse the fire.

"All right." She pushed back from the window, the dizziness passing. "Bring it down. I can do that."

She had dealt with dams before.

There had been a time when a law-abiding person could purchase dynamite at a hardware store. Blasting caps and stump powder were also there for the asking. But times had changed, and a self-reliant woman now had to look elsewhere for supplies.

Sam's resource for such things was Kentucky Grace, aka Tucky, a farm child from southern West Virginia who had struck out for San Francisco during the Summer of Love, hitchhiking west as far as Nashville, where she hooked up with a band in a VW microbus. But the band wasn't heading to the coast, and by the fall of 1967 she was living in a farmhouse commune on the western edge of Pennsylvania, 2,500 miles from Haight-Ashbury, but nonetheless transformed. She bloomed, put down roots, never left.

Over the years, Tucky's counter-culture connections put her in touch with all manner of things, including three cases of vintage dynamite that she kept in a freezer chest behind her home. She sold the sticks to like-minded people, ex-hippie farmers who knew that dynamite was still the best way to uproot tree stumps or dislodge beaver dams. And she provided other services as well, things a person couldn't find by looking in the yellow pages.

Over the years, Tucky had come to Sam's aid on a number of occasions. The first being when Sam had awakened to find herself in a dark room eighteen hours out of Denver, in a highway motel near Columbus, Ohio.

Sam awoke with no idea of who or where she was.

The room was hot and stuffy. Her head throbbed with strange dreams: snakes, electric cables, stolen goods.

She climbed out of bed and walked through darkness until carpet gave way to bare tile. A switch glowed on the wall. She flipped it. Light came on, illuminating the bite on her hand, the burns on her wrist.

I wasn't dreaming!

She left the bathroom, the light fanning behind her as she returned to the bed. The stolen gear from Camp Survival lay piled against a wall. Ray's gun leaned against the nightstand.

She thought of the Jeep, abandoned in a parking lot.

I can't leave it there!

The cops would trace it to Ray. Her name was on the Camp Survival roster, and the address she had given was barely 100 miles east of Columbus. Eventually, if she left that Jeep where it was, the authorities would come for her. She needed to find a way to make the Jeep disappear.

Her knapsack contained a book with dog-eared pages and highlighted text. Its title, *The Survivalist's Mission: Independence in a Dependant World*. Its author, Incendiary Ray.

She had read the book twice before enrolling at Ray's camp, becoming familiar with his world view, his nuts-and-bolts approach to living outside the law. The book had taught her self-reliance, and one of her favorite chapters was "Underground Networking," which covered the ways that off-grid businesses identified themselves to like-minded free thinkers. "Off-grid businesses are everywhere," the book claimed.

> *They operate in plain sight, providing marginal services for the unenlightened, everything from dry cleaning to lawn care. But their true reason for being is to serve Amerika's growing underground, the off-grid Nation that requires goods and services beyond the knowledge of the gridlocked masses.*

Thus, a dry cleaner might rent law-enforcement uniforms, a lawn-care company might sell bomb-grade nitrates, and an out-of-the-way produce farm might be just the place to make a stolen Jeep vanish from the face of the earth.

The book's techniques led Sam to a Columbus scrap yard, which in turn directed her to Tucky, who now owned what remained of the farm that had given her refuge back in the 60s.

The place was in Claudia, Pennsylvania, a mining town whose first-generation inhabitants had named it for the industry that employed them: *Cloddio*, Welsh for *mine*. Within a few generations, the name had evolved through a series of mispronunciations and typographical errors, finally emerging as Claudia some time in the late nineteenth century.

Tucky's front business was organic produce, mostly zucchini and tomatoes, but her real livelihood was in tax-free tobacco, unregulated pharmaceuticals, and making things disappear.

Sam drove the Jeep to Claudia where she and Tucky spent an afternoon talking politics and self-reliance. Then, with the sky turning red along the western horizon, Tucky drove Sam back to Morgantown, assuring Sam that neither she nor anyone else would ever see Ray's Jeep again.

"What'll you do with it?" Sam asked.

"That's my business," Tucky said, her tone making it clear that she had nothing more to say on the matter.

When they got to Morgantown, Tucky helped Sam carry her gear into her apartment. "You a shooter?" she asked, noting Ray's sniper rifle.

"Yeah," Sam said.

"Any good?"

Sam shrugged. "Good enough."

"Good enough to go pro?"

"Shoot for money?"

"That's right."

"Shoot what?"

"Whatever pays," Tucky said. "Think on it. If you're interested, come visit. Show me what you can do. I maybe can put you in touch with someone."

Months later, Tucky sent Sam to a farmer who knew a lawyer who knew a businessman named Kirill Vorarov, who in turn provided Sam with the means for living a fully self-reliant life.

In time, Sam purchased a stretch of land in the West Virginia woods, acquired some off-grid supplies, and began living the dream described in the pages of Incendiary Ray's book. After that, she rarely left the wilds, and then only to purchase supplies or go on assignments.

Eighteen months ago, when one assignment kept her out of town long enough for a colony of beavers to dam up the stream beside her property, Sam knew just who to call.

There was a phone on Kirill's nightstand. Sam picked it up, dialed, sat on the bed.

Tucky answered on the second ring, voice aged with half a century of unlicensed smokes. It was a reassuring sound, the sound of the mother that Sam felt she should have had.

"Hi, Tucky."

A pause, and then: "Sam?"

"Yeah."

"Sam!" Tucky coughed. "Long time! How you been, girl?"

"About half. You?"

"Hanging in."

Sam got up, started pacing. She didn't have time for small talk. "I've got a problem, Tucky."

"That's the only time you call, you know? Last time it was beavers."

Sam forced a laugh. "And you helped me good, too. Can you do it again?"

"Need more of the same?"

"Yes," Sam said. "Lots more. All you've got."

"That's a lot of beavers, honey."

"Yeah." Sam stopped pacing, shifted her weight to the good leg. "Big beavers, too."

The line got quiet.

"Tucky?"

"Still here. I'm just not sure I got anything you can use, is all."

"Out of stock?"

"No. Not exactly out of stock. I've got two cases. But there's a problem with them." Tucky coughed. "You might do better calling Critter Control. Safer that way."

"I like doing things myself."

"Yep, that's you. The self-reliant woman. But I'm just saying—"

"Two cases?"

"Right," Tucky said. "That's all that's left."

"And it's still good?"

"Good?"

"It'll work?"

"Honey, it'll work. No question about that. Only question is, will it hold off working till you're ready? And that's about all I'm going to say on these government-controlled lines. You understand?"

"I'm coming out then."

"Always glad to see you, Sam. But other than that, it might be a wasted trip."

"I'll be there in an hour."

Tucky coughed. "You coming from home?"

"No. Closer north. Just across the line."

"That's not much closer, girl. How you going to make it in an hour?"

Sam looked out the window. The Viper sat in the driveway. Kirill was still nowhere in sight.

"Are you going to fly?" Tucky asked.

"Yeah. See you in an hour." She hung up and returned to the bathroom where her filthy trousers still lay on the floor. She took the payment envelope from the thigh pocket, stuffed it into the top of the sock on her good leg, and limped from the room. The angel's imperative burned inside her, compelling her on.

She returned to the driveway, backed her Jeep to the front of the house, and parked in the front yard.

The strange figure was still there, watching from down the street.

She checked him out in the sideview mirror, realizing he was just a boy, sixteen maybe, seventeen max. He had kicked dirt over his little fire, was standing beside it now.

Just a boy.

And yet there was still something in the narrow slope of his face that recalled the angel from her vision. What was she to make of that? Coincidence?

She climbed out, looking directly at him now.

He didn't look away. He simply stared, apparently amused. What must she look like to him: backward cap, polo-shirt dress, thigh-high tube socks, combat boots.

He waved.

She turned away and went to work removing gear from the Jeep: GPS, radar detector, plastic med kit, and the case containing the pistol she had used to even the score with Jason. She locked the Jeep and carried everything back to Kirill's Viper. The car was almost all engine, a V10 encased in a front end that flared like the head of a snake. The cockpit was considerably smaller, the trunk almost nonexistent.

That cargo area, she wondered. *Is it big enough?*

She put her gear on the passenger seat and transferred her payment envelope from her sock to the glove compartment. Then she went back to have a look in the trunk. An overnight bag sat inside. She lifted it out, set it between her feet, and studied the empty space. There was enough room for one case of dynamite. Would one case be enough?

"Hey!"

She turned.

The kid from up the street stood on the edge of the driveway. "I saw you out front," he said. He was razor thin, but now, up close, he seemed less like an angel and more like the bastard who had raped her . . . or tried to. There was little physical resemblance, of course. This boy was well proportioned and considerably younger. But he was still a male, and at the moment Sam's old insecurities were back on the surface, festering like the wound on her slashed hand.

She looked away, steadying herself on the Viper's trunk.

Relax. This kid can't hurt you. If he tries, you can take him.

The kid seemed oblivious to her fear. "Are you a dancer?" he asked.

"A what?"

"You know, like, at the club."

She tensed. The fat bastard had asked the same thing.

"Are you?" he asked.

Relax! He's not like the other one. He can't hurt you.

She picked up the overnight bag. It felt heavy, too heavy to be just clothes. She wanted to look inside, but not with the kid watching.

"Are you one of them?" the kid asked.

"One of Vorarov's strippers?"

"Yeah."

"Do I look like a stripper?"

He thought a moment. "No."

She closed the trunk.

The boy moved closer.

She backed away, rounding the car.

"Are you his daughter?"

"Whose daughter?" She kept her eyes on him as she walked along the driver's side. "Vorarov's?"

"Yeah."

"Do I look like his daughter?"

"I don't know his daughter. Don't even know if he *has* a daughter. But if he does, I don't think she would look like you." There was no aggression in his voice. She sensed he wasn't coming on to her so much as speaking his mind.

"You're better looking than he is."

"Lucky for me."

"You look like Gogo."

"Who?"

"Gogo. You know, that Asian prep-school chick? In *Kill Bill?*"

"I'm not Asian."

"Yeah, but besides that."

She studied him, decided he was harmless.

"So what are you?" he asked. "What are you to Mr. Vorarov?"

"Just a friend."

"Yeah? Me too."

"You're his friend?"

"He works with my stepdad," he said. "So we're, like, connected."

"We?"

"You and me," he said. "You know, degrees of separation. We both know him. That makes us, like, what?"

"Strangers."

"I'm Pax." He moved closer.

She let him come, no longer afraid.

"Are you looking for him?" Pax asked.

"Vorarov?"

"Yeah. Him. Because he just left, right before you got here. He left in my stepdad's van."

"You *saw* him leave?"

"Yeah. Sort of saw."

She threw Kirill's overnight bag onto the passenger seat.

"Anyway," Pax said, "I haven't seen him since the van left." He stared at her. "Are you taking his car?"

"Thinking about it."

"It's a sweet ride. It's like mine."

"Yours? You drive a Viper?"

"Yeah. Drove one all last night, me and a Japanese kid. *Burnout!*"

"You're losing me."

"It's a game. We play online. He drives all kinds of cars, but I always go with a Viper. He's got another in the garage."

"Who does? Your Japanese friend?"

"No. Mr. Vorarov. He keeps it all locked up in the garage. I saw it one time. I was coming up the street, he had the garage open, and there it was."

Sam checked Kirill's key chain. There were five keys in all: two door keys, one security key, two Viper keys.

"It's copperhead orange," Pax said. "You ever see a car that color?"

She looked in Kirill's glove box. The garage-door opener was there. She took it out and looked at Pax, thinking again about how he had reminded her of Kasdeja. What if that was intentional? What if the similarity was a sign? "Can I ask you something, Pax?"

"Sure."

"What were you doing when I pulled in?"

"Me?"

"It looked like you were burning something."

"Yeah. I was."

"The neighbors don't mind you doing that? Lighting fires?"

He grinned. "What neighbors? This is, like, a ghost town. No one cares . . . just the snakes."

"So I saw that right? You were burning a snake?"

"Yeah." He didn't seem to think there was anything odd about that. It was as if she had asked if he liked pizza.

"You got a grudge against snakes?"

He shrugged. "They're copperheads."

"So they're venomous?"

"Yeah."

"So you're protecting your family, killing the snakes so no one gets bitten?"

"No." He answered matter-of-factly. "I just like burning them."

"You don't worry about getting bitten?"

"No." Now he paused. "Maybe. I guess that makes it interesting. It's like a contest, me and them."

"You like danger?"

"Yeah."

"Guess you don't get much excitement around here."

"No," he said. "Just my PlayStation, the snakes—" He looked at her, seemed about to say something else, but stopped.

She held his gaze. "How old are you?"

"Eighteen."

"*Almost* eighteen?"

"No. *Completely* eighteen. My birthday was the ninth. How about you?"

She looked at the garage door opener. "Can you drive a stick?"

"A stick? You mean in a car? Like *this* car?"

"Yeah."

"Sure. My stepdad has a Porsche. I drive it sometimes. Why?"

She hit the button on the remote.

The garage door rumbled open.

27

S atan shook himself dry, spattering Tony DeAngelis, who was already soaked from the thighs down.

The other officers were still crossing the creek. Fisher in the lead, then Rose and Leroy.

The air reeked of coal, indicating that the haze surrounding them was more than localized fog.

The mine is burning.

DeAngelis had seen the flashing lights in the smoky crater on his way in, and he'd lived in coal country long enough to recognize the stink. Windslow was going to have its hands full in the days to come. Underground fires were difficult to contain. In the extreme, they destroyed towns—not with fire, but with smoke that fouled the air, blotted the sun, and covered the ground with drifting ash.

Satan sniffed the weeds that grew along the bank. Tugging the leash, he led DeAngelis a few yards downstream, paused, then turned. The rhythm of his panting was almost a language, a code.

He's got something.

Satan turned again, cocked his ears. His breathing changed, coming faster. And then he was moving, dragging DeAngelis, not even pausing as he neared a rat-covered log that angled down along the bank.

"You see that?" Leroy said. "You see those rats? That's not normal."

The others kept moving, running until Satan turned and shot up along a slope.

DeAngelis followed, using his free hand to check his balance. Satan didn't seem to notice the steepness. He kept climbing, pulling DeAngelis out of the smoke and toward a crest lined with weedy grass. Something appeared beyond the rise, a wedge of blistered wood, covered windows, sagging porch. . . .

A moment later, he saw the devils.

Satan paused with him, ears up, listening as the plastic wings on the junk statues fluttered in the shifting air. Then he lowered his head, shoulders tense, nose pointed toward a cloth-covered entrance 30 feet away. The house apparently had no door, just that hanging cloth, nailed in place along the top of the frame.

Rose came up behind him. "Damn!"

Fisher was next. "The hell is this shit?"

Leroy came last, panting, sweating. "Junk art!" He coughed. "Someone's got a thing for devils."

Fisher keyed his mike. "Blaston Nine-Oh. We've tracked to a derelict farmhouse, half mile north."

"Roger that, Blaston. 7:19."

The closest statue had a truck radiator for a body. Its legs were swing-set poles, anchored in sandcrete. The arms were braided coat hangers, as were the skeletal arcs of the wings. More braided hangers composed the head and face, with bits of glass wedged among the twisted wire to serve as eyes.

The other statues were much the same, although a few had wooden slats for legs, and one had an old 13-inch television for a head, rabbit-ear antennas for horns. Strange as they were, their workmanship was impressive.

DeAngelis noticed all of these things in an instant, letting the details register in the time it took for Fisher to finish his report to dispatch. By then, Leroy was advancing toward something coiled in a stand of high grass.

"Check this out!" Leroy bent down. "A radio mike!" He picked it up. "Got to belong to Zabek or Jenkins." He looked at the house. "They might be in there."

Fisher drew his pistol, glanced at Rose. "Check the back."

She was already moving, Glock drawn, sprinting down the yard.

Fisher called toward the house. "Zabek!" His voice echoed from the eaves. "Jenkins!"

DeAngelis kept his grip on Satan's leash.

"Zabek! You in there?"

Satan sat, ears pricked like devil horns, muscles tense, eyes staring at the cloth-covered door.

Fisher and Leroy spread out, advancing toward the porch.

DeAngelis held back a moment. He glanced at the statue beside him. Was it his imagination, or was the damn thing moving?

Bird and Kwetis sat beside the pool, at the foot of a sloping garden, behind the mansion's north wing. Kwetis had wanted to be near the water. The scene seemed real enough. Bird smelled the pool's chlorine, heard the rhythmic plop that the water made when it clapped against the drains, and felt the iron lattice of his chair pressing his back. He trusted these things. They were part of his world, but the presence of Kwetis meant it was all illusion, a dream.

"How long do we sit here?" Bird asked.

Kwetis shifted, raised a hand, signaled for silence. He was a strange-looking creature, composed of the sort of jumbled details that one would expect to find in a dream. But there was also logic to his form, the kind of efficient symmetry that occurred at the end of a complex evolutionary chain.

His head was long, flared like that of a hawk, although its black fur gave it a distinctly wolfish aspect, especially when the eyes were closed, as they were now.

The shoulders were powerful, cantilevered with crisscrossing muscles that worked both the arms and wings. Sitting in the chair forced him to drape those wings over the backrest, an uncomfortable pose that offered his shoulders little support. And yet Kwetis seemed to sleep.

It was hard to tell where the fur of his body ended and the feathers of his wings began. There was no clear division, just a gradual shifting of texture, color, and grain that progressed from pelt to quills. But more remarkable was the bare skin of his lower arms and hands, chest and belly, legs and feet. Here, the patterns of his flesh resembled tree bark and stone. *Camouflage*, Bird thought. *For hiding in the wilderness of dreams.*

But here, behind the mansion, Kwetis sat in plain sight, posed against the white deck, reflected in the blue of the pool.

"I know you're looking at me," Kwetis said. "I feel the weight of your eyes." He spoke without sound. His voice was in the shifting of his feathers, tension in his arms. And yet within the silent speech, Bird thought he detected the cadence of Axle's voice—a reminder that Axle was more than the physical vessel of the dream spirit called *Kwetis*. The two—Axle and Kwetis—were connected in complex ways, each an integral part of the other.

"I'm trying to understand," Bird said.

Kwetis turned. Then, as he had done in the room upstairs, he opened his eyes to look at Bird. The eyes shimmered, glowing with the light of burning coal. The right was golden. The left was white hot and painful to look at.

Bird squinted. "We're dreaming this, right? Axle and I are both asleep, sharing this dream?"

"Is that what you think?"

"It's what I'm asking."

"You and Axle?" Kwetis stared at him. "I see you." He looked around. "Where's Axle?"

"Upstairs. Sleeping."

"You were just up there. Did you see him?"

"No. You were there instead, but that was in the dream. If I wake up and look, he'll be in bed."

"And where will you be?"

Bird looked around, up along the sloping garden toward a terrace just outside the west wing's French doors. The antique chair was still there, an untouched glass of single malt sitting on a table beside it. But the chair was as empty as Axle's bed had been when Bird had gone upstairs to check on him.

"When I wake up," Bird said, "I'll be on the patio. I'm not there now because I'm here, inside myself, dreaming with Axle."

"Really?" Kwetis said. "I suppose that's one way of putting it. A child's way. But it's more complex than that."

"I suppose it is," Bird said. "But I have another question. A moment ago you seemed to be sleeping . . . dreaming within Axle's dream. Is that what you were doing?"

"Perhaps." Kwetis spoke with a flicker of his golden eye. "I suppose you could call it that. Concentric dreaming. It's all layered, you know—a stratified cosmos. One won't find deep meaning by mining the surface." A table between them shifted as he rested against it. "You can do it, too, you know? Maybe you can't control other people's dreams, but you can delve deeply through your own."

"Plumb my depths?"

"That's right."

"No thanks. I'd rather leave that to you. You be the plumber, send me the bill."

Kwetis cocked his head. A look of amusement? Disdain? Sometimes his poses were hard to read. But the look in his golden eye remained clear. He was troubled. "All right, then. Pay attention." His left eye darkened. "Here's what you need to know." He extended a four-jointed finger, pressed it against the table. "Here's the bill." His nail clicked the tabletop. "Our plan is being challenged."

"*Our* plan?"

"That's right."

"The *oohaate*?"

Kwetis seemed to nod. "The path that must be followed." He sat back. "We knew it might happen. That's why we created you."

"Created me?"

"We planned you long ago. Even before your birth, we knew we might need you—an idle man of means: intelligent, impulsive, reckless."

Bird grinned. "You've read my résumé?"

Kwetis turned away, looked at the pool. "I *wrote* it." He got up and walked to the water's edge. "But our rivals have made counter plans." He set his hand on the water, palm flat, fingers splayed—letting it rest on the surface. "They've enlisted a woman, and now she's heading north." The water stilled beneath his touch, its surface growing taut, as if the pressure of the palm were pressing it flat. Curves formed around the edges of the hand. Farther out, the curves straightened, forming a grid of intersecting lines.

Bird sat forward. "Is that a map?"

Kwetis took his hand from the pool. "Not a map." Water trickled along one of his fingers, gathering into a drop beneath the curved nail of his thumb. He tilted the hand. The drop fell, struck a line, and rolled along it. "You're too far away," Kwetis said. "Come closer."

Bird got up, moved to the pool, crouched by the water. But it wasn't water any longer. It was trees, houses, roads, mountains, valleys. Not pictures of them, but the things themselves—as if he and Kwetis were perched on the rim of a cloud, looking down at the earth.

"Whoa!" Bird said. "Looks real."

"Because it is." Kwetis flicked his hand again. A second drop fell, landing behind the first. The drops became cars: one a silver convertible, the other an orange hardtop. They weaved between mountains, following a road that dipped and curved as it headed north. "Dodge Vipers." Kwetis pointed to the drops. "V10s. Plastic bodies with truck engines. Fast and maneuverable." He looked at Bird. "And you need to catch them."

Bird gripped the side of the pool, bracing against the illusion of height. "Kirill's Vipers?"

"Yes."

The image seemed to rush toward them, the tiny cars expanding. A woman drove the silver car. Her short-cropped hair blew back from a wound above one eye. On the seat beside her, a golf cap and an overnight bag.

"Who's the driver?" Bird asked.

"A tool," Kwetis said. "Enlisted by our rivals. And she in turn has enlisted the driver of the second car. Layers upon layers." Portions of the map darkened, dimming back from a section of highway that wound past farms and industrial wastelands. Bird looked along that route to a turnoff that led to smaller roads and finally a patch of green that abutted a wide tract of barren earth. "She plans on picking up two cases of frozen dynamite from a farm in Claudia."

"Frozen?"

"Safest way to store and transport it. But the stuff she's picking up is old. It'll turn unstable as it thaws. Stopping her shouldn't be too difficult."

"That's what you want me to do?" Bird said. "Stop her?"

"I want you to help me stop her . . . and the car that's following her."

"How—"

"By getting close enough for me to reach them."

"You're coming with me?" Bird asked.

"I'll join you in spirit, use you as a conduit, reach them through you: appear to them, distract them, startle them if I can."

"You want to make them wreck?"

"I want to get them off the road, preferably before the stuff in their trunks thaws enough to explode. We have nothing against them personally, only what they're trying to do."

"And what exactly are they trying to do with two cases of dynamite?"

Kwetis swept his hand across the image of hills, trees, and roads. The landscape shattered. For a moment, the pool's rippling surface returned. Blue water like a blue screen. Then the water darkened, filling with an overhead view of Windslow, looking much as it had a few hours earlier when Bird had awakened to find himself falling from the sky. As he had done then, he found himself making out familiar landmarks: Silver Lake, Windslow Mine, downtown Windslow—and all around them a network of roads, creeks, and streams.

"The great heart is rising." Kwetis touched Windslow Mine, dabbing the crater with his finger, withdrawing it to reveal a smoking hole at the base of the highwall. "Burning ground," he said. "*Our* plan. The first step toward a better world." Something shifted along the edge of the hole, a curved shadow, like the coils of a glowing snake.

"Doesn't look better," Bird said.

"Because you're looking with momentary vision. The better world lies beyond this moment, beyond the burning ground." His wings shifted. He seemed impatient, eager to end the dream. But he continued, driving his point home.

"I'm talking paradise," he said. "Earthly paradise. A return to balance."

"Balance for whom?"

"Not our rivals," Kwetis said. "They've told the woman in the car that our plan will destroy the earth. They've told her the only salvation lies in stopping us. That's what she plans to do."

"By blowing up the burning hole in the crater?"

"No." He tapped the southern tip of Silver Lake, pushing his finger against the thin gray line of the earthen dam. "By dousing it." He drew his hand back. The dam gave way. Waters rushed out, flowing south, spilling into the mine. "Centuries of waiting, patient planning smothered in an instant."

The waters swirled, bubbled, erupted into roaring steam.

"So she's going to blow up Silver Lake Dam?" Bird said.

"No." Kwetis pushed his hand through a layer of clouds that now spread like a thin film above the pool. He stirred the water. An instant later, the pool was a pool again: blue water flecked with sunlight. "She is not going to blow it up because we're going to stop her."

"And if I fail—"

"Then there's still the chance that the dynamite won't detonate, or that the dam won't collapse. And even if it collapses, there's a chance that the flood may not follow its projected path. There are many forces at play here. Some are beyond our control. But if we can stop those cars, there's a good chance we'll succeed." His wings rustled. He straightened up, turned, and walked away until he reached the sloping garden at the edge of the deck. "We're the first line of defense. It will be best if it ends with us." He looked up along the slope, toward the curtained window, toward the room where, in the world beyond the dream, Axle was still in bed, dreaming the dream that he and Bird were now sharing. "Your friend is a powerful host," Kwetis said. "His spirit is strong. I should have no trouble reaching you as you drive." He arched his shoulders, leaning back as a breeze coursed through the garden, swirled at his feet, caught his wings. "But first Axle needs to practice on an easier subject. If it goes well, I'll come to you, pass through you, stop the Vipers." He clapped his wings, bringing them down hard against the gathering wind.

A moment later Kwetis was flying, shooting skyward on the updraft of dreams.

enjie huddled in a weedy ravine, crouching on the bank of a creek, hiding beneath overhanging vines. His face and hands had been cut by jaggers, but he ignored the pain, imagining he was a piece of stone, an outcrop anchored in the valley wall, the upper edge of a mass of buried shale—locked in place, incapable of moving. But still . . . he trembled.

Even with his eyes closed he saw the sex-club parking lot where Jason, Vinny, and R.D. had been killed by a monster whose invisible feet had left deep gouges in the asphalt, whose roars had seemed to come seconds after striking R.D.'s shoulder, Vinny's back, Jason's head.

But the monster hadn't followed Benjie. Benjie knew this. Now the only sound was the slow hiss of the creek, the chirp of sparrows, and the sound of distant voices beyond the jaggers at the top of the rise.

Cars had pulled up Strip Mine Drive a few minutes ago, and although Benjie had feared for the lives of the drivers, he now worried more about what would happen if those people came into the ravine to look for him.

I can't stay here.

He opened his eyes, realizing that doing so shattered his invisibility. By looking at the world, he transformed himself from a slab of rock to a frightened boy—visible and vulnerable.

He stood up. Specks of light moved through his vision. The world blurred. He felt light headed, the kind of dizziness that came with stress. Resting usually helped, but he couldn't rest here. It wasn't enough to pretend he couldn't be seen. He needed to hide for real, or at least move farther away from the voices.

Upstream, a corrugated metal culvert extended from a slope. If he walked through it, he'd find himself at the base of Boundary Street, in the shadow of Gusky Tower. In the other direction, the slow currents continued south toward Windslow Bottoms, a district that had suffered serious flooding a few weeks back, when torrential rains had turned the creek into an overflowing river.

Which way?

He decided to follow the water.

The landscape changed as he walked, becoming uglier, dirtier. Debris littered the banks, clogged the currents. At one point, a shopping cart lay half submerged between a pair of boulders, its basket matted with branches, paper, and glass. Garbage bags clung to its frame, swaying like algae. It looked like a good place to cross, so he climbed onto the closest boulder, going on all fours, scurrying over rock and metal until he reached the opposite bank. Then he climbed: over a mass of discarded tires, through a patch of jaggers, and into view of a cinderblock building that stood with its back to the creek.

Mud clung to the walls, marking the point where floodwaters had crested a foot above the slope earlier in the summer. Plywood covered the backdoor, buckling at one edge to reveal a dark interior. He peeked inside: hydraulic lift, power tools, metal sheets, chrome hubcaps.

Car shop!

The plywood shifted as Benjie pushed against it. The nails had been hammered directly into the cinderblock. He stepped back and tugged the wood. The aggregate crumbled. A nail broke free, landing at his feet. He pulled again, creating an opening wide enough to squeeze through. He could hide here, rest a while, then head north toward Jason's house. His medicine was there. And there was food, too. He could hide out at Jason's for days, maybe weeks. But he needed to compose himself first, stop the dizziness, rest his legs.

He squeezed inside.

The place smelled of paint and mildew, but the air felt cool, refreshing after the hot sun. A small apartment lay beyond the service bay. He walked toward it. There was a refrigerator, desk, chair, bed.

Someone lives here.

He moved past a pool of oval darkness in the center of the bay. A spill of oil? No, it looked more like a patch of black rubber. Or maybe . . . something else. When he looked again, the darkness resembled a deep void, a bottomless pit.

He stepped back. The pit widened, forcing him against the hubcap-covered wall. He stopped. The abyss did the same, its brink a few inches from his toes. And deep within the pit, something moved. It was a terrible version of the thing he had seen in the woods behind Jason's house, a winged man with a wolf's face and glowing eyes that screamed without sound.

Benjie raced along the wall, stumbling into the apartment, heading toward a door beyond the foot of the bed. He grabbed the knob. It was locked. He fumbled with the deadbolt, sliding it back. The door opened, swinging wide. Sunlight stabbed his eyes. He covered his face and ran: through a tar-patched lot, over a curb, into a street.

Brakes squealed, a car skidded, stopping inches away.

"Asshole!"

Benjie ran.

"Retard!"

Benjie tripped over the far curb, fell on his hands, got up and kept running—determined to keep moving until his legs gave way. Then he would collapse, turn to stone, and never get up.

ird stood in his garage. He was awake now, but an aura of dream still surrounded him. Or was it his sense of heightened reality? Though filled with shadows, the garage seemed to glow with the light of his new vision. He sensed that, if he wanted, he could see the garage as it had been in his father's time, full of horses rather than cars, the air heavy with the scent of manure and straw. And beyond that, he might perceive the space as uncut forest, or ice-age glacier, or Precambrian marsh with fallen trees beginning the slow transformation to fossil fuel. He sensed those things were important, worth pondering, but right now what mattered were the things of the moment: three mothballed Vipers, one beat-to-shit Escalade, a pickup truck, and a customized Firebird. Which one could he use to catch two northbound Vipers with a 30 minute head start?

He turned in place.

Could there be any doubt?

He looked at the car beside him. With its forward-tilting nose, sloping roofline, and fastback design, the '73 Firebird resembled a wingless jet. Even without its enhancements, the car was one of the fastest of the vintage muscle cars. Super-Duty 455 engine. Three-hundred-seventy horsepower. Zero to sixty in 5.4 seconds. Those stats were amazing, but with a full bottle of nitrous oxide in the trunk and a state-of-the-art injection system under the hood, this Firebird could easily outrun a V10 Viper on a straightaway. And its enhanced suspension not only guaranteed he could corner better on interstate curves, but he could also—with the help of a custom set of hydraulics—increase his bottom clearance for off-road terrain.

This was the car.

He climbed in, buckled up, and turned the key. The engine roared like a caged lion. He touched the gas. The sound turned primeval—a King-Kong scream echoing around him as he pulled from the garage. He put in the clutch and revved, flushing a cloud of sparrows from a hedgerow at the mouth of the drive. The birds flew along the house, fluttering in iridescent arcs past the window where Axle was sleeping.

Or had Axle awakened?

One of the windows stood open, shutters and casements swung wide. There was no screen. Heavy curtains swayed in the slow wind of morning.

Bird considered checking on Axle, but Kwetis's urgency had been clear.

Stop the Vipers!

He put the Firebird in gear and took off down the winding drive, toward the serpentine bends of Windslow Road.

xle awoke in a four-poster bed. Cold sweat slicked his head, chest, and shoulders. Footsteps echoed in his ears, the sound of a boy running on pavement, stopping cars as he fled through Windslow Bottoms.

"That boy was easy, Axle."

Axle turned toward the voice.

"That boy was addled."

The shutters and casements of the bedroom window had been thrown wide. Heavy drapes wafted inward. A winged creature sat on the sill.

"Don't expect the Viper drivers to be so simple."

The creature resembled Kwetis, but with coarser flesh, broader bones. He was the dream spirit's flesh-and-blood counterpart, the one who worked the physical world as Kwetis worked the world of dreams. And just as Kwetis required a symbiotic mind, this creature, an earthborn guardian, could not exist without a host body.

"You're my father, aren't you?"

"Was."

"No, not *was*," Axle said. "You're still him. I feel it."

"That's your desire talking. There's emptiness inside you, a father-shaped hole that needs to be filled. It will be easier for both of us if you don't try forcing me into it." The creature straightened up, flexing his shoulders. "It won't be a comfortable fit. Trust me."

"But you're what he became."

"No. He *was*. I *am*. Let's leave it at that." There was sadness in the voice, guarded distance. Axle had been looking forward to this meeting, had known it was coming, and wondered what it would be like to finally come face-to-face with the father he had never known—the man who had died in a long-ago accident at Windslow Mine. Axle had hoped the meeting would be one of fulfillment, of spiritual reunion. But evidently the transformed man had no intention of playing the role of father.

"So what do I call you?" Axle asked. "*Earthborn guardian?*"

"That's not a name."

"*Hayestani?*"

"Teacher-man?" The creature's dark face remained hidden, backlit by the sun, yet Axle thought he detected a smile. "Your great-grandmother would have called me that. She looked for meaning in old words. But I'm older than words . . . and so are you."

"So you're saying—"

"I'm saying you can call me what you like. Anything but *father*."

"Hayestani."

"That'll do. For now." He extended a multi-jointed leg. Then, folding his wings, he stepped into the room, moving with a sense of physical strength, weighty power. Floorboards creaked beneath him. Dust swirled about his head. A fly darted at his back, attracted by the sheen of his wings. Such weighty physicality set him apart from the ethereal Kwetis, but the most striking difference between the two lay in their faces. Hayestani's was partly human, particularly around the mouth.

"I'm here with two concerns," Hayestani said. "One small, the other vast. We'll handle the small one first. It'll prepare you for the other." He crouched before the bed, pivoting on high ankles. "I have made a nest for myself above the mine, in the kitchen of a ruined farmhouse, a property purchased and partly bulldozed by the Frieburg Coal Company."

"How long?" Axle asked.

Hayestani paused, considering the question. "How long have I lived there?" He spread his arms, a gesture that seemed to reference his physical shape. "Always. Ever since this form emerged from the rockslide that killed your father. I became earthborn the day he died."

"And you've been up there all this time?" Axle shook his head. "So close?" He pushed a hand through his hair, combing back the sweat-slicked strands. "I felt it, you know? I always sensed you were close, watching out for me, caring for me."

"But that wasn't me, Axle. What you felt was yourself, the pieces of your father that live inside you. I've always made a point of staying away."

"But I heard you," Axle said. "The wind when there wasn't any, the hissing of leaves—*teyunies.*"

"That's another one of your great-grandmother's words, another fable. I'm not a fable, Axle. I'm real. And today we have real problems. One of them can be handled quickly. The other . . . maybe not at all . . . but we have to try just the same."

"You're talking about the transformation, the heart of the world? I've already sent Bird—"

"I know what you've already done," Hayestani said. "I'm here to tell you what still needs doing, a new complication that needs to be corrected so that the bigger pieces can fall together." He shifted, lowering himself onto the floor, sitting like a nesting bird. "Three months ago, a man on the run nearly died in my farmhouse. He was bitten by snakes. I helped him, but after that I couldn't get rid of him. He made a home for himself in a front room, decorating it and the ground outside the house to conform to some mad vision. I let him stay. But now he has brought two more people to the house. They're there now. He begged me to help them."

"Help them how?"

Hayestani raised a long-fingered hand, the dark palm crosshatched with pale veins. "The same way I helped you. Remember? Last night. You had a bullet in the brain. I touched the wound, kept you alive. I've done the same with them, but they can't be moved just yet. And since conditions aren't right for two more skybirths, they will remain in a state of incomplete transformation, at once more- and less-than human. And they'll be scarred, too. Nothing to do about that. If I could have taken them to the mine, gotten them closer to the great heart . . ." He looked away. "But I doubt even that would have made a difference. So much has changed since last night. "

"But you've kept them alive."

"In a manner of speaking, yes. But they're still too weak to move. They need time, and I need you to help me buy it for them. "

"How does this serve the *oohaate*?" Axle asked.

"*Oohaate?*"

"The path into the future, the way that must be followed, the spirit plan that will reclaim the world."

Hayestani shook his head, a slow rolling motion—like the shifting of a heavy stone. "It's not that simple, Axle. Nothing is. You'll see, but right now I have people to deal with. And people still matter."

"You know these people?"

"They are complete strangers."

"Then why—"

"It's the right thing to do, Axle."

"So there's still humanity in you. You say you aren't my father, but he's still—"

"Consider it practice, Axle. The dream you shared with Bird proves you can sustain a presence in one man's dream, but what if a person is awake?"

"The boy in my body shop," Axle said. "I appeared to him, scared him away. That was my practice."

"That boy was addled, Axle. What about more formidable subjects?" He set his hands on Axle's shoulders. His palms were stone cold. "Cast your spirit to the northwest, across the mine, between crater and dam."

The chill from the stone-cold palms flowed through Axle, entered his mind.

Axle closed his eyes.

"Ride the spirit wind, Axle."

Axle flew over the flashing lights of fire trucks, past the glow of a widening pit, toward the remnants of an isolated farmhouse.

Once again, he had become Kwetis.

He folded his wings, dove toward the house, and landed on a bare beam that angled above a bed with a truck grill for a headboard.

A man stood beside the bed. He was bald and nearly naked. Smeared markings covered his scalp and shoulders.

Two people lay on the bed, faces black, arms swollen. The painted man had been looking at them, but now he turned away. He seemed to sense something, but instead of looking up toward the second-floor beams, he turned his attention to a cloth-draped door, tensing as a voice called from outside.

"Come out slowly. Hands on your head. Do it now!"

Kwetis looked toward the voice, and as he did the dream vision shifted. He was now in the front of the house, looking at three police officers. One officer had a dog. He stood a few steps back from a seven-foot sculpture—a trash-art devil with iron limbs and plastic wings. A car radiator served as the devil's torso, and the radiator vanes seemed to be moving, shifting in the sunlight as if the metal were coming alive.

Kwetis sharpened his gaze, bringing the statue's body into focus. A moment later, he saw the snakes coiled amid the metal slats. And a moment after that, he knew what he needed to do.

32

The wind shifted, turning cooler as fog moved in, dimming the hard edges of the junk-art demons. DeAngelis moved toward one of them. A moment ago, it had seemed to twitch. Now he realized that the movement came not from the statue but from something on its neck.

Satan growled.

"Easy, boy."

It was a snake, a black racer—three-feet long and shimmering as it crawled along the wire shoulders.

Satan strained at the leash.

"No." DeAngelis pulled. "It's OK." He looked around. There were snakes on some of the other statues too, coiled in the twisted wire, taking refuge on the sculpted arms, shoulders, necks. As Leroy might say: *Not normal.*

He looked toward Leroy and Fisher, still approaching the house, partly hidden in the mist. He considered telling them about the snakes, but then something moved behind him: creaking metal, snapping plastic. It came from a few yards away, from the statue with a radiator chest and Coke-bottle eyes. DeAngelis remembered how it had looked when he'd first seen it: standing upright, metal legs anchored in concrete-filled holes. But now the radiator body looked off balance, ready to fall . . . ready to lunge.

I'm getting jumpy.

But it was more than that. He felt disoriented, as if the gathering mist were getting inside him, clouding his vision, fogging his senses.

"DeAngelis!"

He turned to see Leroy stepping away from the porch.

"Snakes," Leroy said. "Fucking snakes!"

"In the statues?"

"No. On the porch. It's covered!"

DeAngelis started toward the house.

Satan walked beside him.

"Big ones," Leroy said.

DeAngelis stopped when he drew close enough to see them. They were fatter than black racers, lighter in color, each capped with an arrow-shaped head. "Coppers." DeAngelis backed away. "Pit vipers."

Satan didn't react. The height of the porch put the vipers out of his line of sight. And snakes had no scent.

Fisher keyed his mike. "Blaston Nine-Oh. We're going to need—*fucking shit!*" The thing in Fisher's hand wasn't a mike. "*Jesus!*" It was a snake. Fisher gripped its neck. "*Goddamn!*" He yanked hard, pulling it from his shoulder. The damn thing had been resting on him, its body coiled beneath his shirt. "Motherfucker!" The snake blurred as Fisher flung it down and smashed its head beneath his heel. The skull cracked.

"How?" DeAngelis asked. "How'd that thing get on you?"

Fisher turned, looking confused, dazed. He seemed about to answer, then his eyes went wild. He lunged at DeAngelis.

Satan barked, rearing up, attack mode.

DeAngelis pulled the dog back. "Fisher? What the hell?"

Fisher grabbed something from DeAngelis's collar. It was another snake, whipping the air as Fisher flung it down. And now Leroy was doing the same, struggling with a timber rattler, pulling it from his shoulder.

"What the fuck's going on?" Fisher screamed.

Leroy didn't stomp on his snake. He threw it down and shot it with his Glock. Twice. *BLAM! BLAM!* The first shot shattered its head. The second was evidently on principle.

"Damnit, Leroy!" Fisher stepped away from the flying dirt. "You got him the first time!"

DeAngelis's ears were ringing now, the partial deafness adding to the strangeness of the moment. *We're all dazed*, he thought, looking at the remains of Leroy's snake, head in fragments, pieces of skull strewn like shattered plastic.

Plastic!

The damn thing wasn't a snake.

"Our radios!" DeAngelis said.

Leroy and Fisher looked at him.

"Christ, Fisher! We've trashed our mikes!"

Fisher squinted at the ground, started to protest, but stopped. His expression made it clear that he saw it too. The things weren't snakes. Just shattered mikes with coiled cords.

The mist shifted, thickening, blotting the sun. The world dimmed, graying out. Surrounding trees lost their color, becoming silhouettes, patterns in the fog. DeAngelis felt as if he were standing in a room, sealed off from the world, locked in a place where logic no longer applied.

"They *were* snakes!" Fisher said. "Hell!" He looked at DeAngelis, eyes wide, pupils dilated. "You saw them! Goddamn snakes, right? You—"

Something squealed in the mist, a harsh metal-on-metal sound.

"Not normal," Leroy said. "This is so not normal."

The sounds repeated, coming from another direction . . . from *all* directions.

The statues were moving.

Leroy raised his Glock. "We need to get out of here."

"I make that call," Fisher said.

The sound grew louder, coming nearer, high pitched, shrill.

"All right!" Fisher turned, facing the fog. "Stay together."

They moved, Fisher and Leroy leading with their Glocks, picking up the pace until a statue appeared directly in front of them, coalescing out of the mist, television head pivoting, turning toward them.

Fisher steadied his weapon.

Leroy fired. The pistol flashed, thumping in the fog. The picture tube shattered. The monster recoiled, reared back, then twisted as if trying to walk. Metal groaned, and then—

FhhooMMMPF!

One of its swing-set legs broke from the ground. Dirt flew from the hole, pattering the grass as the leg swung forward.

THUMP!

The foot came down, bracing as the statue wrenched the other leg free.

FhhooMMMPF!

Fisher fell in beside Leroy, both retreating. And suddenly they were all running, stumbling as the ground shook with the thud of sandcrete hooves. But through it all, DeAngelis sensed something odd about the dog. *He thinks we're playing.* He looked at Satan, noticed the angle of his ears, the ease of his gait. He seemed unafraid, as if the statues were no more alive than the smashed mikes had been.

Something's wrong, and it's not the statues.

DeAngelis forced himself to slow down. He glanced back. Nothing was after them. Nothing back there but mist and shadows. And the shadows weren't moving.

He tugged Satan's leash. "Stop."

Satan responded. No hesitation.

"Sit."

Satan eased down, panting, looking toward the retreating officers, then up at DeAngelis.

"What's going on, boy? What do you see?"

Satan closed his mouth, swallowed, went back to panting, all the while keeping his eyes on DeAngelis. The body language was clear: *That was fun! Can we do it again!*

"Hey!" Fisher called from the edge of the field, nearly hidden in mist. "DeAngelis!"

Satan glanced at Fisher.

"DeAngelis! What're you—"

"Look at the statues!" DeAngelis said.

"What?"

"The statues, Fisher. They haven't moved."

"The fuck you saying?"

"Look at them."

"But we saw—"

"*Thought* we saw."

"What the hell's that mean, *thought*?"

"We *thought* we saw them moving. Just like we *thought* we saw snakes instead of radios."

"That's not normal," Leroy said. "That's not anywhere near—"

"I know what I saw," Fisher said.

"Do you?" DeAngelis approached him. The dog kept pace, trotting along. "Is it just me, or are you feeling . . . I don't know . . . out of it, confused, disoriented?" His voice rang flat in the mist. "Like you're dreaming?"

Leroy frowned. "Sleeping?"

"Not thinking clearly."

"You mean, like, seeing things?"

"Yeah," DeAngelis said. "Like we're sharing some kind of—"

"I *know* what I *saw*," Fisher said. "We all saw it. Just because we can't explain it don't mean—" He spun abruptly as a shadow raced toward them. In a flash, both he and Leroy leveled their Glocks, ready to fire. And now Satan was barking. He saw it too.

"Hey!" The shadow kept charging, arms waving. "It's me!"

They lowered their weapons.

Rose appeared, panting, face blanched. She pulled in close, weapon drawn, epaulette dangling from her shoulder. She too had trashed her radio. "You clearing out?" she said. "Leaving me?"

"No!" Fisher said. "Hell no." As commanding officer, he couldn't admit to forgetting she had been behind the house. But he had. They all had. And Rose knew it. She moved in close, trembling. "I was lost, couldn't see anything. If it hadn't been for your voices—"

"We need to get out of here," Leroy said.

Fisher ran a hand over his bald head, looking around. "And go where?" He extended an arm, the hand fading to a gray shadow. "Can't see for shit now, and it's getting worse by the second."

"This is so fucking not normal."

"Hold on!" DeAngelis said. "I want to try something." He peered into the mist, toward what he believed was the direction of the house. "I want to go back."

Fisher frowned. "To the house?"

"Yeah."

"Just you?"

"Me and Satan."

"You'll get lost," Rose said. "You think it's easy, think you know where you're going, but trust me. It's—"

"There's a scent trail leading to the porch. Satan'll guide me."

"Past those statues?" Fisher said.

"Satan didn't see them moving."

"You know that for sure?"

"Yeah . . . I know it. I know him, know his reactions. He'll follow the scent trail, guide me back to the porch. If he senses danger, I'll turn around. If he doesn't—"

"What about the porch?" Leroy asked. "The snakes on the—"

"Don't see why they'd be more real than anything else."

"Giant statues are one thing," Fisher said. "But snakes—"

"If they're there, Satan'll see them."

"Not till you climb the steps. Not till you're right on top of them."

"Maybe we should all go," Rose said. "Stick together."

"I'll go alone." DeAngelis set a hand on Satan's head, stroking his ears. "One person means fewer distractions. If Satan senses something, I'll want to know for sure that it's not one of you." He looked at Fisher. "You all right with this?"

Fisher just stared.

"This is screwed up," Leroy said. "This is, like, it's—"

"Not normal?" Rose said.

Leroy frowned. "Fucked," he said. "Abnormally fucked."

Fisher put a hand on DeAngelis's shoulder. "You call to us when you get there. Keep calling. We'll come to you then. Go inside together."

"Count on that." DeAngelis tightened his grip on Satan's leash. "All right, boy. Track!"

The dog moved forward, following the human scent into the veil of mist.

33

Sam knew the interstate: the rural straightaways, the reduced-speed stretches, and the pull offs where police lay in wait for speeders. She drove strategically: speeding when she could, gearing back when she reached a suspicious stretch of road. She watched her detector, too. But most of all, she watched the trucks. No one knows roads better than the professionals. When they highballed, she cut loose.

Pax kept pace. He was surprisingly good behind the wheel, his response times honed from playing computer games. What his generation lacked in intelligence they made up for in reflexes. She watched him in the rearview, sometimes slowing when he fell behind, but mostly trusting him to keep up.

Forty miles out of Windslow, they left the interstate for a rural freeway. Then it was a few more miles on backcountry roads that straightened when they hit Claudia. It wasn't much of a town: three blocks, two lights, one lane going north, another south. They lost time at the lights, and then a little more when they stopped to top off their tanks at a corner station. But they sped up again on the final leg outside town, coming at last to a hump of land capped by a weathered fence with an open gate.

A wood-frame house appeared as they cleared the hump: dark windows, sagging gutters, blistered paint. Most of the structure seemed poised at the brink of ruin—all except for a portion of the first floor. Here there were curtains, clean glass, painted shutters. The front steps were clean. Potted impatiens bloomed on a porch rail. This was the occupied corner of the house, the portion that Tucky had settled into long after the members of the commune had abandoned their ideals for a cookie-cutter existence beyond the farm. But Tucky had remained, inheriting the estate from her common-law mate, gradually sealing off unused rooms as she settled into the house's southeast corner.

The farm was much the same. Except for a whitewashed barn and an acre of cultivated vines, the bulk of the property lay tangled in weeds that extended along the rising ground behind the house. Beyond the weeds, hills of overburden rose from a wide wasteland, acres of abandoned property that had once belonged to heavy industry. There was still coal back there, but not enough to sustain a mine. The machines had moved out, leaving a stretch of land so dead that even weeds had a hard time reclaiming it.

Sam parked along the inside of the fence. She took her med kit from the seat beside her, tucking it into the top of one of her socks. Then she got out.

Her leg cramped as she gave it her weight. She leaned on the door, trying to look nonchalant as Pax pulled up beside her.

He grinned through the windshield, adjusting the sunglasses that she had bought for him at a fuel stop back in Waynesburg. She had bought a pair for herself, too, but the polarized lenses blurred her vision. Her senses still weren't right. *Probably a concussion.* Nothing she could do about that. It would either get worse or better. Either way, in a couple hours it wouldn't matter.

She gestured for Pax to lower his window. "I need you to sit tight while I go inside," she said.

"You're the boss!"

"And turn off the engine. You can survive a few minutes without the AC."

He did as she said. "Is this a farm?" he asked.

"Among other things."

"They sell construction supplies?"

"Yeah." She slapped the roof of his car, the way boys did when they wanted to signal that they'd be right back. Then she turned and started away.

She probably should never have told him that they were picking up construction supplies for Kirill's engineer. Lies always complicated things, and she was pretty sure Pax didn't care what they were doing. Driving the Viper was enough for him.

Tucky stepped out onto the porch. She had aged since their last meeting. Her face looked sunken, pinched around the lips and eyes. She wore a calico dress, threadbare along the elbows, frayed at the hem. The sun caught her face as she stepped to the rail. "What do you call that dress, Sam?"

"Temporary."

Tucky frowned as Sam started up the steps. "You're limping."

"Only a little." Sam reached the porch.

"That's not a little. And I don't like the look of those bandages."

"Cuts on my hands, Tucky. From rock climbing."

"Since when are you a rock climber?" Tucky put out her arms, pulling Sam close. "What kind of trouble you in, child?"

"Nothing much, just what I told you. The beavers are back."

"Really?"

"Something like that." Sam let her face linger on Tucky's shoulder, eyes closed, nose to the calico. Tucky's smell recalled Sam's childhood, the early days before her mother had pushed her away and embraced Jesus.

"Those cars yours?" Tucky asked.

"Borrowed."

"What happened to your Jeep?"

Sam slid free from Tucky's arms. "Wrecked."

"And that driver?" Tucky gestured toward Pax. "You going to invite him in?"

"No," Sam said. "He's just helping."

Tucky opened the door. "You have time for some tea?"

"No. Just water." She set her hand on her right thigh, feeling the plastic container through Kirill's polo shirt, making sure it wasn't sliding loose. "And I need to use the bathroom."

The kitchen was warm, with a fan humming in a back window and another spinning in the ceiling. The next room in had become a combination living- and bedroom, arranged like an efficiency apartment: bed, chairs, TV.

A short hall led to the bathroom.

"I'll get the water," Tucky said. "You know where to find the other."

Sam headed toward the short hall.

"How about that driver boy outside?" Tucky said.

"He doesn't need a drink. I bought him a pop in Waynesburg."

"Might have to pee."

"He's a boy. He'll make do."

The refrigerator clicked open as Sam entered the bathroom and shut the door. The space was tight, barely room enough to turn around between sink and toilet, little more between toilet and tub. She leaned against the sink, raised the polo-shirt, and removed the med kit. She considered the preloaded syringe of morphine, but as much as she wanted to kill the pain, she couldn't risk losing her edge. She would inject that later if she had to. Right now she needed something to counteract her growing fatigue, a couple of black pills to go with the water that Tucky was getting in the kitchen.

Sam took out two of the methamphetamine capsules, set them on the side of the sink, and pushed the med kit back into the top of her right sock. Then, carefully, she rolled down the left one and looked at her wounded leg.

It was all bruise now, everything from hip to knee. And the swelling was worse than ever. The bone may not be broken, but muscle trauma was deep and severe.

She lowered herself onto the toilet, sitting on the lid, head in her hands. She didn't need to pee. Just think.

Why am I doing this?

The answer had seemed obvious at Kirill's house. Now it felt ill-formed, delusional.

My mother's sickness. I'm like her now. Trusting visions.

A hand touched her shoulder. She straightened up, expecting to find the bathroom door open and Tucky leaning in. But the door was still closed. Instead of Tucky, Kasdeja stood beside her, the hint of a frown on his sculpted face.

She straightened up.

"You're letting me down, Samuelle."

"No." She tried standing. "Just resting—" Her leg twinged. She slumped back, striking the tank.

"No time for resting." He took her arm, pulled her to her feet. "Resting brings doubt. Doubt delays actions." He turned toward a plaster wall. Lights flashed within the swirls, pulses of red and blue beating in time with Sam's throbbing head. "You need convincing," he said. "Let me show you something."

They stepped forward, not into the wall, but into a swirl of mist that smelled of burning rock. The pulsing lights slipped behind them. Straight ahead, a new glow bloomed red-orange, coming from the ground, growing wider as they advanced.

"The sinkhole?" she said. "We're back in Windslow."

His grip tightened, holding her fast as they reached the brink. At their feet, the earth plunged into a funnel of glowing red.

"Careful now." He spread his wings. "Grip my shoulders, and hold on. We're going in."

She glanced behind her, looking for traces of Tucky's home in the flashing haze. There was none. The farmhouse in Claudia was miles away . . . if it even existed at all.

"Doubt delays action, Samuelle."

She turned and threw her arms around his shoulders. His skin was smooth, like the down of a chick. Or was it fine wool—cashmere, angora? She pressed her face against it.

He extended his wings to catch the wind.

Then, together, they drifted down.

"You're an angel, aren't you?" she said.

"If you like."

"But are you?"

"Knowing what I am is not as important as recognizing the threat that will rise if you don't act swiftly." He banked to one side, bringing them toward a glowing wall, close enough to see variegated bands of rock: yellow sandstone, gray shale, brown siltstone, red-hot coal.

The coal was burning. She felt its heat against her skin, saw patterns in its glow. The patterns looked familiar, like the markings of a snake.

"They're almost ready, Samuelle. That's why you need to act swiftly . . . stop them before they rise."

"But what are they?"

He folded his wings. The stratified wall blurred as he plunged. The air grew hotter. She could hardly breathe. And then, with a concussive snap, he extended his wings again, grabbed the air, swung in close to another glowing vein of superheated coal. This time the shape in the rock was fully formed. She saw a triangular head, hooded eyes, banded body, and something else: a folded appendage draped with translucent skin.

"Wings!" she said. "It's sprouting wings."

The rock rumbled. A molten snakehead pulled free, crackling as it swung into the smoky air, big as a bus, suspended on a neck that moved like a jointed crane.

"Can you imagine, Samuelle? Can you imagine what such creatures could do if loosed upon the world?"

The head swung toward them, flicked its tongue, studied them with glowing eyes. Then, with a force that shook the wall, it pulled free, tumbled away and extended its wings.

Sam feared it might come for them, but instead it spiraled downward, descending until it vanished in the smoky air.

"They're not ready to leave the nest," Kasdeja said. "When they are, their flight will mark the end of days."

"What will they do?"

"Do? It's not what they will do. It's what they will herald. Something more insidious is taking shape in the depths below." He folded his wings. Strata blurred as they dove. "I'll show you." They fell, deeper—plunging toward something that crackled in the depths of the abyss. She saw it first as a glowing mass, pulsing with the color of arterial blood.

"Hold on!" Kasdeja extended his wings, breaking their fall. Then he circled, riding the waves of heat that radiated from a thing that resembled a red-hot tree—no leaves, just pulsing branches and glowing snakes that dangled from their tails, heads hanging like smoldering fruit.

The tree seemed to expand as she looked at it, swelling until she turned away for fear that it would overwhelm the world.

"Sam?"

She looked up.

The bathroom door swung open. Tucky stood within it, water glass in her hand. "What's going on?"

"Sorry. I'm OK."

"Don't seem OK." Tucky glanced at the sink. Saw the capsules. "What's that?"

Sam grabbed the pills, cupped them in her hand. "My business." She said it as if she meant it to be the final word.

"Maybe they are," Tucky said. "But you don't need them. What you need is rest, a decent meal."

"No time." Sam stood up, took the glass, downed the meth. "I'll be fine." She took another drink, handed the glass back to Tucky.

"You need to tell me what's wrong, Sam."

"No. I don't *have* to. You told me that. The first night I came here, you told me a woman's business is for her to keep or share as she wishes. You said you'd always respect that, and that's what I need, Tucky. That and those two cases of Hercules you've got in the freezer."

Tucky frowned. She clearly didn't like having her own rules turned back on her. But she was a woman of her word. "All right, Sam." She backed out of the doorway. "But about that Hercules . . . there's something you need to know . . . something I couldn't tell you over the phone line." She started toward the living room, looking back to make sure Sam was following. "I'll show you what I have. If you still want it after that, it's all yours."

They walked out onto the little front porch to find Pax stretched out on the hood of Kirill's copperhead-orange Viper, resting on a couple of floor mats. Shirtless, shoeless, and still wearing his shades, he seemed to be sleeping. At any rate, he didn't look up as the screen door creaked open and banged shut.

"He's a looker, Sam."

"I wouldn't know." She followed Tucky down the steps, around to the side of the house.

"You don't see it?"

"I've got other things on my mind, Tucky."

"You're not much for relationships, are you?"

"There's you and me," Sam said. "We get along."

"You know what I mean. One of these days, you're going to have to fall in love. Seriously, Sam. It'll change your life."

Sam winced.

"Did I say something wrong?" Tucky asked.

"No," Sam said, putting an edge in her voice, making it clear the topic was out of bounds. "I hear you. Maybe someday."

"What happened to that man and his two sons, the ones who helped you build that cabin in the woods?"

"That was my business, Tucky."

Tucky looked away. "Then let me tell you about the dynamite." She glanced toward a utility pole as they neared the back of the house. "It has to do with my electric service. I still get it from the government, fool that I am." She gestured toward the power line that ran toward the barn. "I'd like to generate my own power, go off grid, but the startup is too steep." She paused beside the barn door, a curtain of corrugated steel that had been retrofitted into the wooden frame. "Anyway, the power lines get surges. The lights go out and come back on. I used to think it was no big deal. But then, a few weeks back, I noticed a problem."

She opened a panel beside the door, uncovering a keypad on which she entered a seven-digit code. Then she threw a switch, stepping back as the door thundered upward to reveal a deep warehouse lined with metal shelves stacked high with cigarettes and pharmaceuticals. This was her real business, warehousing and shipping untaxed and unlicensed goods. Orders arrived via fax machine, sent by a clearinghouse operation that relied on a network of independent warehouses and shipping centers. Tucky never had to order stock. Trucks simply arrived at irregular intervals. The operation paid better than farming, and it was something she could do on her own. That, and making things disappear, which she achieved with the help of huge tracts of forgotten land beyond the western edge of her farm.

"I know that people with computers worry about surges," Tucky said. "But I've never much cared for computers. I've got my phone and my fax. That's all I need."

They moved past the shelves, toward a stall near the back of the barn. The space was dark. She flipped a switch. A light came on. "I'm a nuts-and-bolts person. Switches and relays. I never understood how people could make real things happen by pressing make-believe buttons."

The stall held an assortment of tools and supplies, mostly things that her extended family had once pilfered from the coal company. It also held an old freezer chest that sat humming to itself in the shadows.

"You wouldn't think a freezer would be much affected by surges," Tucky said. "It's a simple machine. Inside gets warm, compressor clicks on. Inside cools down, compressor clicks off. If the power goes out, it keeps its cool until the lights come back. At least, you'd think that'd be the case. But then something happened . . . must have been a power surge. It knocked out the circuit to this stall. Nothing else. Just that circuit." She set her hand on the freezer's lid. "If the stall were a space I used everyday, I would have noticed it a lot sooner." She looked at Sam. "See what I'm saying?"

Sam was getting the picture. "How long was the power out?"

"Don't know. I almost never come back here. No one's much interested in dynamite these days. It's all ammonium nitrate, which doesn't pack anywhere near the same punch—especially if you're looking to move earth and rock."

"So what you're saying is?"

"This freezer lost its power, Sam. I noticed it a few weeks back. An old farmer from up north wanted a stick to blast a stump. I came back here, opened the lid, and then I shut it again—real slow."

"The dynamite was thawed?"

"Thawed and warm. The freezer was the same temperature inside as out."

"You think the nitro separated?"

"I *know* it did," Tucky said. "I could smell it. Only safe thing to do was reset the circuit and freeze it solid again."

"Weren't you afraid the compressor might set it off?"

"The thought crossed my mind, but what choice did I have? Call Hazmat? Tell those government boys to come out and hope they don't notice my cache of meds and Jin-Lings?"

"So you refroze it."

"I did, and it's been that way ever since. Sleeping here, minding its business, waiting for me to figure out what to do with it." She raised the lid. The crates sat side by side, wrapped in plastic sheeting. She peeled back one of the wrappers, letting Sam see the stenciled logo on the wood-grain. "It's stable as long as it's frozen solid," Tucky said. "But once it starts thawing—"

"Is it useable?"

"Useable? Do you mean, will it explode? That it will. Concussion, open flame, electric spark—just about anything will set it off. One thing's for sure. You won't need detonators."

Sam stood a moment, looking down into the mist that gathered in the open freezer.

"My advice," Tucky said. "Whatever it is you need this for, you consider using fertilizer instead."

Sam shook her head. The mist in the freezer reminded her of the haze from her vision: smoking sinkhole, burning rock, flying snakes. "No. You said it yourself. Dynamite's the only thing for earth and rock. The only *sure* thing."

"Earth and rock?" Tucky said. "How much earth and rock you talking?"

"Lots."

"Two cases worth?" Tucky looked at Sam. "We're not talking beaver dams here, are we?"

"No. Not beaver dams." She left it at that.

They lifted out the cases, set them on a dolly, and carted them to the cars.

"We never talked price," Sam said.

"No price. I don't charge for damaged goods."

"I want to pay you," Sam said. She had taken a look inside Kirill's overnight bag while gassing the cars in Waynesburg. She had seen the shrink-wrapped brick of twenty-dollar bills. That brick, combined with the cash she had earned last night, put her in a position to pay Tucky handsomely for her help. "I have money."

"And I don't want it."

Sam let it drop. She had another issue to deal with now. "Hey, Pax!"

Pax sat up on the hood of his Viper.

"Put those mats back on the floor, get dressed, and get in the car."

He stood up, slipped into his shoes, grabbed his shirt. "I can help you with those cases!"

"You can help by doing what I said. Now, sweetheart!"

He hopped to it.

"Sweetheart?" Tucky said.

"He likes me," Sam said. "Sometimes I play along."

Tucky eased the dolly behind the silver Viper while Sam popped the trunk.

Pax put the mats back in the car. "I really don't mind helping!"

"Then get in the car and pop your trunk."

She didn't know what he would do if he knew they were hauling dynamite. There was a good chance he'd believe her if she told him there was no risk, that the stuff was stable, that he could drive fast and not worry about it going off. But there was also a chance he'd get scared, drive like a wimp, maybe refuse to drive at all. Of course, she'd have to level with him when they reached the dam. She'd need his help getting the stuff into the culvert. She'd tell him they were storing it for Kirill, that the engineers were going to need it for their reconstruction. He'd probably believe that. He was a trusting kid. She was almost sorry she was going to have to kill him when it was all over.

Sam and Tucky loaded the first crate into the silver Viper, pushing it in tight between the wheel wells. Then they closed the lid and moved to the back of Pax's car.

Pax was behind the wheel, strapped in, looking at himself in the mirror.

"Hey!" Sam slapped the trunk. "I told you to pop it, Pax."

"I did."

"It's not open. Do it again." She waited. Nothing happened. She rounded the side of the car. "The hell you doing, Pax?"

"I popped it!"

She reached inside, hit the release, and looked back at Tucky who shook her head.

"Could be disconnected," Pax said.

"Give me the key."

He pulled it from the ignition, passed it to her.

"Nothing's easy." She returned to the back of the car, slid in the key, turned it. Nothing happened.

"Wrong key?" Tucky asked.

"It's an all-in-one." She tried again. It turned the cylinder, but the trunk remained locked. "It has to be right." She pulled it out. The key was cut the same on both sides. Nevertheless, she flipped it and tried again. Still no good.

"Maybe you'll have to settle for one case," Tucky said.

"Might not be enough." Sam tried to think.

"Hot out here," Tucky said. "Maybe we'd best put this case back in the freezer while—"

"Hold on!" Sam noticed a second lock on the edge of the trunk. It was a security lock, shaped to take a barrel security key. "Wait a second." Sam stood up, thinking. Her leg cramped. She hardly noticed. The meth was kicking in now, her mind racing. "There's another key!" She walked back to the silver Viper, pulled Kirill's keychain from the ignition, and returned to the trunk.

"Another key?" Tucky asked.

Sam held up the security key.

"Looks like it goes to an alarm," Tucky said.

Sam slid it into the second lock. Turned it. Still nothing. The trunk remained close. She kept the barrel key in place and tried the other key again.

The lock popped. The trunk disengaged.

"That did it!" Tucky said.

Sam stood up. "Doesn't make sense." She gripped the trunk, swinging it upward. "Why does a trunk need two—" She caught her breath when she saw what lay inside. "Jesus H. Christ!"

Tucky sidestepped, looked past her, gave a loud shriek.

"What?" Pax opened the door, started climbing out. "What is it?"

"Nothing!" Sam shouted, voice going ragged.

"Didn't sound like nothing." Pax pointed at Tucky. "She screamed!"

"And now I'm screaming at you, Pax. Back in the fucking car!"

Pax stood, glancing at the raised trunk.

"Goddamnit, Pax!" Sam lowered the lid, pushing it down without engaging the latches, hiding the contents. "Mind your goddamn business!"

"I was just—"

"Get in the fucking car!"

He turned. "Whatever!" He climbed in, slammed the door.

Sam raised the trunk again, looked in, wishing she'd find it empty this time. No such luck.

"You said you borrowed these cars?" Tucky said.

"Yeah."

"From a friend?"

"From a client."

"You mean—"

"No questions, Tucky. Please." Sam reached inside the trunk, setting her hand on the transparent plastic sheeting, looking at the faces beneath her fingers. Lots of faces. Grants and Jacksons mostly, but some Franklins, too—all bundled into shrink-wrapped bricks.

"That's an enormous lot of money, Sam."

Sam leaned forward, bracing herself on the bills, noticing a gap among the bricks—a space where a square of twenties had been removed. Her mind flashed to the shrink-wrapped cash in Kirill's overnight bag.

"Interesting place to keep a stash of money," Tucky said.

"Yeah. But you got to admit, there's logic to it."

Sam had a couple of hordes of her own back at the cabin, both hidden in pits behind her shed: one pit for paper currency, another for gold coins in the event the economy turned really nasty. She had never thought of keeping a large reserve in the trunk of a car, but it made sense for Kirill. The spare Viper was always locked in his garage, and if Kirill ever needed to leave town for good, he wouldn't need to worry about emptying a safe. The safe would be ready to roll.

Sam studied the bricks. Her leg throbbed. She needed to sit down, but work came first. "Help me, Tucky."

"Help you?"

Sam grabbed one of the bricks. "Help me unload this shit."

"The money?"

Sam picked up the brick and dropped it on the pavement. "Come on," she said. "Get it out of here!" She picked up another.

"And do what with it, Sam?"

Another brick hit the pavement. "Just pile it up for now. Make room."

They piled the bricks by the dolly, working quickly while a puddle formed around the plastic-wrapped crate of Hercules. Seeing the puddle made Sam work faster, pushing herself in spite of the pain. Then, when the trunk was clear, they lifted the case. It was still cold, but they worked it more carefully than the last one, pushing the wood gently between the wheel wells.

Tucky knelt beside the puddle on the ground, dabbed it with her finger, pressed the finger to her tongue. "Just water." She spat. "Nitro's got a sweet, burny taste. Smells sweet and burny, too." She stood up, speaking softly so Pax wouldn't hear. "When it starts thawing, the separated nitro will probably stay inside the case, in the wrapper. Stuff that gets past the paper will run into the wood before it drains out to make a puddle. What I'm saying is, you might not see any seepage right away. But you'll smell it. And once you do, you'll know you're on borrowed time. In the wrapper or in a puddle, it's going to be completely unpredictable. You might bump it hard and have nothing happen. But that's the real danger, getting over confident, thinking it's stable when it isn't. Sometimes the gentlest tap will do the trick."

"I get the picture, Tucky. I'll be careful."

"But will you be careful enough? Are you being careful now?"

"What do you mean?"

Tucky squinted at the sun. "It's hot, Sam. Going to be even hotter on the freeway."

"What if we insulate it?" Sam looked at the shrink-wrapped bricks. "We'll put the money around the crates." She picked up one of the bricks. "Come on. Help me." She put it in the trunk, wedging it in against the wet plastic. "As many as will fit."

They filled Pax's trunk, then did the same to hers. Then Sam shut Pax's trunk, bearing down, latching it with weight rather than force. Then she removed the keys.

"One way or the other," Tucky said. "It's going to be tough to handle. But like you say." She folded her arms. "It's your business."

"The stuff's still frozen, right?"

"As far as I can tell."

"So we'll be fine then."

"I suppose," Tucky said. "Unless someone rear ends you."

"We'll be careful."

"And I'd keep away from open flames. Fire might not explode dynamite, but if it melts the nitro—"

"Like I said, we'll be careful." She gave Pax his key, moving alongside the car to pass it through the window.

"We going now?"

"Yeah." She limped toward the silver Viper. "We're going."

Pax started the engine.

Sam climbed behind her wheel.

Tucky came up beside her.

Sam frowned. "I have to go, Tucky." She put the car in gear.

"Be safe." Tucky leaned in, hugged her. There was that smell again, the loving-mother smell. And then it was gone, walking away toward the small pile of money bricks that still remained on the pavement.

Pax lowered his window, called over to Sam: "Expensive supplies, huh?"

"What?"

"I saw you paying her."

"You saw nothing, Pax."

"All right. I know. I see nothing!" He gunned the engine.

"Stay close, Pax. Don't stop unless I do." She let out the clutch and raced toward the gate, glancing in the rearview to make sure he was following . . . and then once more to see Tucky standing by the bricks, hand in the air, waving good bye.

34

Bird cruised north, guided by his memory of the map that Kwetis had shown him in the waters of the west-wing pool. It was as if the route, glimpsed once within the dream, had been imprinted in his mind. But there was more to it than that. The roads seemed to speak to him, letting him know when the way was clear, when he was free to floor it and push the needle into the red. Even on the two-lane roads that dipped and wound between the interstate and downtown Claudia, he felt in complete control. It was as if he were seeing the world in slow motion, able to react with hair-trigger swiftness to the changing terrain. And so he flew, watching the road unfurl until he realized it was time to gas up.

Claudia appeared, a dead-looking town of boarded windows and struggling shops. A Sunoco sign rose in the distance. He cut his speed, ran a light, and steered into the service lot. There were no other cars. The little station seemed on the brink of closing, barely hanging on in a town that had already lost its economic grip. He got out, and then it hit him.

"Shit!" He checked his pockets, knowing they were empty. "Fuck me!" He didn't have a wallet, hadn't had one since Axle's friends had taken it at Windslow Mine. He hadn't forgotten about that, but everything had been happening so fast that until now he hadn't considered the implications of travelling without credit cards. "Goddamnit, Axle! I thought you had this all planned." He leaned back against the car, closed his eyes. "A little help, Axle. Come on, man! What am I supposed to do?"

He heard a roar, a sudden breeze blowing his hair, pushing his collar. But it was only a truck highballing through a green light. The stink of its exhaust swirled around him, overloading his senses, distracting him. And there were other things too: the smell of the sun, the texture of the air, the sound the pavement made as it shifted in the warming morning, the color of the heat waves rising from the Firebird's hood. As focused and in control as he had been while driving, he now felt completely distracted, at once omnisciently aware and totally overwhelmed.

"Think! Need to think! Focus!"

He glanced at the pump. What if he just filled up and drove off? He looked around for security cameras. There weren't any, at least none that he could see. *Do it!* He removed his gas cap, put in the nozzle, tried the pump. No good. The thing wouldn't switch on.

A sticker beside the credit card slot told the story.

PLEASE PREPAY

"I'm wasting time!"

He stepped away from the pump and looked at the mini-mart, glass walls covered with posters and stickers, brightly colored ads that screamed in the sunlight. Someone was looking out between those ads, watching him, probably waiting for him to insert his card and activate the pump. He sensed it was a woman. Perhaps he could play on her sympathies, get her to help.

He started across the lot.

The woman moved away from the glass as Bird reached the door, pulled it open, and stepped into a gale of sensory overload. Wrappers, bags, bottles, cans, boxes, and tins—shelves and shelves of them—each designed to attract the attention of jaded consumers. Before today, he had been able to tune them out, but now he had no recourse but to cover his eyes and steady himself on the door as it closed behind him.

"Sir?" It was the woman behind the counter. "Are you all right, sir?"

He turned toward her, squinting, struggling to bring her into focus: dark skin, darker eyes, braided hair. She was Indian. Not American Indian, but Indian-American.

"Sir? Can I help you?"

Her accent was thick.

"Sir? Are you all right, sir."

She stood in a Plexiglas booth, the kind that could be closed in the face of danger. So far, she hadn't closed it.

He went to the window, braced himself on the counter.

A fisheye mirror in the corner reflected someone in the back of the store, stacking shelves, possibly the woman's son.

"Listen," Bird said. He licked his lips. "I'm having some trouble. Just listen, OK." He had no idea where to begin. Telling the truth was out of the question. A simple sob story might work best, that and the promise of a reward once he got back home.

The woman stared, saying nothing.

The man in the mirror was doing the same, leaning forward, waiting for him to continue.

"Yes?" the woman said.

Bird just stared. *Yes?* What did she mean, *Yes?*

"I'm listening," she said.

He had asked her to listen, and now she was.

"Sorry," he said. "I lost my wallet."

The woman didn't react, just kept staring, waiting for more.

"I need gas. I can't pay for it . . . not now. But I will. I can send you a check. Can you—"

She turned away.

So much for skyborn mojo.

He leaned over the counter, calling after her. "I'll pay you double. I know I don't look it, but I'm good for it. My family's—"

She reached beneath the counter. Something clicked. She looked back. "Go ahead, sir."

"Excuse me?"

"Pump five, sir."

He glanced at the mirror. The young man had gone back to stacking shelves.

Bird stepped toward the door. "Thank you."

"Not at all, sir."

He turned and hurried into the humming sun.

The tank full, he returned to the road and continued north.

He came to a turnoff, a drive of oiled gravel leading up to an open gate, and it was here that he heard the igniting roar of a V10 engine. A second ignition followed.

"All right, Axle. I'll do my part. You better do yours." He spoke the words to empty air. If the dream spirit were close, Bird couldn't detect him. What he could detect was the roar of two V10s just above the rise, accelerating toward the narrow drive. He had to pull over, let them by. The Vipers would pass close, within a few feet. If Axle needed a conduit to reach the drivers, this was his chance.

Bird closed his eyes. "Come on, Axle!"

The engines thundered. Then, in a flash of chrome, a silver Viper shot onto the drive. The second car followed, copper finish flashing in the sun.

Vrrrrrooo0OOOMMMM!

Vrrrrrooo0OOOMMMM!

They shot past in a haze of dust, speeding down the rural road, leaving Bird choking in their wake.

"Goddamnit, Axle!" He looked at the sky. "What the fuck?"

The sun beamed down. No Axle. No Kwetis. Bird was alone, left with no instructions beyond the ones he had already received. *Find the Vipers, get close, wait for Kwetis*—it had all sounded so easy at poolside.

He spun the wheel, gunned the engine, and took off in a hail of oiled gravel. The chase was on.

35

With the pain in his neck worsening, Kirill was lucky to follow half of what Arnold Gusky was saying. All he knew was that bank statements now filled the screen behind Gusky's desk. Color-coded arrows showed how checks in one account had been written to cover checks in another. The arrows curved, forming arcs, becoming circles: Gusky Investments paid Windslow Enterprises, who paid AG Construction, who paid Gusky Hardware, who paid ArGus Paving, who paid Gusky Investments. Round and round, rivers of paper flowing between bank accounts, all of it intended to make it seem as if Arnold Gusky was solvent, when, in fact, he was broke.

Gusky set the digital pad on his desk. "You see the problem, Kirill?"

Kirill blinked, trying to focus. "I see. I understand. I listened, Arnold. Now have that doctor bring me something for this pain."

Gusky tapped his Bluetooth and turned away, appearing to talk to the air. "We need some morphine up here."

"Tell her to hurry!"

Gusky listened to the thing in his ear, then looked at Kirill. "All right." He lowered his hand. "She's coming."

"So we're finished?"

"Not quite." Gusky scooted forward, still sitting on the wheeled stool. "Look. I've confided in you. Now it's important that you understand. I started the scheme to buy time, just a little time at first . . . then a little more. At first I thought it would be a matter of weeks before property values rose. Now . . . with Peterson dead—"

"You don't know he's dead!"

"Please, Kirill. I may be impulsive. I may be a risk taker. But I'm no one's fool . . . least of all yours." He stood up, walked back to the desk, picked up Kirill's gun. "So I'll put it to you straight. No more graphs and charts. Just a simple question, a proposition." He frowned at the gun. "How do I cock this thing?"

"You don't know guns, Arnold. You should put it down."

Gusky spun the cylinder.

"You need to think about what you're doing," Kirill said.

"I have. Now it's your turn. I need you to think hard, answer my question."

"What question?"

"Can you help?"

"Help?"

"Help, Kirill. Can you help me?"

"Help you how?"

"Jesus Christ, Kirill!" Gusky glanced back at the screen. "Haven't you been listening? I need money. Seven-hundred thousand to staunch the flow of bad paper. That'll buy me two, maybe three days, at which time I'll need $1.3 million."

Kirill flinched. The pain was getting worse, coming in waves.

"So here's my question, Kirill."

Kirill glanced toward the door.

"Look at me, Kirill. Focus. This is important."

"Where's that doctor?" Kirill asked.

"Be patient. She said she was coming, bringing morphine."

"You're sure?"

"What?" Gusky said. "You don't believe me? I wouldn't lie to you, Kirill—even if I *am* an expert liar." He grinned, momentarily full of himself. "It's a gift, you know, the ability to lie. I'm two million dollars in the hole, but everyone believes I'm the richest man in Windslow." He looked at the gun. "But it's a curse too. Lying bought me time, but the banks are catching on. They're about to call my bluff, so here's my question." He raised the gun. "Can you get me $700,000?"

Kirill just stared.

"Kirill?"

"*Perestan' mne jabat' mozgi svojimi voprosami!*"

"Come again?"

"Stop screwing with me and get me some morphine!"

"Answer the question, Kirill. Can you get me the money?"

"No. Hell no. What do you think—"

"Is that your final answer?" Gusky took aim at Kirill's face.

Kirill blinked, tried to focus. He could see the bullet resting in its chamber, ready to come for him in a blinding flash.

"I know you have deep pockets," Gusky said. "It's time to skim a little off the top for your good friend Arnold." He sighted across the barrel.

"What do you say, Kirill? We can use my computer, make a bank transfer—from your account to mine."

"I don't have access—"

"Then you can call your uncle. I know he's got cash. Tell him you need a favor."

"He won't do it."

"Come on, Kirill. Use your lifeline."

Kirill closed his eyes.

"You're my only hope, Kirill. If you don't help me, I lose everything. Absolutely everything. I lose nothing more by killing you."

The pain around the base of Kirill's skull was now so exquisite that he almost wished Gusky would go ahead and shoot him. *Almost* wished it. Not quite. The will to live long enough to rip out the little prick's liver was just a little stronger. "All right," Kirill said.

"All right?"

"But we can't do it with your computer. We have to go back to the lake."

"Why?"

"It's at the house."

"The money?"

"Yes."

"Cash?"

"That's right."

"You have $700,000 in cash? In your house?"

"Not *in* the house," Kirill said. "I never store money in the house. Bad luck."

Gusky lowered the gun.

"Let Dr. Was give me that morphine," Kirill said. "Then take me back to the lake, back to my home. I'll show you where I keep the money."

36

Bird caught sight of the Vipers as he reached the highway. The intersection reeked with exhaust, but the cars were a quarter mile ahead, with the silver convertible passing out of sight beyond an underpass.

The land was level, rolling plains dotted with pastures, crop fields, and isolated clumps of forest, all registering with crystal clarity in his peripheral vision as the road unfurled beneath the Firebird's hood.

The road veered left beyond the underpass. Bird shot through, the screaming V8 echoing from the girders and beams. He could see the cars again: copper hardtop 2,000 feet away, the silver convertible not much farther. They were accelerating, V10s thundering along a two-mile straightaway.

He glanced at the dash, eyeing the toggle switch and button for the N2O injector. The system was new. The mechanic that installed it had given Bird a demonstration, the two of them watching while the Firebird sat on a rack, engine screaming, rear wheels spinning in empty air. Bird had wanted to give it a test drive, but the problem was finding enough straight back roads around Windslow to do the system justice.

Now, with the Vipers becoming dots of glare on the long straightaway, Bird threw the toggle switch. It snapped smartly beneath his finger, arming the system. A diode glowed. All he had to do now was push the button.

He hesitated, looking ahead as a truck rumbled toward him in the southbound lane. There was a car behind it, a yellow Nissan. He glimpsed it for a moment, then it was gone, hidden behind the truck. What if that car tried passing? There'd be no breaking or swerving once he'd noxed the engine. Once he did that, the Firebird would be a bullet, a projectile on wheels. In the few seconds it would take for the N2O to burn through his engine, he'd be at the mercy of physics and chemistry. But the hell with that. The Vipers were getting away, and his skyborn mojo had to be good for something.

He placed his thumb on the button, gripped the wheel, and pushed.

The engine screamed.

"Holy shit!"

Dashboard needles jerked to the right, tachometer flying into the red, speedometer crossing 100 . . . 110 . . . 120.

"Sheeeeiiiit!"

The approaching truck expanded like a balloon, and just behind it, nosing across the center line, the little Nissan prepared to pass.

Bird leaned on the horn.

The Firebird screamed—engine whistling, horn blaring, Bird shouting.

The Nissan driver must have heard him.

The yellow car swung back behind the truck.

Bird shot past him—racing by so close that they might have shaken hands, if such a thing would have been possible at a combined speed of 180 mph.

An instant later, truck and Nissan were gone. And straight ahead, the snakehead logo on the copper Viper seemed to rear up and say hello.

The kid behind the wheel glanced in his rearview.

The Firebird tacked down.

The cars were close now, separated by less than a dozen feet of howling wind.

"Can't run, you son of a bitch! Can't run from the Bird!"

A few hundred feet away, the silver Viper screamed toward the interstate entrance ramp.

37

DeAngelis moved into the fog, gripping the leash as Satan followed the trail of human scent that should have led them both to the house. But it didn't.

"Sit!"

Satan stopped, drew back on his haunches, pricked his ears.

DeAngelis looked around, the fog thicker than ever. No sign of anything. No house. No statues. No forest. It was as if the world had gone up in smoke. He looked back over his shoulder. "Fisher!"

"Right here!" Fisher's voice came from the left, muffled by heavy air, but sounding close. "You at the house?"

"No. I think Satan's been tracking in a circle." He turned in place. The mist shifted. A shadow appeared, vanished, reappeared. It looked like the house, walls out of plumb, rickety steps leading to a porch. "Hold on." He stared through the mist. "I think I see it."

Satan whined, deep and breathy—the sound that he made when he sensed something bad.

"What is it?" DeAngelis asked.

Satan stared straight ahead, growling low and deep, reacting to something in the mist.

And now the house seemed to be changing, the straight lines giving way to organic curves that pulsed as the haze thickened and thinned. He couldn't tell what he was seeing, only that it was huge . . . and clearly alive.

He drew back, pulling Satan with him.

Fisher called, his voice right behind him now. "DeAngelis!"

The shadow shifted, started to unfurl, and then vanished.

"DeAngelis!"

DeAngelis turned toward the voice. "Keep talking. I'm coming to you."

"No!" There was an edge in Fisher's tone, the sound of panic.

"Not this way." It was Rose talking now.

"We're coming to you," Fisher said. "I think I see you."

A shadow coalesced. Broad shoulders, shaved head—Fisher. He was running.

"I see you," DeAngelis said.

Two smaller shadows appeared behind Fisher, also running.

Satan barked.

A fourth shadow appeared, larger than the others. It wasn't running.

It was flying.

"Move!" Fisher yelled.

They ran together, charging through the mist as the thing screamed behind them. The ground sloped downward. They followed it, sliding and falling into the smog-filled valley. And there they crouched, looking back as the shadow soared over them, curving in the air like a winged serpent, circling within the point where the mist thickened to form a ceiling of impenetrable gray. DeAngelis glanced at the others. No one spoke, but their eyes made it clear they were all thinking the same thing.

The snake was real.

38

A xle felt pressure on his hand, the stone-cold grip of the earthborn guardian. And yet, within that inhuman touch, Axle sensed the warmth of something human, the vestige of the person who had once been his father.

"That's enough," Hayestani said. "That'll do for now."

Sunlight streamed into the room, stinging Axle's eyes as he left the dream of blinding mist.

"Putting those officers in a mist was a good touch," Hayestani said. "An effective way of shaping their dream."

Axle rubbed his eyes. The mist still clung to his thoughts, blurring his vision.

"And I'm impressed with how you handled the dog. Animal dreams are tricky, but you did well."

Axle was still sitting on the bed, naked but for the sheet that wrapped his loins. And in spite of the sun in the window, he felt cold—chilled to the soul. "I think I'm getting sick."

"You can't get sick. Not anymore. You're more spirit than flesh, and what flesh you have has already died. Trust me, you're not sick."

"But I feel like crap."

"That may be. But that's a different thing entirely." Hayestani rose to his feet and moved to a claw-footed chair across from the bed. "Did you think this would be easy?"

"What?"

"Living between realms, shaping the world through dreams."

"No," Axle said. "I never thought it would be anything. I never thought about it at all."

"But your great-grandmother told you about it."

"She told me stories," he said. "I never paid attention to them, not until after she died."

"But then you listened to her."

"No. I *remembered* the things she said. That's hardly the same as listening."

"Actually, it's closer than you think." Hayestani sat on the chair, folding his legs under him, gripping the seat with his finger-like toes. "Memory is spirit. She must have told you that."

Axle nodded. "Memory is spirit, spirit is dream." His arms shimmered in the sunlight. *Sweat! I'm covered with sweat again!* He grabbed the corner of a sheet, dried himself off. "I didn't sign on for this," he said.

"Neither did I." Hayestani folded his arms against his knees. "Existence isn't a choice, you know. No one asks to be born. Why should rebirth be any different? The best you can do is work with what you're given, do what needs doing. And right now your skyborn servant needs your assistance. You promised him, remember? Promised to help him."

"Bird!" Axle got up, crossed to the window, looked toward the garage.

"He left some time ago, while you were dreaming with the officers. There was no holding him back once you told him there were rival forces at play. He might be reborn, but he's still an alpha personality."

"Putting it that way makes it sound so petty," Axle said. "Are you testing me?"

"No. Just telling it as it is. The spirit world isn't all that different from the human one—a little more rarified, a bit trickier to navigate, but nonetheless selfish. It took me years of reading and meditation to realize that, but I'm only earthborn, reanimated clay. You're skyborn. I can't imagine what disenchantments are waiting for you."

Axle gripped the windowsill. The sun was hot against his skin, but still he felt cold. "How long?" he asked. "How long ago did Bird leave?"

"Long enough to think you've forgotten him. As I said, he needs your help."

"Now?"

"A few minutes ago would have been better, but now will do." The chair creaked as Hayestani got up. He crossed the room, set his hands on Axle's shoulders, turned him toward the bed. "You've stretched your body. Now let's get back to working the spirit."

Axle stepped out of the sunlight, back into the shadows of the bed. "Shouldn't be too hard." He sat on the rumpled sheets, crossed his legs beneath him. "Physically, he's farther away than the officers were. But he's closer in spirit, right? And his dreams are already open to me. He's expecting me."

Hayestani stepped away from the bed. "All of that's true enough," he said. "But don't underestimate the obstacle of physical distance and unfamiliar terrain. And then you'll have to maneuver through Bird, catch the wind of his spirit, tack against him to reach the Viper drivers. It's doable, but first times are always iffy."

"If those drivers were asleep, I could reach them easily enough."

"But they aren't." Hayestani turned to the window. "But no matter, you may only need to appear to them for the blink of an eye. If Bird is close enough, you should be able to do that much." He looked back into the room, face in shadow.

"Are you leaving me?" Axle asked.

"Yes."

"To go where?"

"Back to my home. That rescue crew won't huddle in the valley for long. Perhaps, if the bitten officers are strong enough, Dalton can escort them outside, get everyone together, and send them on their way." He stepped onto the sill.

"But—"

Hayestani extended his wings as a sudden gust rose from the courtyard. A moment later, Axle was alone, head spinning, mind full of questions, spirit full of doubt.

39

Pax saw the Firebird screaming toward him in the rearview, racing so close that it appeared to be inches from his tail. It was the same car he had passed when leaving the farm. What did it mean? Did this guy know Sam? Did he want something? If that was the case, too bad. Nobody was stopping unless Sam stopped first, and she was moving faster than ever, smoking the pavement like something out of *Burnout*.

God! She's amazing!

He imagined the two of them getting it on when they returned to the lake. That would be cool. Maybe they could do it in Mr. Vorarov's house, or maybe out in the woods, or maybe in one of the unoccupied houses. Yes! That would be best. He'd broken into some of those houses before. It wasn't hard to do. Some of them didn't even have windows yet. He imagined how it would be, doing the naked monkey on a hardwood floor. That would rock.

But right now, there was a Firebird to outrun.

Pax hit the gas, leaving his pursuer in a burst of exhaust, watching the flaming raptor logo dwindle in the rearview as his Viper shot forward. "Eat my dust!" he said, letting his gaze linger on the mirror a little too long. When he glanced back at the windshield, he saw that Sam had cut her speed as she neared the freeway onramp. Her trunk swelled before him. He hit the brakes, forcing the pedal to the floor, throwing the Viper into a rubber-scorching skid.

"*Noooooooooooo!*"

He gripped the wheel, swerving left as Sam banked onto the ramp. Then he lost control, doing a 180 across the center line. He took his foot from the brake, racing backward now, going south in the northbound lane. He knew the maneuver. He'd done it many times playing *Burnout*. Controls were different. Theory was the same. He slammed the brake, cutting his speed. Then he downshifted, eased up on the clutch, and hit the gas. Tires screamed like smoking rockets. Heat rose around him, reeking with the sweet stink of burning treads. And then he shot back toward the ramp.

The Firebird driver was right there. He'd closed the gap again and was leaning forward on his wheel, looking right at Pax.

"Going to cut you!" Pax stared him right in the eyes. "Got you!" He steered toward the ramp, swerving in front of the Firebird, missing him by inches. A second later, he was at the top of the ramp. A truck horn blared. Pax looked left to see his reflection rippling in the chrome of a highballing Kenworth. It was cutting time again, time to get in front of the truck, put one more obstacle between him and the Firebird.

He hit the gas, shooting ahead of the truck, preparing to pass. It should have worked. It should have been so smooth . . . so perfect. But then, as he prepared to swerve in front of the diesel, something leaped in front of him. He glimpsed it for a moment, a man in the road: leaning forward, eyes glowing, wings spread.

Wings?!

Pax swerved onto the shoulder, treads whistling over grooved pavement. Then he was airborne, flying over grass and rock, landing hard—

WHAM!

The trunk bottomed out, slamming with a metallic crunch that reverberated through the car, and then, as he rebounded, something leaped behind him. The winged man? He lost sight of it as the Viper spun around, slashing the high grass before lurching to a stop. Pax was facing the interstate now, traffic racing 100 feet away. And suddenly the thing that had leaped up behind him appeared again, in front of him now, falling through the air to strike the grass with a hollow thump. It wasn't the winged man. It was the Viper's bumper, the wide strip of molded plastic that had been connected to the base of the trunk. It had broken free, bounced over him as he'd spun around.

Up on the interstate, a car pulled over. It wasn't Sam. Wasn't the Firebird man. They were both gone, racing south.

This car was a Cobalt, four-cylinder with a spoiler.

A woman stepped out. "Hey!" Traffic raced behind her. She held a cell phone in one hand, gestured with the other. "I'll call for help!" She opened the phone. "Get—" Her words vanished beneath the whoosh of passing traffic.

The grass between the Viper and the shoulder looked wet and shiny.

Pax smelled gasoline.

"Get out of that car!" the woman yelled.

Something crackled beneath the Viper. Smoke rose, thickening as it curled beneath the hood.

The woman kept yelling. "Get out! Get out of that car!"

He unfastened his seatbelt, climbed out, and stumbled away through the grass. He got the picture now. The fuel tank had ruptured when he'd bottomed out. Then he had spun, spreading gas over the ground. The heat of the engine had ignited the grass . . . and now the fire was moving beneath the car, raising thick black smoke as it spread toward the trunk.

"Get away!" the woman yelled. "Get away before it blows."

Pax backed away.

Before it blows!

He walked backward, not wanting to miss seeing the explosion if it happened.

The trunk buckled, plastic melting. Whatever was in the trunk, it was toast now.

"Get away!" the woman shouted. "You're too close!"

The trunk popped open, everything burning now: grass, gasoline, tires, molded plastic body. The trunk was burning too, flames capped in papery ash. He felt the heat on his face and took a few more steps back.

The woman kept screaming for him to get away.

The burning stink grew stronger, and with it came a new smell—the sweet scent of wood smoke.

"Get away from there before—"

This time, it wasn't the whoosh of passing traffic that drowned out the woman's voice.

This time, the world exploded.

40

Sam was over a mile east when she saw the blast in her rearview. It was incredible, a black-veined fireball rising behind an overpass. A few seconds later she felt the concussion.

Her mind raced. One case lost! Could she do the job with only one?

She glanced again at the rising smoke, contemplating the combined power of nitro and gasoline.

I can still do this. I'll tank up in Windslow. Get a jerry can. Fill it. It'll work. I can make it work!

The Firebird was gaining on her. She had gotten a look at the driver out at Tucky's farm. There was something about him. Something familiar. She had never seen him before, but she had heard about someone like him last night, when Kirill had described his eccentric business partner: *Braided hair, sleeveless vest, tattooed arms. He's hard to miss.*

The driver was wearing a long-sleeve shirt. If he had tattoos, there was no way to see them. And his hair, though not braided, had the wild crimped look of hair that had been. Perhaps it was her meth-logic working, but it seemed to make sense. What if the man had a message from Kirill?

Her head throbbed.

"What do I do?"

Something stirred beside her, wind swirling in the passenger seat, speaking close to her ear.

He's the Devil's servant, the wind said. *Keep away. If he stops you, everything is lost.*

She accelerated, swerving around a tractor trailer in the right lane, then around a camper in the other—cutting back and forth until she saw an exit for State Route 519. She could take it south to US Route 40. The trip would be longer, but right now losing the Firebird was more important.

She took the exit, hurtling down the ramp and through an intersection.

Sirens blared on the freeway, racing toward the remains of Pax and

Kirill's copperhead-orange Viper.

She pulled to the shoulder and climbed out, staggering, bracing herself on the door and fender as she walked to the back. Then, gently, she unlocked the trunk and looked inside. The plastic wrapping on the money looked wet. Condensation from the frozen crate? She lifted out one of the shrink-wrapped bricks, sniffed it. Oily? Or was that the smell of the plastic?

Play it safe. Take it slow.

She lowered the trunk, pressing down until it latched. Then she climbed back behind the wheel and drove south.

41

Bird had lost the Viper.

Now, rounding a bend that led to a straight shot between rolling fields, he had a clear view of nearly a mile of two-lane road. No Viper in sight.

"Damn!"

It had taken the state-route exit.

He braked hard, pulling to the shoulder. A truck raced by, shaking the Firebird, whipping his hair. What now? Backtrack? And what if he was wrong?

"Damnit, Axle! I could use some help here!"

Roadside branches stirred, hissing, becoming a voice: "Trust your instincts."

Bird looked toward the trees, and there was Kwetis, perched on the side of the car.

"It's about time," Bird said.

"I've been busy." Kwetis spoke with the glow of his eyes. "And you don't need me to confirm the obvious."

"The Viper took the exit?"

"Where else would it be?"

Another truck passed, whooshing by a few feet from Bird's head. The Firebird shook. Bird put in the clutch, shifted to reverse.

"Hold on," Kwetis said. "There's a better way." He touched Bird's hand, taking hold, sliding the car out of gear. "We won't catch her by backtracking. She's too far ahead of you. But you're on a faster route. Stay the course, and you'll reach Windslow before she does."

"And do what? Wait at the dam?"

"No. Once she gets that far, all bets are off. You need to wait for her at the edge of town. If you park at the off ramp, I can stop her there."

"What'll you do?"

"Stand in the road, startle her, make her swerve."

"That'll work?"

"It worked with the kid."

"If you call that working," Bird said. "The idea wasn't to kill them."

"The idea is to do whatever it takes."

Bird considered the size of the fireball he had seen in his rearview. "An explosion like that, on the edge of Windslow—"

Kwetis squeezed Bird's hand. "Don't over think this, Maynard." He let go, speaking now with his shifting wings. "Just get yourself there. I'll follow." The trees shifted again, moving with the spirit wind. "Drive!"

"But what if—"

Too late.

The trees had stopped shaking, and Kwetis was gone.

42

Kirill got his morphine. But he didn't go to the lake to get the money for Gusky. Instead, Gusky sent Joe and waited for his call. By the time it came, Kirill was asleep, propped on Gusky's couch, dreaming about kicking Gusky's ass.

It was a strange dream. Neither he nor Gusky were wearing pants, just oversized polo shirts that extended to their thighs. Gusky lay on the floor with his butt in the air. *Wham!* Kirill kicked hard. Gusky screamed. Kirill kicked again, leg flying high, like he was doing the can-can. *Wham!* Not wearing pants made the kicks freer, more powerful.

A dress, Kirill thought. *It's like wearing a dress.*

"What?" Gusky said. "What's that?"

Kirill stopped kicking.

Gusky frowned. "A dress?"

"I didn't say it," Kirill said. "I only thought it."

"What?"

"About the dress," Kirill said. "I didn't—"

"What address?"

Kirill opened his eyes.

Gusky sat before him, leaning into his headset. "Christ, Joe!" Gusky said. "You don't need no address! It's the same address you went to before! Kirill's house!"

Kirill straightened up. His head spun, partly from the morphine, mostly from the dream.

"Right," Gusky said, cupping his ear, shouting. "The same house!" Gusky looked at Kirill. "Is that right, Kirill? You said *your* house?"

Kirill swallowed. What the hell was going on? "My house?"

"You said the money was at your house?"

"No," Kirill said. "My *garage*. Beside the house. The remote for the garage is in the Viper. The Viper's parked in the drive—"

"Right." Gusky turned away, talking to Joe. "The opener's in the Viper. The *gowdahm* Viper, Joe." His voice shrilled. "*Whadja* mean there's no *gawdahm* Viper?" He looked at Kirill. "What're you pulling, Kirill?"

"Just tell him to look in the Viper."

"Joe says there ain't no Viper, Kirill! He says all there is is a bashed up Jeep!"

"Sam?"

Gusky picked up the gun.

"Sam must have taken it," Kirill said.

"Sam?" Gusky came up beside the couch, pushed the gun to Kirill's ear. "Sam who?"

Kirill tried leaning away.

Gusky grabbed his head, holding it in place.

"She took the Viper, not the cash," Kirill said. "There's a second Viper in the garage. The money's in the trunk. Trust me."

"You're stalling."

"I'm not! I swear—"

Gusky pulled the gun from Kirill's head and turned away. "Joe!" He cupped his ear. "Listen, Joe. I want you to break into that garage."

The earpiece buzzed, Joe protesting.

"Hell yes I'm serious!" Gusky said. "I don't care how. Drive the freaking van through the door if you have to. I need that money."

More buzzing.

"Just do it, Joe!" He tapped the earpiece, breaking the connection. "You're playing me, Kirill."

"No."

"Stalling for time."

"I'm not."

"I will kill you, Kirill." He leveled the gun. "If that money's not in that garage, I will *so* kill you."

43

By the time Sam returned to the interstate, the pain in her head had become nearly unbearable, spreading from behind her eyes, into her right ear, and out onto the seat beside her. She could almost see it sitting on the edge of her vision, out of focus, hunched against the door. She glanced toward it. It hardened, becoming real, assuming the form of Kasdeja.

"Stay focused," he said.

"Easy for you to say."

"The pain's that bad?"

"Worse than ever."

"You need to get above it." He shifted. The Viper's seats were form fitted for human shoulders, not angel wings. "This is no time for distractions, Samuelle."

A sign approached, announcing that Blaston was ten miles ahead. From there she could pick up the back road that cut behind the mine, get to the dam that way.

"Don't get off at Blaston," Kasdeja said. "Those back roads aren't safe."

The interstate rose before her, a steep straightaway slicked with glare. The glare looked like water. A mirage. They were everywhere.

"I've got a case of thawing nitro in my trunk, and you want me to continue south to the Windslow Exit? That's miles out of my way."

"But the roads will be smoother in Windslow. Fewer bumps, a lot safer."

Ahead of her, a rig downshifted, cutting its speed on the steep grade.

Sam shot around it.

"Safer," he said. "But not without risk. Your adversary is waiting for you in Windslow."

"The man in the Firebird?"

"Not a man," Kasdeja said. "*Was* a man. He's a demon now, and he's parked beneath the overpass, just off the exit ramp. He's there to channel his master."

"Lucifer?"

"Yes, if you must name him, call him *Lucifer*."

"What will he do?"

"The master? He'll come at you as you descend the exit ramp."

"And that's the exit you want me to take?"

"Forewarned is forearmed, Samuelle. All you have to do is keep driving."

"Run down Lucifer?"

"That would be a nice trick if you could do it," Kasdeja said. "But he'll be an illusion. Stay the course, he'll vanish."

"And the demon in the Firebird?"

"Not an illusion."

"Flesh and blood?"

"Not exactly."

She wanted to know more about the Firebird demon, but at the moment she had something else to consider. "There's a mini-mart beyond the Windslow underpass," she said. "Will I have time to stop, gas up?"

"No. You'll need to keep driving, straight to the dam."

Fresh pain stabbed her temples. She inhaled deeply, let it out slowly. "You're telling me the dynamite alone will be enough?" She studied him from the corner of her eye. "You see, I'm not sure it is. I planned on using two cases for this job. With only one left, I'd feel better if this car's tank were full."

"Really?" he said. "How does a tank of gas compare to a case of dynamite?"

She didn't like the sound of that question. "You don't know?"

"That's your area, Samuelle."

"But you're supposed to know things."

"I do," he said. "But not all things."

"But you're an angel, right?"

He didn't answer. For a moment she felt alone with the whipping wind. But when she looked around, he was still there, leaning uncomfortably against the backrest, one arm on the door, the other gripping the windshield. It occurred to her that he was sitting on Kirill's overnight bag, a tight fit with both that and a pair of wings to contend with. "It's complicated," he said at last. "But tell me, do you intend on blowing up the car, driving it into the culvert, setting it off with the dynamite in the trunk?"

She hesitated. Until now, the plan had been little more than a nonverbal sense of what she needed to do. But hearing him say it gave it form. "Yes," she said. "That's it. Everything goes. Dynamite, gasoline, car—the whole shebang."

"And you?" he asked. "You'll stay with the car?"

She watched the road, considering. "No. Not if I can help it." They cleared the top of the rise, descending now, the Blaston exit less than two miles away. "I'm not a martyr," she said. "Nothing's worth dying for."

"And a full tank of gasoline," Kasdeja said. "Tell me what you know. Will it make a difference?"

"What I know?" She remembered the force she had felt when the copperhead-orange Viper exploded. It had been far behind her by then, but still she had felt the concussion in her bones. The gasoline certainly seemed to have heightened the blast. But *seeming* wasn't *science*. "What I know?" she glanced at him. "It's complicated," she said, unable to resist using his words against him. "But basically, a gallon of gas has 300 times the energy of a stick of dynamite."

"Three hundred?"

"Give or take."

"So why bother with dynamite, Samuelle?"

"Because dynamite's faster. It releases its energy all at once, and that's what you need when you're moving earth and rock, an instantaneous blast, not a slow release."

"Gasoline's slow?"

"Comparatively."

"But you think a full tank will make a difference?"

"The dynamite will accelerate the gasoline, give it more force than it would have if it were just going off on its own." Again she remembered the fireball from the orange Viper. "So . . . yeah. I think so. If we've only got one shot at this, it's got to be with a full tank in addition to the Hercules." She looked at him. "Am I teaching you now? Do you mean to tell me you really did not know these things?"

"Perhaps I didn't know them fully," he said. "But then neither did you. You had to speak them first, sort them out, bring them forward in your mind."

"All right," she said. "So now we both know what I think. Any more questions?"

The Blaston exit was ahead of them now, only a few hundred feet away, coming up fast.

"Are there any service stations in Blaston?" he asked.

"Yeah," she said. "An Exxon and a 7-Eleven."

The exit raced by.

He looked back.

"What?" she said. "Change your mind? Should I have gotten off there?"

"No." He turned back around. "Stick to your plan. Get off at Windslow. Gas up at the mini-mart."

"And the Firebird demon?"

"He thinks he's just there to channel his master. He won't even consider approaching you until he sees that illusions can't force you from the road. By continuing down the exit ramp and pulling into the mini-mart, you'll force him to try using his own special power on you."

"His own special power?"

"The power of his words."

"Words?" she said. "Talking?"

"That's his power, Samuelle. His words are lies, but they'll get inside you, bend your will."

She considered that. "All right," she said. "I can deal." She thought of the magnum under the seat. "I've got some power of my own."

"You do. Just remember, he's more than human. You can't kill him, but you can hurt him. He feels pain. And something else, a contradiction of sorts. He'll wish to avoid violence. He thinks he's seen enough of it. But he has no idea . . . no grasp of the pain his actions will cause in the long run. That's where you're different, Samuelle. You understand the importance of single deaths, the selective slaughter for the advancement of a plan."

"Yeah," she said. "All right. But one question. You said he thinks he's seen enough violence. When? Last night? Was he one of the people from last night? Kirill's partner, maybe?"

"What he was doesn't concern you, Samuelle. What matters is what he is. You'll need to keep your wits about you, play a few moves ahead, and . . . above all . . . do not listen to him when he speaks. The very sound of his voice can derail everything."

"I'll remember that. I'll take care. Like you said, forewarned is fore-armed." She gripped the wheel. "And you'll be with me, right? Guarding me, staying close?"

She cleared another rise, shooting up toward the heat-rippling waters of a new mirage, cresting the hill to find smoke rising from the trees a few miles away. The pain in her head was subsiding, settling down to a dull ache behind her eyes.

"Right?" She glanced beside her. He was gone, nothing there but Kirill's bag on the seat, the gun case on the floor.

"Damnit! I hate when you do that!" She wondered if something she had said had driven him away, if maybe her tenacious sense of self-reliance had made it seem as if she wanted to go it alone. She was often like that. Even when she felt vulnerable, she had a need to talk the talk, as if pretending confidence were a self-fulfilling prophecy.

But it is self-fulfilling!

She grabbed Kirill's overnight bag, upending it as she came out of a downhill turn, dumping the contents onto the seat beside her: clothes, vodka, aspirin, money brick. She brushed it all onto the floor, then waited for a straightaway before reaching beneath the seat to retrieve the gun case. Six pounds. It thumped when she dropped it on the seat.

"Like I said." She opened the lid. "I've got some power of my own."

The ear plugs rolled out. She swept them onto the mat with the rest of the crap and put the gun into the bag, concealed but ready.

Forearmed!

The straightaway ended. She went back to concentrating on the road, taking a bend at 70 mph.

A sign emerged, swinging out from the roadside trees, letters hot with glare:

**WINDSLOW
2 MILES**

44

DeAngelis sensed the snake was still up there, circling just above the slope. He heard its wings slicing the air, but the mist had swallowed its shadow just as it had obliterated everything else. He could still see his companions—Fisher, Rose, Leroy, Satan—but even they were fading, becoming vague shapes as they crouched beside him.

"We need to get out of here," Leroy said. "Follow the creek to that leaning log, cross there, climb back to the clearing."

DeAngelis looked toward the sound of the circling snake. He glimpsed a curve in the mist, an arched shadow that might have been the edge of a wing. It vanished almost instantly, but it looked closer than ever—no more than twenty feet above their heads.

"I don't think the creek's there anymore," Fisher said.

DeAngelis had been thinking the same thing. It wasn't just that he couldn't hear it. The fog could account for that. It muted everything. But DeAngelis's awareness of the creek—his sense that it even existed—was also gone. He couldn't define the feeling, but it was as if the world had shrunk until it held nothing more than him, his companions, the ground beneath them, and the snake above.

"You want to try finding the way back?" Fisher asked. "Go ahead. I'm not moving till this fog lifts."

"I think it's lifting," Rose said. She was looking up along the slope, toward the top of the rise. "You can see the trees now."

DeAngelis looked up to where the snake had been circling in the fog. The curved shadow was still there, but it was clearer now, coming into focus as the mist broke apart. The shape wasn't the body of a flying monster. It was merely a tree branch, curved and gnarled, swaying twenty feet above them. Then, from a few yards behind them, came the sound of flowing water.

"It is breaking up," Fisher said. "Goddamn."

But DeAngelis had a different sense. The fog wasn't breaking up. Instead, the world was reassembling.

Satan whined, nose pointing up the slope, breath coming in short bursts, beating out its unmistakable code.

"Something's coming," DeAngelis said.

They heard footsteps—heavy, unsteady, moving through the grass above the slope.

"The devil statues?" Leroy said.

DeAngelis looked at Satan, noting the slant of his ears. "No. I don't think—"

"Hey!" A voice called from beyond the rise. It was a breathy sound, low and rasped. "Hey! Someone down there?"

DeAngelis looked at the others. No one spoke.

Another voice called, a woman's this time. "Help us!"

45

S am glimpsed the parking lot of the Strip Mine Gentlemen's Club as she cut her speed to take the Windslow Exit. The Chevy truck, bodies, and even the bloodstains were already gone, cleaned up in time for Amateur Lunch, business as usual at the Strip Mine. Danny Love was nothing if not efficient. The scene registered as a snapshot, a momentary image that vanished as she approached the bottom of the ramp.

That's when Lucifer came for her, leaping up from the asphalt, flying toward the front of the Viper. She gripped the wheel, stayed the course, waited for the thing to vanish like a heat mirage. It didn't. It grew larger, more pronounced, wings thumping at the air, catching the wind as she slammed into it.

WhoooMMMMPFFFF!

The hood cut through it. Then it was gone, scattered like smoke as she roared toward the sunlight beyond the overpass. The Firebird was to her left now, parked at the side of the road, the driver watching. Wild hair. Fixed stare. She didn't look at him, but she felt his gaze, pounding against her as she sped toward the mini-mart 100 feet down the road. She downshifted, coming around a readerboard sign placed at the edge of the lot, and drove to an outside pump where a Ford Focus was pulling away. There were no other cars in the lot.

She adjusted her mirror, turning it to get a look at the Firebird. The demon was still there, behind the wheel, alternately glaring at her and glancing at the seat beside him. She couldn't be sure from the distance, but he seemed to be talking to himself . . . or to an invisible master.

The crap from Kirill's bag was still scattered over the floor. She covered the money brick, gun case, and vodka with a large shirt and pair of slacks. Then she opened the glove box and took out the envelope Danny Love had given her back at the club. Kirill always made payment in banded twenties. She reached inside, pulled out three bills, crumpled them in her hand. Then she grabbed the overnight bag and climbed from the car.

Her leg was worse than ever, the stiffness spreading down into the knee, up into the hip. She steadied herself on the door and worked the leg, bringing it back to life as she surveyed her location. Freeway to the east, strip club to the north. The mini-mart lot lay on a patch of low ground between them. At the moment, the only one looking was the demon, parked at the bottom of the exit ramp, staring right at her, planning his move.

The gun shifted in her bag as she stepped away from the car.

"Please let this place stay empty," she said, speaking to Kasdeja, trusting he was close. Invisible but close. He had to be watching. He was her guardian.

"Three minutes. That's all I need. Let the demon come, but keep this lot empty."

On those terms, her exit strategy would work.

She limped into the store, carrying Kirill's bag like an industrial-size purse. She had seen women carrying stranger things, but it wasn't until she caught a double take from the cashier that she remembered what she was wearing.

He sat behind the counter, reading a book. "Costume party?" he asked.

"Yeah." She noted the book. William Goldman's *Adventures in the Screen Trade*. She sized him up as she approached the counter: soul patch, bleached hair, pierced ear, Gen Con T-shirt. *Undergraduate media major. Summer job.* "I'm Gogo," she said.

He put down the book, open against the counter.

"From *Kill Bill*," he said. "But Gogo's Asian."

"Besides that." She took a Bic lighter from a display beside the register. "I need one of these." She looked around. "And one of those." She pointed to a line of one-gallon jerry cans behind the counter. "And a fill up." She handed him the twenties and then turned to look out the window, making sure no one else had pulled up. No one had. The Viper was still the only car in the lot. The demon was out of sight beyond the side of the store.

"Pump four." He rang her up. "Don't forget to come back for your change."

She took the can and limped toward the door.

"You all right?" he said.

"Yeah." She spoke without turning. "Just the way I walk."

"I mean your hands. Your head."

"Part of the costume." She pushed through the door and crossed the lot, pretending to focus on her car, but watching as the parked Firebird reappeared in her peripheral vision. The demon was getting out, the click of his unlatching door echoing from the overpass.

She put the jerry can on the pavement, inserted the nozzle, started filling.

"Protect me, Kasdeja. Guide my plan. Make it work."

A car approached on Windslow Road, slowing as it neared the lot.

"I'll do my part," she said, louder, more desperate. "You do yours."

The car stopped at the intersection, then continued on, heading left toward the interstate.

The nozzle clicked off. She took it from the jerry can, slid it into the Viper, started the flow and locked the valve. Nice and easy.

The demon was in the lot now, moving toward her in long strides. "Hey," he called.

Kasdeja's voice came to her, not so much speaking anew as rising from her memory: *"His words . . . they'll get inside you, bend your will."*

She slipped her hand into the bag, took hold of the gun, but kept it hidden as she turned and hurried back into the store.

The Firebird demon called again. "Hey! Miss? I need—"

The door banged closed behind her.

The kid had gone back to reading. He looked up.

She took out the gun, aimed it at him. "Fast," she said. "Out from behind that counter!"

He dropped the book.

"Now!"

He did as she said, trembling, coming out into the store.

She slipped behind him, wrapped one arm around his chest, raised the gun, and fired.

ird heard the shot as he approached the store. It resounded through the air, muted by glass and cinderblock, but nonetheless powerful. He ran, past the refueling Viper, and through the front door. Again, as he had back in Claudia, he found himself suddenly surrounded by screaming displays, posters, and packaging. This time, however, his senses were focused, vision narrowing on the woman at the far end of the counter. She had her arm around a college-age kid, holding him in a vice grip as she aimed across the store.

Once again, as he had last night, Bird found himself staring down the borehole of a gun, only this time the barrel was huge, dwarfing the woman who held it in a bandaged hand. Her arm flexed as she steadied her aim. She was small, but her muscles were toned. The gun almost seemed part of her.

"Easy." Bird raised his hands, surprised to find that the kid in her arm was apparently uninjured. A crackling light above his head told the story. The woman had fired the gun straight up, not at the kid, but at the ceiling. What the hell was that about? What had she been shooting at? Not that such things really mattered at the moment. What did matter was that the woman was aiming at him. "Easy." He held his hands higher, not for fear of being killed. He was pretty sure he was beyond that. But immortal or not, he had no desire to find out what a bullet from a magnum would feel like to his heightened sense of touch. "Listen." He spoke as he had to the Indian woman in the Sunoco mini-mart, looking her straight on, commanding without aggression. "Listen to me. Are you listening?"

She waved the gun. "Get away from that door." Her voice was flat, unnatural.

"Listen!" he said. "Are you listening? That gun can't kill me, can't stop me. And even if it could, you don't want to use it. You want to put it down. Let the kid go. Do you understand?" He started toward her.

She swung the gun away from him, pushing its barrel against the kid's jaw.

The kid screamed.

"Easy," Bird said. "Just put that gun down, all right. Listen to me. Do it now." Something was wrong. Had he lost his power? "Please, lady. Are you listening?"

"Get away from the door," she said.

This time he understood why her voice sounded as it did, flat and unnatural. "Aw, fuck me!" He stopped advancing. "Shit!"

"I'll shoot him!" she said. "Blow his head off. Then I'll start shooting at you."

He backed up, amazed at her ingenuity.

"She's on to me, Axle. She knows my power, and she's canceled it." He glanced again at the sputtering light in the ceiling, grasping the sonic consequences of discharging a hand cannon in the tight confines of a mini-mart. "She's deaf, Axle. They're both deaf. What now?"

Something rumbled outside, a shadow gliding past the door. Bird didn't need to look back to know it was a car, steering through the lot, pulling to a pump.

"I can make a real mess here," the woman said, jamming the gun harder against the kid's face. "I don't give a shit about people, just the common good." She glared at Bird. "Do you understand?" She stepped toward him. "Do *you* hear *me*?"

She was nuts. Totally gone.

Bird realized he had no choice but to step away, give Axle another chance to derail her on Windslow Road . . . or Cliff Mine Run, if she got that far. After all, this was Axle's game, not his. He was just the helper, the peon doing the dirty work while Kwetis rode the spirit wind. "All right." Bird stepped aside. "Whatever."

She walked the kid to the door, pushed through it, and headed toward her car.

Bird followed, stepping out to see a second car parked at the opposite pump. The guy had his back to them, oblivious.

The woman pushed the kid away, toward the front of the Viper, where she could keep the gun on him as she hung up the nozzle. Then she secured her gas cap and climbed behind the wheel.

The man at the other island looked around. She swung the gun toward him. He slumped against his car, then put up his hands.

She started her engine.

"All right, Axle." Bird watched her pull away. "She's all yours." But unwilling to give up the chase, he turned and took off through the lot, racing toward the Firebird.

"Hey!" the guy at the other pump said. His hands were still raised, trembling as Bird raced past him. "What was that? What's going on?"

Bird kept running, bounding toward the underpass as the Viper's engine roared north on Windslow Road.

47

Dalton made sure that the rescue party was still cowering in the ravine before he turned and hurried back toward the house. He heard the lady cop call out as he ran from her.

"Help us!"

And suddenly there was rustling on the slope: boots, hands, and paws scrambling upward.

Dalton looked back, peering past the statues, each shaped in the likeness of the winged creature that had saved his life three months earlier—his guardian devil.

The K-9 officer climbed into view. He gripped a dog leash in one hand, reaching toward the woman officer with the other. Her knees buckled. She slumped forward, collapsing against the man as the other officers emerged from the ravine. Not one of them looked toward the house. They behaved as if they saw only their immediate surroundings. The devil had arranged that, filled their eyes with mist, engulfing them in fog that wasn't there. And even though that mist had begun fading from their collective vision, the house remained hidden.

Dalton watched from the foot of the porch, confident that he couldn't be seen, but then he looked at the dog, noting its posture: stiff shoulders, pricked ears, staring eyes. It was looking at him.

Dalton turned and hurried away, up the steps and onto the porch. Only a few snakes remained there. The others had slipped into the house to take refuge in the debris beneath the open roof—far away from the ground that was turning against them.

The dog barked.

Dalton kept moving, through the door and into a hail of flying dust. Plaster, dirt, and grit swirled through the parlor, apparently blowing from the room that had once been the kitchen.

"Hey!" He called to the devil. "What's going on?"

No answer.

He rounded the junk-art bed: truck-grill headboard, cardboard sheets, grass mattress. He paused beside it, looking up past the hanging snake skins that were now coming apart in the wind, scales shimmering in the sunlight as they blew away through the open roof. It was the spirit wind, the one that always accompanied the devil's flight. But Dalton had never known it to blow in a sustained gale from within the house. He pushed on, moving past the mound of debris in the center of the house, the pile of wood, plaster, and slate that stood between his bed and the room where the devil kept his nest and book collection. The devil often sat in there reading during the day, but he wasn't reading now. Instead, he was cowering in the corner, wings wrapped tightly around his body, head hidden beneath black feathers that flexed and trembled with the force of a terrible wind.

"Hey!" Dalton entered the kitchen, slipping into a far corner where the air was comparatively still. He crouched, looking at the devil. "What's going on?"

The devil lifted his face until one eye peeked above the joint of a trembling wing. His face was dark, somber, possibly frightened. That face, at least the portion of it that Dalton could see, looked anything but devilish. Of course, the creature had never claimed to be the Devil. Indeed, he had never claimed to be anything, neither confirming nor denying Dalton's hunches.

"Did you take care of it?" the devil asked. "Are the wounded officers with the rescue team?"

"Yeah," Dalton said. "But the dog saw me."

"He won't bother you. Not now. Not ever, the way things are going."

"What do you mean?"

"I mean one way or the other, it's coming to an end. If this house stays here, cops will be back, different ones to verify the reports of the ones you brought here." The wind gusted. The devil struggled against it, clenching his wings. "You should never have brought that snake-bit officer here, Dalton. That was a mistake."

"But she would have died—"

"People die all the time, Dalton. It's what they do. You can't change that." The devil sounded angry, voice like grinding stone.

"But she was young. I knew you could help her."

"Help her? Is that what I did? Do you think I *helped* her? She's changed, Dalton. The other officer, too. I had to change them to keep them alive."

"But being changed isn't as bad as being dead."

"For you, maybe. Not for some. Most people wouldn't be content painting themselves with mud, living in the woods." His voice softened as he spoke, shifting until it seemed to come from some deep and private place. "Trust me, Dalton. I know."

The wind whipped again, pushing up against the devil's wings. He seemed to be struggling to keep them closed, trembling as the gale rose along the hair of his face and head, making it whip and crackle like a black flame.

"What're you doing?" Dalton asked.

"Me? Nothing. I'm doing nothing. It's the wind that's *doing*. I'm being forced back into service by the powers that made me." The devil seldom spoke of his origins. When he did, his words were vague, evasive. But now he seemed poised to elaborate, if only the wind weren't pulling at him, trying to lift him from the floor, through the roof, into the sky. "I have to go," he said. "There's one more complication to deal with."

"What complication?"

"A woman. I need to block her path."

"Why?"

"Because I have to. There's no reason beyond that, none that I know. I'm tired of waiting for reasons. I'm tired. . . ." His voice trailed off, lost in the wind.

Dalton felt he should say something. He had never seen the devil like this. It was as if something had broken inside him.

"I'd die if I could," the devil said at last. "I'd dive back into the earth, die like a man, dead and buried." He raised his head, the gale changing pitch, whistling around his jaw. "Maybe someday." His wings twitched, seemed about to open, then snapped back, tighter than before.

"What're you saying?"

"Nothing, Dalton. There's noting to say. Except maybe . . . if you want to live . . . you should stay in this house. Inside if you can. On what's left of the roof if it comes to that."

"The roof?"

"If the house becomes unstable, go to the roof."

"Is that some kind of riddle?"

"No . . . not a riddle." He glanced toward a pipe that rose from the floor, remnants of plumbing that had once carried water from a well beneath the house. It branched about a foot from the floor, forming a copper cross against the wall. "Hold on to that," he said. "I can't fight this anymore. I'm leaving."

Dalton gripped the pipe.

The devil opened his wings, releasing an updraft that ripped the breath from Dalton's lungs.

FhhhhooooOOOOMMMM!

The devil's bookshelves exploded: boards rising, cinderblocks toppling, books scattering like paper birds. Dalton rose into the air, feet kicking at the ceiling. He hugged the pipe, hanging on until the gale spilled from the room, carrying the devil through the front of the house, where he grabbed one of the exposed beams. "Stay with the house," he said, looking back, voice almost lost in the tumult. "You might survive." And then he spread his wings wide, caught the wind, and leaped into the sky.

48

Sam saw someone standing in the downhill lane as she approached the turnoff to the coal-hauling road. It was a cop, positioned beside a flashing cruiser. He gestured for her to slow down, but she couldn't do that—not with the Firebird on her tail. And she had no doubt it was back there. The demon would certainly not let her off the hook so easily.

Mind racing, she gauged the situation, realizing that the cop wouldn't give chase if she raced past him. Manning the roadblock alone, he would be forced to hold his position and call for assistance. By the time anyone responded, she'd be at the dam.

She leaned on her horn and hit the gas.

The officer leaped aside.

She squealed around the next bend. She didn't hear the sound, only felt it. *Like a snake*, she thought. *I hear with my body.* She took the next turn even faster, steering by reflex until the pavement split three ways: Cliff Mine Run continuing to the right, Lakefront Drive and Old River Trail branching to the left. She took the harder of the two lefts, downshifting toward the bridge that led to another intersection: one road winding through the trees, the other descending toward the base of the dam.

The car scraped bottom as she left Cliff Mine Run. She toed the brake, cutting her speed.

Her front end scraped again.

ScccrrrcccCCCHHH!

Metal on rock, felt but not heard—but still it put her nerves on edge.

She swerved to the left as she approached a pothole, then to the right again as the road rose to meet the bridge that spanned the valley. The dam was beside her now, its slope high enough to hide the surface of the lake. But she smelled the water, fresh and cool on the southeast breeze.

The bridge deck thumped beneath her, resonating with the cadence of speech. The steering wheel vibrated, speaking to her hands: *Slow and steady*, the vibrations said. *Almost there . . . steady and slow.*

Her rearview remained clear. The Firebird was still out of sight. Perhaps the cop had stopped the demon. But she couldn't count on that, and the fear of seeing it rounding the bend behind her compelled her to speed up as she left the bridge and steered onto the unpaved utility road. And it was there that she felt a cold blast from overhead, spiraling down into the valley. Dust rose. She covered her face, blinking away the grit, and when she looked again, she saw something black crouching at the base of the trail. It hunkered down as it landed, pressed its hands against the ground, and then reared back.

She kept driving.

The thing spread its arms, then its wings, blocking her way. But she wasn't buying it. She'd called his bluff before. No reason not to do it again. All it took was a steady grip, a lead foot, and a willingness to deny what her eyes told her.

She accelerated, realizing as she did that she might simplify her plan by driving full speed into the culvert. If the nitro had thawed, the force of slamming the collapsed rock would detonate both nitro and gasoline. It'd be over in a flash. The dam would fail. Water would flow. And she would fly to the realm of sexless angels . . . free at last.

Do it!

She reached the base of the slope, the point where the utility road angled upward toward the culvert. The winged devil leaned forward, arched its wings.

"You're not real." She looked him in his glowing eyes and shifted to low. "Coming through!" She hit the gas, let out the clutch.

The devil stared right at her, eyes burning. She tried looking past him, keeping the Viper aimed at the stone culvert—the low tunnel just wide and high enough for the Viper to pass through. She didn't brace for a collision. She kept driving, waiting for the thing to vanish.

It didn't.

She struck it hard, feeling the concussion of polymer against bone as the front end rammed the devil. He fell forward, slammed the hood, threw his hands against the windshield. His wings closed around the open cockpit, enveloping her, cloaking the car. She couldn't see the culvert now, only the monster's face leering through the windshield. Up close, he looked strangely human, jaw clenched in pain, mouth drawn back from uneven teeth. But the eyes . . . the eyes didn't lie. They glowed with the light of hellfire, dark red like burning rock, like the tree of evil in the sinkhole of Windslow Mine.

I see the truth in your eyes.

She kept accelerating.

You will crawl on your belly . . . eat dust . . . and I WILL CRUSH YOU!
She closed her eyes. She thought of paradise. She thought of Kasdeja.
WHAM!

The culvert's entrance struck the wings. She felt them snap, bones break-ing, feathers scraping stone, coming loose as they grated against the tunnel walls. The car slowed. Tires lost traction, filling the tight space with the stink of burning treads. And then, with an anticlimactic jolt that left her sitting in the glow of the Viper's dashboard icons and the devil's blood-red eyes, the engine stalled.

49

The cop was pissed. Bird saw that as he rounded the bend. The bastard had his weapon drawn, swinging it toward the racing Firebird.

He hit the brakes, burning a skid in the uphill lane, swerving to a stop a few feet from the parked cruiser.

The cop leveled his gun, steadied his aim. "Shut her down!"

Bird kept his hands on the wheel, up high where the cop could see them.

The cop approached, leading with his weapon. "Now! Turn it off. Get out!"

Bird looked at the gun. Glock. 40 caliber. Once again, as he had in the Windslow mini-mart, he wondered how impervious his skyborn flesh would be to a direct hit. It might not kill him, but it was bound to hurt like a bastard . . . and pain like that might mess him up, keep him from catching the bitch in the Viper.

"Listen," Bird said. "Do you—"

"Out of the fucking car!" Spit flew from the cop's mouth. Veins pulsed in his neck and temples. He was one fired-up son of a bitch, and he sure as shit wasn't inclined to listen to anyone.

What the hell did she do to you?

Bird kept his eyes on the cop while his peripheral vision scanned the scene, picking up details, putting the story together. The cop's hat lay in the center of the road, crushed flat like some kind of blue-black road kill. The situation was clear enough. The speeding Viper had surprised him, almost hit him as it raced by. Now the bastard figured the Viper driver and Bird were a matched set, highballing lovers racing through the Pennsylvania highlands in a kind of muscle-car mating ritual.

"Keep your hands where I can see them and get the fuck out of that car!"

Bird wished he could sprout wings, transform his face, make his eyes glow from within. But those were Axle's tricks, not his. He was just the servant, the spiritual gofer, and if he was going to get out of this jam in time to catch the Viper, he was going to have to get the cop to calm down and listen.

"Now!" the cop roared. "Do not make me tell you again!"

Bird looked the man straight on, into his eyes, focusing on the dark hollow in the center of each. "Hey," he whispered, trying to speak with his eyes as well as his voice. "Look at me. Think. You know who I am. Look."

The cop flinched.

"See?"

The cop stared.

"Look! Look hard! Recognize me."

"Mr. Frieburg?"

"Yeah." Bird kept his voice flat, expressionless. "Just me." He held the cop's gaze, focused his thoughts, speaking with just his eyes now: *I own this county. Own you. Give me shit and I'll take your badge.* He kept staring. "Sorry about the speeding, officer."

The cop didn't lower his gun.

This is taking too long.

The cop flinched, stepped forward.

Shit! Focus!

"Out of the car, Mr. Frieburg!"

"No!" Bird roared. "Listen to me!"

The cop froze.

All right. So now I've got your attention.

The cop stared.

"Listen!" Bird looked at the man, into his eyes, into his soul. "I'm Maynard Frieburg. You know that name . . . know its power."

The cop didn't answer. Didn't move.

"My family owns this town, your job, your life. And my Okwe blood transcends your laws." He didn't need to add that last part, but it felt right . . . felt powerful . . . like an incantation.

The cop lowered his gun.

"Let me pass," Bird said. "Look away and forget I was here."

The cop holstered his gun, turned, looked up the road to where his hat lay crushed against the center line.

Slowly, Bird put in the clutch, slipped the Firebird into gear. "I'm going to drive," he said, speaking softly. "Going to ease past you. Nothing important. Not worth noticing . . . not worth remembering."

The cop started toward his hat.

Bird steered onto the shoulder, then eased back into the uphill lane. When he looked back, the cop was bending over the center line, picking up his hat, shaking grit from the brim.

A second later, the road turned.

The cop vanished behind roadside weeds.

Bird gunned the engine and burned rubber toward the Silver Lake Dam.

50

She was still in one piece, sitting in the Viper, leaning back as the devil clawed at the hood, pinned between rock and car.

The nitro hadn't exploded.

The devil roared, a pathetic sound that she felt in her bones, more pained than angry. The headlights had come on and were now blazing against the rock, throwing an aura over his broken wings. His face was less than a foot from hers, just beyond the windshield. Eyes glowing. Lips contorting. She could see his words: *Go on!* the black lips said. *Finish it!*

She unfastened her restraining belt and climbed from the seat, out from under the broken wings. The feathers felt cold and tingly against her back as she crawled beneath them. A breeze seemed to emanate from them, swirling around her as she lowered herself to the culvert's floor. She looked again at his face through the windshield, lips still moving, still speaking: *Hurry! Finish it! Now! Before it starts again!*

She opened the trunk. The smell of nitro rose around her as she looked inside. Tucky's words came back to her.

. . . you might bump it hard and have nothing happen, but . . . sometimes the gentlest tap . . .

The car shifted. She stepped back, looking toward the devil. He was still shouting at her, pounding the hood with his fist. *Finish it!* he seemed to be saying. *Go on! Finish it!*

Why was he telling her that? First he had blocked her path. Now he was goading her on.

"Are you with me?" she asked.

I'm with no one!

"So why—" She stopped, realizing the futility of talking to a devil. He would try to confuse her, distract her. The best thing was to ignore him, finish what she had started.

She leaned back into the cockpit, pushing beneath the blowing feathers until she found the jerry can. She grabbed the handle, lifted it out. Gasoline sloshed inside. One gallon, six pounds—it strained her leg as she set it down beside the bumper. Then she reached into the trunk and peeled the plastic sheeting from the wooden crate. The lid came off easily. She set it on the ground and began ripping the plastic bricks, crumbling the bills, scattering them around the dynamite. The nitro smell was stronger now, choking her. She was already dizzy by the time she opened the jerry can and doused the crumpled bills.

The breeze came again, gusting from the front of the car as she lit a crumpled bill and dropped it into the trunk. The fumes caught first, igniting as the bill fell, billowing behind her as she turned and ran toward the semicircle of light at the end of the culvert.

She almost made it before the nitro exploded.

ird reached Old River Trail in time to see fire shooting from the culvert. He stopped the car.

The dam shook. For an instant, its face looked fluid, rippling as shockwaves moved outward from its center, reached the valley walls, then rebounded. After that, the air turned still. The fire went out. The world fell silent but for the rumble of the Firebird and the far-off hiss of water flowing from the spillway.

The dam held!

And then, from the valley, someone screamed.

Bird drove toward the bridge, looking down at slopes strewn with wreckage from a blasted car. A body writhed amid the debris. It was the woman, the Viper driver. She'd been caught in the blast, shot like a cannonball from the culvert's mouth. Now she lay near the base of the bridge, screaming as Bird reached the utility road. She seemed to be praying, calling to God and Jesus . . . and someone else. "Kasdeja!" Her voice rasped. "*Kasdeja!*"

It's done. The dam held. Time to clear out.

The woman screamed louder, but she was nothing to him . . . less than nothing. And yet something Kwetis had said came back to him.

We have nothing against them, only what they are trying to do.

"Shit." He put his hand on the gear shift. *What would Kwetis do? What would he want me to do?*

He noticed a strange darkness surrounding her, deep purple like an ultra-violet bruise. *Her pain*, he thought, the realization hitting him with the kind of intuitive certainty he had previously only known in dreams. *I can see her pain.*

The color darkened as she tried moving, clawing at the slope, trying to pull herself up on broken legs.

I need to get to her, put her in the car, drive her to a hospital.

He studied the trail that led into the valley. The woman was a good 50 feet away from it, lying on a rocky bank that would rip up the bottom of an ordinary car. But Bird didn't drive one of those, and when the color of the woman's pain deepened to glowing black, he hit the switches that activated the Firebird's hydraulics. The car lurched, tilting to the left, then to the right, rising up on its struts as fluid flowed from the canisters in the trunk and into the suspension system above the wheels. Then, with the chassis elevated, he drove down the trail and onto the bank, rolling forward until he reached the woman in the weeds.

Her hair and clothes had been burned away. Skin hung in tatters from her hands, or were those the remnants of the bandages he had noticed in the mini-mart? She looked at him, blood running from her nose, mouth, and ears. If she couldn't hear before, she certainly couldn't hear shit now.

He leaped down from the elevated cab, hit the ground running, raced toward her.

She waved him away. "No!" Blood bubbled from her mouth. "*No!*"

He reached for her.

"*No!*" She swung at him, her arms arcing with streamers of pain.

He grabbed her wrist, letting go when he felt her scorched flesh slipping against her bones.

"*No!*"

He stepped back, looking up as a new sound entered the valley, the hiss of water flowing from the center of the dam. The lake had breached the top and was now flowing in a glassy ribbon over a section of subsided road. It ran down the slope, around the culvert, and then continued on to join the runoff from the spillway.

"It's happening!" the woman screamed, her voice as ragged as her body. "You didn't stop me. It's happening!"

The dam groaned, shifting under the weight of the spill, and then . . . slowly . . . the culvert collapsed, closing like a stone eye, crushed by the weight of subsiding rock. And now there were two spillways, one on the east bank, the other surging from the center of the dam.

Bird approached the woman again, coming up behind her.

She spun, swinging at him, raking his face.

"Christ, lady!" He stumbled, feet splashing in ankle-deep water. The stream was swelling. He looked back at the Firebird, water rising around its wheels. That did it! The hell with her. Kwetis could speak platitudes from Axle's dreams, but down here in the trenches it was every man for himself. It wasn't that he feared drowning. His skyborn mojo would protect him from that. But there was the Firebird to consider.

He hurried back to the open door, climbed in, and tried steering out the way he had come. But he stopped when he saw that the route was now completely submerged. The only thing left was to drive downstream, look for a way out. There had to be one.

The woman rasped again. She was back to praying, calling to God, Jesus, Kasdeja.

Bird cut the wheel, hit the gas, and steered up along the bank until his tires cleared the rising water. And it was then, glancing in his rearview, that he saw a fist of water punch out the top of the dam. The sound of it reached him a second later, a thunderous roar that quaked in his bones. And suddenly the woman was kneeling in waist-high rapids—arms spread toward an advancing wall of foam and debris. An instant later she was gone, her agony guttering out like a purple flame.

And the wave kept coming.

"Axle!" Bird gripped the wheel, accelerating between near vertical walls. "Goddamnit, Axle! Get me out of here!"

52

Dalton sat on his mattress of cardboard, plastic, leaves, and grass. He was leaning back against the wall, looking up at the sky beyond the beams, and trying to make sense of the devil's final words when he heard a thunderclap to the north. It shook the beams, reverberated from the hills.

A copperhead peeked out from the pile of roof debris. It flicked its tongue, looked at Dalton, then slipped down into another opening among the shingles. That pile of slate, wood, and plaster was full of snakes now. But Dalton didn't mind. The snakes didn't bother him anymore. Perhaps it was because he had learned to avoid pissing them off, but he liked to think it had more to do with the way the devil had healed him. The healing touch had made him something other than human. The snakes seemed to respect that.

The thunder stopped. The air turned still. And yet Dalton sensed something happening to the north. He couldn't say exactly what it was, but like a snake he had developed a sensitivity to vibrations, to the background hum of his environment.

He got up and went outside.

The sun blazed overhead. No clouds. Only the lingering haze from Windslow Mine. He walked out among the devil statues, crouched among them, and set his hands against the ground.

"Something's coming."

He leaned forward, butt in the air, ear to the dirt. The sound was there, whining like a racing engine. He stretched his legs, lying flat now, listening with his entire body. It *was* an engine, a car racing somewhere close. He held his breath, detecting the deep throb of something else. He closed his eyes. *Water*, he thought. *Sounds like water . . . a wave . . . coming this way.*

The engine sound grew more distinct as he pushed back from the ground. It came from the ravine, racing south along the bank of the stream. He got up and walked to the slope, pausing amid the flattened grass where he had left the two snake-bitten cops a short time ago. Now, crouching, he looked down into the valley as a glint of color flashed into view. He squinted, focusing on the thing, trying to make sense of it. It looked like a bird—a painted bird with flaming wings bounding atop a screaming hood.

Firebird!

But the car's wheels were all wrong. The suspension looked like it belonged to an off-road dirt buggy . . . or maybe a monster truck. And the man behind the wheel looked just as wild, with a mane of tangled hair whipping behind him, cracking in the wind as the car roared nearer.

VvvvrrrroooOOOMMMMMMM!

It raced by, shaking the weeds, throwing up mud, splashing through the edge of the stream. And then it was gone, speeding around the next bend in the valley, leaving behind the stink of its exhaust. The engine's roar dwindled, yielding now to a deeper sound, like the rumble of an approaching train or a convoy of low-gearing tractor trailers. He looked toward the thunder, leaning out over the brink as a wall of dirt, rock, and trees rumbled into view. It churned as it advanced, roiling like the edge of a cyclone, shaking the ground that now seemed to be breaking apart beneath him.

A crack formed near his feet.

He turned and ran, looking back as he scrambled toward the house, up the stairs, and into the parlor. The devil had told him to stay with the house, inside if possible, on the roof if necessary.

He climbed onto the pile of debris in the center of the room, up along the fallen shingles and planks until he reached one of the overhead beams. From there he lifted himself up to the remnants of the second floor, where a ladder angled down from a still-intact section of roof. He took the rungs three at a time, leaping up and out onto the sun-baked slates.

He scuttled like a bug on a skillet, retreating to the shadow of the chimney. Here he turned, looking down to see the wave clawing at the bend in the valley. One of the devil statues fell, then another, then a third—each vanishing under an avalanche of churning dirt and weeds as the front yard collapsed.

The house shifted. He leaned back against the chimney, hugging it as the porch broke apart. Boards flew into the air. And then, slowly, inexorably, the house lilted, pitching like a ship without a keel, picking up speed as the walls gave way and the intact section of roof crashed against the torrent.

Beams groaned, slates creaked, but the shingles held together. He dropped to his knees, gripping the eaves, sailing now—riding the wave through the valley, heading south toward Windslow Mine.

53

Sharo Jenkins heard the blast. It had the cadence of rolling thunder, a slow and steady rumble that echoed through the hills.

I've heard this before.

The sound moved through her. It was part of her.

I'm dreaming.

She tried opening her eyes, realizing as she did that they were already open. She was awake, surrounded by people she seemed to remember from somewhere. One of them held her arm, guiding her through a wooded valley.

The thundering roar grew louder, shaking the ground, making her stumble.

Yes . . . I know this sound . . . I've heard it before!

The blast had started it all. She remembered hearing it for the first time, driving toward it, then veering out of her life and into a nightmare: smoke and snakes and flashing lights. She remembered these things. And she remembered something else . . . an aching desire to return to her son.

She tried calling his name, but her throat felt raw, swollen. The best she could manage was a whisper. *"Jordan."* But the whisper was enough. She spoke it, and his face appeared, blurring as a screen door closed in front of him.

"Mommy!" He held his ear with one hand, reached for her with the other. For a moment, it all seemed real. Then it faded, back into memory.

"He needs me!" she muttered. "I have to go to him! He's sick." The words felt thick, as if she were speaking from a dream. "He needs me!"

Thunder roared, louder than before.

"The hell is that?" a man said. He was a cop, heavy-set and black. He walked ahead of her. She had seen him around. Or perhaps she simply remembered him from a dream. "Is that thunder?"

"Not thunder," another said. He held a leash, leading a dog. She knew him too. K-9 from Hamilton. But what was his name? "Not thunder," K-9 said again. "It's coming from the ground."

They climbed a slope, emerging into a clearing that looked at once familiar and strange. A Dodge Viper was there, wrecked and bloody. Sharo's cruiser sat near it, the passenger window shattered. And there were other cruisers, too. From Cokesburg, Blaston, Windslow.

"Zabek." She recognized his car, remembering. "Robert was coming for me," she said.

A voice answered. "He's here."

Sharo looked at the woman who walked beside her. She had a pretty face, high cheeks, coffee skin. *Tiffany Rose.* She walked close to Sharo's side, gripping her arm.

"He's behind us," Rose said. "You're both going to be fine. It's over. We're all going home."

Sharo glanced back to see two more officers stumbling behind her. One of the officers was Robert Zabek. His legs looked swollen, straining against the fabric of his pants.

"You're going to be fine." Rose's voice faltered. "Both of you."

Sharo looked down at her own discolored arm. She remembered now, the snakes in the cruiser, the horror coming back to her as the thunder came again, louder than before. And this time it seemed to come from two directions: north from Silver Lake, south from the crater of Windslow Mine. A thought stirred within her, resonating with the certainty of a dream: *Something's happening to the ground . . . to the rocks . . . to the earth.*

Paramedics approached, wheeling a gurney. "I'll take her." One of them extended a gloved hand. "I'll take—"

Thunder. Deafening now. So close that the sound of it crossed over into a physical thing, striking Sharo's ears like fists to the side of the head. Then the world pitched, tilting sideways. Sharo fell, past the paramedic, onto the side of the gurney, then down against the ground. She put out her hands, breaking her fall. Then, with her palms pressing the ground, she felt the earth shifting, rocks breaking, heat rising. A crack opened beside her hand. Thin as a hair, it continued beneath her palm, zigzagged under the gurney, and widened as it approached her cruiser. The crack glowed as it spread, radiating beams of blood-red light that swirled with jets of soot and ash.

People panicked, shouting together, one voice rising above the others. "Listen! Everybody! Stay calm!" It was a Blaston officer. She'd seen him before, but what was his name? Roy *something.* Maybe *something* Roy.

"This isn't happening!" he yelled, turning in place.

Leroy. His name is Leroy.

The ground kept shaking.

"You know what I'm saying!" Leroy looked at the K-9 officer. "Those things we *thought* we saw. Shared hallucinations, right?"

"Like our radios?" K-9 said. "The statues?"

Their words sounded random, a conversation from a dream.

The K-9 officer's dog was going nuts, barking, straining at the leash.

Leroy looked around at the others, keeping his back to a widening fissure, the underground glow radiating around him. "We need to keep our heads." He turned to the paramedics. "Get the wounded out of here. Don't rush. It's all right."

Sharo stared at Leroy as the paramedics lifted her from the ground. Then she looked past him, toward a twisting shadow within the glowing fissure, an undulating darkness that was even now jutting into the smoking air. It was the length of a man's arm. *A snake?* She blinked as it vanished and reappeared, seeing it more clearly this time. It looked like a snake, a large one leaping straight up from the widening chasm. But it wasn't a snake. Not a whole one. Only a piece of one . . . only the flicking tongue of a monster whose truck-size head was even now emerging into view.

The dog kept barking.

Leroy turned as the snake arced above him.

People shouted, stumbling toward their vehicles.

The paramedics picked up Sharo, dropped her onto the gurney, and wheeled her toward the back of the ambulance.

She tried sitting up.

Leroy shouted louder. "We've seen stuff like this before! Everybody, listen. Please!"

The snake opened its jaws. Its mouth glowed, red around the edges, orange near the back of the throat. And then—

The ambulance door swung wide, blocking Sharo's view. She called to Leroy, seeing him through the window of the swinging door, catching his wide-eyed expression as the glowing jaws closed over him, lifted him from the ground. And for a moment the snake had a new tongue, forked and kicking as the truck-size head reared back. Someone discharged a weapon. One shot. Then another. The reports resounded through the clearing as the snake jerked its head and swallowed the man. And then Sharo was in the ambulance, kicking and screaming as the doors closed behind her, sitting up as a paramedic tried restraining her. "Did I see that?" She was shouting now. Her words tasted like blood. "Did I see—"

The ambulance turned, siren wailing, lights strobing against the trees. And then, forcing herself up one last time, she managed a quick glance through the back windows. Outside, a glowing shape leaped upward. It was pointed like an arrow, but bisected by a pair of fiery wings. And then she was down again, lying flat on the gurney while people drew straps across her chest, arms, and legs.

"I saw it!"

Faces hovered over her.

She closed her eyes. The flying snake was there, blazing behind her lids. She watched it climb into the air, and as she did she heard a new sound rising beyond the screaming siren. It sounded like a race car, engine howling from the ravine below the clearing . . . and right behind it, welling louder and louder, the crash of an advancing wave.

54

Kirill was pretty sure that Arnold Gusky was going to end up shooting him. It had been that kind of day.

"You got to admit," Gusky said, waving the revolver. "It's a *slippy* slope, Kirill. A *rilly slippy* slope!"

"You mean *slippery*," Kirill said. "You mean *really slippery*."

Gusky didn't acknowledge the correction. He was listening to himself, not Kirill.

"First the Viper in your driveway is gone. Then Joe breaks into the garage and there's no Viper in their neither. No Viper, no money."

"I told you," Kirill said. "Let me call my uncle."

"No, Kirill. Seriously. I'm tired of *jagging witchew*. You know what I'm saying?"

"*Jagging witchew?*"

"With you, all right? Jagging around with you! Christ almighty. You're a freaking Russian, Kirill. Stop with telling me how to talk English!"

The building shivered as he spoke. Or maybe it only seemed to. Kirill couldn't be sure of anything anymore. But when he turned his eyes toward the plate-glass window, he saw that something new was happening out near the crater of Windslow Mine.

Gusky saw it, too. "The hell was that?" He got up, walked toward the glass, leaned against it. "Like a goddamn earthquake." Gusky looked back at Kirill. "What's up with that? Two in one day? What are the odds—" He cocked his head, apparently listening to his in-ear headset, his lips compressing to a bloodless line as if he were holding something back. Then, with an explosive burst, he let it out. "Please! Not now!" He broke the connection.

"Who was that?" Kirill asked.

Gusky frowned. "Goddamn drunk," he said.

"Your wife?" Kirill asked, realizing that it was probably the wrong thing to say.

"The hell?" Gusky said. "You saying my wife's a goddamn drunk?"

"So who was it?"

Gusky shook his head. "My wife," he said. "But that don't give you the right to assume." He glared at Kirill. "That goddamn *jagoff* of hers is missing again."

"Your son?"

"Damnit, Kirill!"

"Sorry. Your son's not a *jagoff*. It's the morphine. I'm not thinking."

"He is a goddamn *jagoff*. But he's *her jagoff*, not mine."

"So what'd he do?"

"Nothing," Gusky said. "She's just telling me he's not in the freaking house. And he's not outside, neither. And then she's telling me there's a dent in the lake."

"A dent."

"That's what she said. A dent—like all the water's sinking down in the middle, like someone pulled the freaking plug from the *warsh* tub. All of which is neither here nor there, right, Kirill?"

"We're talking about money again?"

"I think we're done talking."

"No, Arnold. Listen. Call my uncle. Or let me call him."

"Right. I let you call him, and the next thing I know there's two *jiagunda* Russian goons coming through my door to blow me away."

"What's *jiagunda*?"

"Big ass. Big-ass goons."

"Ilya doesn't work that way, Arnold. Trust me. I think we both need a little help today. Let me call him."

Gusky turned away.

Kirill looked out the window, past the mine, toward the highlands. Out there, beyond the smoke that still rose from the crater, some *jiagunda* thing was rising through the trees. And then came a sound that told Kirill that all bets were off. It started low, more like a sense of movement than a sound. Then it swelled, growing louder, deep and resonate like the roar of something primal. The windows shook, trembling in their frames. And then, just when the roar seemed about to tear the building apart, it fell back—still there, rumbling in the distance, but approaching . . . ready to swell again.

"The fuck," Gusky said. "What the fuck was that?"

ird watched the wave as he drove, gaze darting from windshield to rear-view. The water was advancing in fits and starts, occasionally pausing to swirl in on itself, other times surging ahead at alarming speed. Bird's progress was much the same. On the straightaways, when the ground was level, he raced ahead—sometimes losing sight of the pursuing wall of roiling debris. Other times he crawled along, climbing over rocks, steering clear of muddy pools, and always looking for a drivable slope to carry him out of the valley.

He seemed to be putting distance between himself and the wave when the path narrowed sharply. Straight ahead, a rusting girder passed over the valley, the remnants of an old rail bridge that had serviced his father's mine. He cut his speed, easing through as the wave appeared behind him.

Up ahead, the stream descended into a V-shaped ravine. The slopes were barren, all silicate and slag. He was approaching the mine, plunging toward a huge half-pipe spillway that ran through the base of a hill. If he could reach that pass, if he could drive through it before the wave caught him, he'd be home free. The spillway would slow the wave, give him the time he needed. All he had to do was cross another hundred yards of relatively smooth terrain.

He didn't need to check the rearview. He felt the wave's breath on his neck, heard its voice in his bones, saw its shadow spreading over the dash. It was above him now, breaking up in the air, preparing to crash down on top of him.

I've got one chance!

He glanced at the N2O controls.

Do it!

Mud and grit rained over him as he flipped the switch. The wave's shadow blotted the sun. The cockpit went dark. He gripped the wheel and thumbed the trigger.

The engine whined. He shot forward, wheel jerking in his hands as the front end veered slightly to the left. The spillway swelled before him, off-center now.

I'm going to miss it!

He steadied the wheel, straightened his approach. And then—

BAM!

He was inside, hurtling through like a bullet in a half-pipe barrel, the squeal of the engine echoing around him as he approached the end. And then—as fast as he had entered—he was through.

And he was flying.

"SheeeeeiiIITTTT!"

There was no ground on the other side. The half-pipe extended out into empty air—sixty feet above the edge of Windslow Mine. Cliff Mine Run was to his left. To his right, beyond a ridge of weedy trees, emergency vehicles surrounded a smoking sinkhole. He was flying over a dry channel that would catch the water from the half-pipe. From his high vantage, he could see how the water would course along the channel, flowing in a wide curve out onto the floor of the mine . . . past the emergency vehicles . . . into the sinkhole. But he wasn't going that way. He was airborne in a nitro-powered Firebird, flying beyond the curve of the channel, toward a plain of hard-packed slag.

He realized he had his foot on the brake pedal. The effort was both reflexive and futile, but he kept bearing down, pressing harder as he soared, not slowing, but losing altitude, nosing toward the ground. . . .

He braced for the collision, straightening his arms, pushing back from the wheel as if increasing the distance between his face and windshield would make a difference.

The Firebird logo on his hood glinted in the sun, wings spread against the racing wind, beak open in a soundless scream as the ground approached.

He was in freefall now—weightless, leaning forward, screaming into the wind.

Sitting on the side of Cliff Mine Run, Benjie saw a bright red car leap from a spillway on the edge of Windslow Mine.

The car screamed as it flew, engine whistling, driver shrieking. The man seemed to be steering, holding the wheel steady as the car angled downward, picking up speed until it struck the floor of the mine and exploded into a rolling fireball.

Benjie stared, amazed at how the man's screams continued even after the car exploded. But then something new appeared, a jet of water bursting from the spillway, spewing out in a foaming cascade. It landed in a channel, becoming a raging river that curved toward the fire trucks that ringed the sinkhole. There were other vehicles down there too, some with news logos on their doors. And now drivers were climbing behind the wheels, revving their engines, racing away as the currents flowed toward them.

They had time. The water seemed to be moving in slow motion. Indeed, the flow from the spillway was falling back, as if the half-pipe had gotten clogged. And now Benjie thought he heard the sound of reversing currents surging backward through the hills.

But down in the mine, the sudden river still flowed, channeled by banks of bulldozed overburden, bypassing the flaming Firebird and swirling into the sinkhole.

Steam rose. Fissures spread, widening as they opened beneath the fire trucks. One of the vehicles tilted. The driver turned the wheel, trying to pull away, but the ground kept opening . . . wider . . . wider. . . .

Benjie didn't want to watch, but the scene had paralyzed him, holding his gaze as trucks slipped into the spreading chasms.

And then he saw the snakes, leaping from the sinkhole like giant flames. They swayed together, tasting the air with flicking tongues. Then, as one, they sprouted wings and threw themselves at the sky.

Dalton rode the farm-house roof along the back of the raging torrent. He knew he was floating on water, but all around him were trees and rocks and weeds—all packed so tightly that nary a drop of water appeared between them. As he flowed on, the slopes on either side of the valley broke apart, filling with cracks that glowed as they opened wide. The water seemed to be doing it, cracking the shell of the earth, exposing something terrible beneath.

The roof's chimney crumbled as the currents jostled him around a bend in the valley. Straight ahead, the rock walls steepened, rising almost straight up to a railroad trestle. The debris seemed to be collecting there, clogging the pass, creating a counter surge, sending some of the waters back the way they had come.

Dalton crawled away from the chimney, scuttling like a lizard as falling bricks banged against the slates, and now he was spinning, roof beams straining beneath him as another section of valley wall opened wide. The splitting earth glowed red, undulating with serpentine shadows. One of the shadows curved toward him, resolving into a head as large as the floating roof. Its tongue flicked. Then it turned away, spread a pair of flaming wings, and leaped skyward. The wind of its flight surged over him. He tried watching, but the roof spun faster, groaning, breaking apart. A moment later he was surging toward Cliff Mine Run—a mountain road that had been named for a stream that had been diverted decades ago by the Frieburg Coal Company.

Windslow, he thought, looking out over the edge of his crumbling raft, looking south. *I'm heading toward downtown Windslow!*

But he didn't make it that far.

The last remnant of his raft shattered. Then he fell, plunged into the churning debris, passed through it, and sank into darkness.

The advancing wall of trees, rocks, cars, trailers, and houses was clearly visible beyond the glass wall of Arnold Gusky's office by the time Uncle Ilya called back. Kirill watched the wave as Arnold cupped his headset.

"Ilya?" Gusky's voice sounded thin, barely audible above the approaching roar. "Not now. I'll call you later." He broke the connection.

"No one talks to him like that," Kirill said.

"Fuck it."

Kirill laughed. He didn't give a shit. *Morphine*, he thought. *Better than vodka.*

The wave was maybe thirty feet high, thundering as it reached the edge of town. It surged over Boundary Street, taking out a small church and its readerboard protesting Mountain Downs. The sign sparked, letters scattered. Then the wave continued on, straight for Gusky Tower.

"This place," Kirill said. "This building. Did your company handle the renovations?"

"Who else would I hire?"

"Did they follow code?"

"What do you think?"

"Just asking."

The wave crested at the second floor, breaking windows and surging through the offices rented by Dr. Was and her team of for-profit doctors. The building swayed.

Gusky caught himself on his desk.

Kirill just stayed where he was, slumped on the couch, watching a glass on the table beside him, noting how the water inside tilted toward the brim, almost spilling before leveling out again.

"It's structurally sound," Gusky said. "Just in case you were implying otherwise, the building is as strong as—"

Something banged beneath the floor, followed by a roar of falling steel. And then, once again, the floor tilted. Papers fell from Gusky's desk, scattering to the floor, while tables and chairs migrated toward the wall of glass. The tumbler on the table beside Kirill toppled, shattering. Then everything was falling, crashing down into a vat of churning debris.

The last thing Kirill saw was Arnold Gusky tapping his earpiece and shouting into his cupped hand. "Damn right!" Gusky said, or maybe it was only Kirill dreaming it. The morphine made it hard to tell what was real, what was simply amusing fantasy. "Damn right I hung up on you! You're goddamn right!"

Then the floor gave way.

Then darkness.

59

"Hey, Bird!"

Bird felt something nudge his side.

"Get up, Bird! It's not over."

Bird opened his eyes.

Kwetis stood beside him, eyes glowing, wings backlit by glowing fog.

"Get up." Kwetis spoke with his shadow. "You can't die. You're skyborn."

Bird sat up. A line of scorched rock lay beside him, stretching away toward the point where his car had crashed and burned. A berm of slag lay beyond the point of impact, rising like a dyke between the plain on which he found himself and a pillar of steam that rose from the base of the collapsed highwall.

He looked again at Kwetis. "Am I dreaming this?"

"No."

"This is real?"

"Afraid so." Kwetis took Bird's wrist, pulling him to his feet. "The barrier's been breached." He spoke with his grip. "The world has changed."

Bird looked again at the pillar of steam. "So she succeeded?"

"Not quite." Kwetis stepped back, still holding Bird's wrist. "I'll show you."

Bird took a step, and suddenly his surroundings changed. The mine vanished. In its place lay a muddy plain dotted with twitching fish. It was Silver Lake, what was left of it, as seen from the edge of the now collapsed Silver Lake Dam.

"Hey!" Bird turned toward Kwetis. "How'd you—"

But Kwetis was gone.

Axle had taken his place.

"I thought you were Kwetis."

"I am."

"Goddamnit, Axle! You're messing with me."

"No," Axle said. "It's you. Your perceptions are changing. Old barriers are coming down. Your currents run free."

"Which means?"

"You're getting stronger, more powerful. More like me. And it's a good thing, too." He turned Bird's attention to the valley that ran behind them, its slopes scoured to bare rock by raging currents. In the distance, beyond a bend in the valley, steam rose from Windslow Mine. "Whatever abilities you're developing, I have a feeling you're going to be needing them real soon."

Shadows drifted in the heavy air above the mine, serpentine bodies on glowing wings.

"I take it this wasn't the plan," Bird said.

"I can't say for sure. Not yet. Maybe soon." His voice dropped to a whisper. "I think . . . I'm afraid I'm starting to see the overarching plan of what my great-grandmother called the *oohaate*. But it isn't that. It's older than people . . . older than Okwe . . . maybe older than life. And I'm afraid of it." He glanced at Bird, then turned away. "I'm afraid it'll drive me mad when I figure it out."

"But you're Kwetis, right?"

"I'm something. And so are you. We're part of a force that people have been trying to name for as long as there's been language. But the force is beyond naming. My father . . . the thing that my father became . . . I think he understood. He knew what was controlling us, what we're up against. That's why he wanted out."

"Out?"

Axle looked down at the wreckage of the dam.

"He's down there." Axle pointed to the jumble of rocks and slag. "And this time he won't be climbing out. He'll stay buried. Not fully dead, but close to it. Before this is over, I'm afraid the same might happen to me."

EPILOGUE

Dalton crawled from the water, lifted himself onto a rock, and waited for the sun to burn strength back into his body. Nearby, on a patch of high ground, a woman sat beside a fire. Across from her, a man was roasting a snake on a spit.

The woman was small and wiry, covered in scales that shimmered in the sun. She looked strong. *Waterborn*, Dalton thought. He had no idea where the term came from. But it felt right. There was a ring of truth in it, intuitive truth, like the kind encountered in dreams.

Then he looked at his own skin. It shimmered too—glowing like the woman's.

The man looked up, raised a long-fingered hand, and beckoned.

Closer, the gesture said. *Come closer*.

Dalton advanced, picking his way up along a slope that the raging waters had scoured to bare rock.

The fire crackled.

Smoke blew toward him, stinging his eyes. He blinked, and this time he saw that the thing being roasted wasn't a snake.

It was an arm, severed midway between elbow and shoulder. A bone protruded from the end, capped in charred gristle.

Dalton backed away.

"No," the man said. "Too late for that. I made this for you." He raised the spit. "Come and eat."

And then, from somewhere over the scarred hollow of Windslow Mine, the sky began to scream.

Read on for an exciting look at

the final book in the Veins Cycle.

PROLOGUE

Sweating against the elastic that bound her chest, wearing a starched blouse that would draw blood if she turned too quickly, gripping a Bible of tissue-thin pages that glowed with the light of the Word, Samuelle Calder watched the preacher paint pictures in the air.

Sometimes he looked right at her, staring deep with flaming eyes. The heat of his gaze made her soft and wet, like dough before you punched it down. Lately she had been feeling that way about a lot of things. "It's your heart," her mother told her. "*Out of the heart come evil thoughts—adulteries and fornications!*" Her mother's voice always moved to the back of her throat when she quoted scripture, like thunder on the horizon.

The preacher spoke in scripture too, but his voice was different, sharp but muted, a sheathed blade. He was telling the story of the flood, of the days when a vengeful God reclaimed the earth, scoured it clean, started again.

"*And behold!*" The preacher spread his arms, hands wide in the angled light. "*I bring a flood upon the earth!*"

He wore a tailored suit and hand-tooled boots, more like a country singer than a preacher, the kind that sang songs about forbidden things. She wondered if Christ had seemed like this to the people who had heard him preach back in the day. That would explain why the early Christians were so willing to follow him even though it meant defying the law. If this man had a following, if he asked her to be his apostle, she would go with him. She would be his Peter, or maybe his Thomas—though she would never doubt or deny him. And she wouldn't need the light of the Holy Spirit to make her a true believer any more than she would need to be a man to be counted among his closest followers. Yes, these things could happen. Maybe. Someday.

But today she simply listened. And watched.

"*Behold! The waters of justice gather into waves!*" He made a sweeping gesture, painting the air.

"See them now! Mighty waves! They gather above the sinful world! Do you see them?"

The people called out, answering as one: "Yes!"

But Mother held back, cold and reserved. She might speak in tongues at home, but in public she was all ice and stone.

"Do you see it?"

Samuelle tensed, wanted to answer, wanted to leap from her chair and tell him yes, wanted to break the elastic that bound her breasts and scream: "I see it! Everything you've said, I see. Tell me more and let me see that too. Everything you have! Show me!"

But she remained as before, starched and bound in her mother's shadow.

He looked at her, held her gaze, and continued in a voice like cool torrents, carrying her away.

She closed her eyes.

The torrents coiled, fast and hard.

Do you know it, sister? Do you feel the waters?

He spoke inside her now, voice breaking in her private spaces.

And the serpent will cast water over the woman, that he might carry her away!

The water roared.

She gasped.

The chill rushed in.

And she was drowning.